To SGT JACK JAMES
EX AIR DISPATCH
6TH AIRBORNE DIVISION
1941 TO 1947

The Reunion

The Reunion

Eric Rankin

© Eric Rankin, 1993

Published by Aeberhard & Partners, Millstones, Egypt Lane, Farnham Common, Bucks SL2 3LF.

All rights reserved. No part of this publication may be reproduced, stored in any retrieval system or transmitted in any form or by any means, electronic, mechanical, photocopying, recording or otherwise, without prior written permission of the copyright holder for which application should be addressed in the first instance to the publishers. No liability shall attach to the author, the copying holder or the publishers for loss or damage of any nature suffered as a result of reliance on the reproduction of any of the contents of this publication or any errors or omissions in its contents.

A CIP catalogue record is available for this book from the British Library.

ISBN 0 9521972 0 0

Designed by Nigel Burt
Production in association with Book Production Consultants, 25–27 High Street, Chesterton, Cambridge CB4 1ND.

Typeset in Baskerville by Rowland Phototypesetting Limited, Bury St Edmunds, Suffolk.
Printed and bound by Biddles Limited, Guildford

DEDICATION

To all Old Comrades. No man can form part of a more caring, mutually supportive and united society than those who have shared their youth and early manhood in combat, no matter what their background. To these brothers and comrades, I dedicate this book.

CONTENTS

Chapter	Page	Chapter	Page
Plate section between pages 136–137		17. Repeated echoes.	119
1. Comrades not in arms.	1	18. The Goat.	123
2. The college.	7	19. The visitation.	131
3. The school.	13	20. The tiger rug.	145
4. The Test.	21	21. The crusade.	153
5. The unholy garden.	31	22. The cavalier.	161
6. Wealth is life.	39	23. The hill of Calvary.	171
7. Job vacancy.	47	24. The trap.	179
8. The birthday party.	55	25. Intermission.	189
9. The camp.	61	26. Search for oblivion.	197
10. War games.	69	27. Winter attack.	207
11. L'amour d'enfance.	75	28. Theatre of the absurd.	217
12. Les Miserables.	85	29. Big men and little men.	225
13. The initiation.	93	30. Games of chance.	231
14. Temporary gentlemen.	99	31. The betrayal.	241
15. An historical view.	109	32. Islands.	249
16. Flashback.	115	33. Reunion.	257

chapter 1

Comrades not in arms

"The Ship and Shovel" is an exceptional name for a pub. It is so liable to misinterpretation, having something to do with an Admiral of the Fleet, one Sir Cloudesley Shovel who went down with his ship off the Scilly Isles, not the shifting of manure. It caught Geoffrey Davis' attention on the road and opened the floodgates of memory.

He was near the sea in Kent, inside the public bar where high-backed pews had been against the walls for centuries and the double number one on the dart board had been pock-marked out of recognition.

The doors had burst open to admit a whole crowd of miners and their wives from the cricket field outside. Their throats were like the bottom of parrot cages, they said, especially through the final overs when they were sure the officers could never win before stumps were drawn. Betteshanger Colliery had not had it so easy for a long time and victory was theirs with Bill Stocks still to go in.

"What can we get you. It's on us." The officers assumed a breezy air of equality, grinning inanely, trying to conceal their embarrassment when they were feeling as ill at ease as if at a feast in an African kraal.

"Port and lemon for the wife and, for me, a pint of bitter, if you don't mind, Sir." Bill Stocks, as fast bowler, had wreaked havoc on the officers and the sweat mixing with coal dust in his skin pores gave off an acidic smell. The "Sir" had come quite naturally even after his opponents had suffered an humiliating defeat in which Davis had been run out after just a single due to Bill's accurate throw in.

They had all been surprised in the mess when the major told them he had taken on the miners. It invited a trouncing in a one-day match with the honours to do in the pub afterwards.

The Reunion

Perhaps it was one of the few ways where, for an hour or so, the English could forget their class differences, rather like the first time at Hambledon. Davis still remembered the score. Hambledon v the Rest of England, with victory for Hambledon by an innings and 168 runs. The Duke of Dorset 0 and Minshull 60 on their side and Lord Tankerville 3, Aylward 167 on the other. There would have been no loss of respect by the players for the gentlemen afterwards.

It was July, 1940 and the Battery had been stationed near the colliery for a week to resist the threatened invasion. Every day brought reports of German barges massing in Boulogne and the preliminaries were testified by thin wisps of trailed vapour from the Spitfires and Focke-Wolf high above.

"Thanks, dearie." The feathers in Ethel's hat waggled appreciatively as she downed the port. "You'll give 'em what for, if the buggers come, pardon the expression. I was saying to Bill, how much safer I feel now we've got the soldiers."

Davis, who better knew the odds, tried not to look dubious, but his uncertainty must have been plain to her.

"Don't worry, love," she went on. "You'll be here with your grandchildren one day, down on the beach, you'll see."

It was as unbelievable as the Second Coming then, but she must have been clairvoyant, because here he was, 50 years on, planning to do just that and now on his way to the regimental reunion.

The reunion is always the first Saturday in October, so that the few who keep diaries can leave the day clear. It is always the same pub in the same town so they can all find their way. This was simple and reassuring to Geoffrey Davis and John McManus who were now of an age when they needed things to be straightforward.

Not that the town itself had stayed unchanged. It had become even more out-of-keeping with its surroundings. Always a blemish within chalk hills, gentle pastures and knife-clear streams, it was now an ugly conglomerate of brick and concrete – the brick from its decayed railway past, the concrete from the reconstituted gut of its shopping precinct.

Here there are supermarkets and furniture shops, Boots, Woolworths and Mothercare. But there are few bookshops, no buildings designated as worth preserving and the place does not figure in the Good Food Guide.

On Saturday afternoons, there are crowds in the shopping centre for the weekly spend-up. There are the sharp-witted and the gullible, the newly married and the newly divorced, skilled men from the car factory with their wives and kids indistinguishable from their contemporaries in Detroit, Malines or Dusseldorf.

The wives are smoking rather more now that part-time jobs are going, but the kids go on demanding a new Airfix and create hell if they don't get it.

This particular year, McManus went with Davis in McManus' car. Next year it would be Davis' turn for transport. They had both been brought up to watch these matters and, as the cost of petrol, food and services went up remorselessly, it gave a touch of desperation to their efforts to save.

The war had affected them deeply, occurring at a formative time in their lives. McManus, an only child, had been prised away from a doting mother by it, while Davis, orphaned early, had been liberated from an almost equally demanding aunt.

They had first met in 1942. Davis was then a subaltern and had discovered that the sergeant-major of his troop came from the same part of London. He had secretly admired the calm solidity of the older man, had respected his judgment and wished he had the other's persistence to go on educating himself.

Physically, they were quite different, but this perhaps was an added reason for their friendship. McManus, tall and thick-set, had the reddish hair of his Scottish border ancestors. His bushy eyebrows gave a certain incongruous comicality to a natural seriousness. He was a romantic at heart and his eyes dreamed a lot.

Davis was always surprised by the width and strength of his friend's shoulders and biceps. McManus would not have been out of place with a buckler and claymore in the ranks of the Bonny Prince. His voice boomed and he talked impulsively, and for far too long, with a declamation that became a teacher, or actor of ham.

He could be relied upon for mighty sixes, or for being clean-bowled.

The Reunion

In contrast was Davis, who was small, dark and quick to seize an advantage. There was a permanent intention to succeed about his eyes and an ironical twist of the mouth as if to say, "I've seen that move before and know well how to counter it."

Complicated, even devious in thinking, Davis was direct in speech. He knew how to time his counter-moves and had the patience not to strike until he judged the time was ripe. He was restrained and concealed his thoughts behind his words. He painted on a smaller canvas, but his brushstrokes were more accurate than those of McManus. He was a good man in a close field and fine in the slips.

After the war, the two men had lost contact with each other for a long time. Then, one day years later, chance had brought them together again across the bar in the main pub of their suburb of origin. McManus in the public had recognised Davis in the saloon.

It had been unusual for McManus to have been there at all. He was not a drinking man, but that day, after a walk in the country, with the kids outside engrossed in their Coke and crisps, he had spotted Davis with some of his cricketing friends. From that time, their acquaintanceship had been renewed and, former differences of rank forgotten, they had found many interests in common. They had become friends.

Both talked of the old regiment, their wives and children, house buying, gardening, politics and their careers – McManus a history teacher and Davis an accountant. It was suburban talk of schools, cars and house decorating, but, most important to them both, they talked cricket.

Cricket was something of an obsession with them both. The county championship, individual and team performances, the Test series, all these were matters of detailed and concerned comment.

Like others of their generation, they shared the recognition that, being alive, they were among the lucky ones. Both had emerged virtually unscathed from the war. Davis had escaped with a superficial wound in the cheek, long since healed. McManus had been physically unhurt, but retained some mental scars, deeper because unrevealed.

It was 50 years ago, but he still dreamed of the horror and darkness of it. He was too sensitive and proud to disclose this to his friend. McManus' wife often said of him that he "took things too much to heart, seeing slights where none were intended," but he had a long memory for occasions of this kind and made heavy weather of them. He still recalled the time when, as a youth, he had blushed and floundered when accused of some misdemeanour, although he knew full well he was innocent.

The car moved quickly out of London. It was the glorious month of June with England at its best. They felt at peace and their friendship had matured to the stage of respecting and tolerating the differences between them. To add to their delight, it was Test match time and the car radio gave a commentary, ball by ball, as a muted accompaniment to their talk.

"I enjoyed cricket at school," Davis was saying. "It wasn't a gentlemen's game then. Tooth and claw among the kids, with the occasional adult coming in to clear the ring, but most of the time you were on your own. The school I went to did at least instil a respect for the game."

Davis recalled Fairlight clearly. They called it locally, "The College."

chapter 2

The college

Having divided Gaul into three parts, Caesar had sent his troops again "causa pabulandi." Presumably they were out foraging once more from the miserable Gauls.

Geoffrey Davis sat in the dark corner of the class, making himself as inconspicuous as possible from old Burbridge. Fifteen boys, each in his own desk, were struggling to tease some meaning from the text.

They all feared Burbridge. He was a stout, sweating man with the pomposity of a hippo and the malicious eyes of a pig: an unfair comparison, since pigs mostly meant no harm and hippos are docile if left alone.

"Tiggers," who deliberately annoyed everyone, including the decent masters, shut up shop and played cave when Burbridge was expected. Geoffrey dreamed about Burbridge in the dorm and would wake up to hear Ferrers whimpering to himself under the bedclothes.

A regular tread with squeaking boots presaged Burbridge. He always flung the door wide and stood there, glinting at his charges, as he called them. The charges knew he was there, but dared not take their eyes one moment from the grubby texts.

"Don't look at me, boy," he would say, revelling in his power over them. "Eyes on Caesar. He will do you much more good." They knew he was lying as he said it. To Burbridge, Burbridge out-Caesared Caesar.

Come to that, he looked like the picture of a Roman senator as he entered and encircled the room with his presence. A beam of sun made a tiny sound as it struck a speck of dust, such was the silence.

Placing his cane on the table, Burbridge would grasp the back of a chair. In his grip, it became as light as furniture from a doll's house. He would then set it on one of its corner legs and twirl it slowly and with menace, watching them with eyes like iron buttons.

They knew well what had to be done. There were ten minutes before he stopped his chair whirlings and room pacings, his window staring and his nail polishing, and then he would say, "Stop, gentlemen. And who shall have the honour of construing today?"

Pause. The piggy eyes, lazy now, would roam. "Now – now Ferrers – you!"

Ferrers stuttered. Burbridge knew he stuttered. Burbridge enjoyed his stutter. Geoffrey Davis and the others were tacitly enticed to enjoy it too.

Ferrers stood. "Caesar et cccopiae approppp-pinquant ad oram exp-pplorant." "What?" "Exp-p-pl . . ." Ferrers agonised.

Burbridge imitated. "Ex-p-ppl . . ." They all tittered, some with shame. "Sit down, you idiot. And what are you laughing at, Davis? What gives you cause to laugh at the imbecilities of Ferrers?" It was a rhino now, with its horns lowered for the charge.

Davis stood up and fumbled. "Dunno, Sir."

"Of course you don't know, Davis. Who could expect you to know. Your aunt has sacrificed good money for you to come to Fairlight to be civilised, to give you a sense of duty, to be disciplined, Davis, to have a proper respect for your natural superiors, rather than to go to the council school where you will end up on the dole, or worse, resort to violence and robbery. And a hard task Fairlight has got, if I may say so. Don't you think you should apologise to Ferrers?"

"Yes, Sir."

"Well, do so, then."

Davis turned to the tearful Ferrers. "Sorry, Ferrers." Ferrers nodded.

"Well, Ferrers, and is that all you can do?"

The college

"That's all right, Davis."

"Manners, manners," Burbridge expanded. "Manners maketh man. And who said that?"

They knew too well who had said it. It was a Burbridge special. But he would ask Bravington whose father was a nob.

"William of Wykeham, Sir, the founder of Winchester College."

"Quite right, and you, Bravington, should get one of the Fairlight scholarships, because you have the right attitude. In Fairlight you can have the benefit of better facilities for games, learn about being members of a team, giving loyalty to the team, how to deal with natural nastiness. And what do I mean by that? Well, the sort of thing one sees far too often these days from the yobbos of the Council school, throwing bricks through windows, bashing up old people, yah, yah."

Burbridge seemed to have difficulty in putting his thoughts into words and returned to safer ground. "Fairlight has gained the cricket cup every year since 1902. Think of that! Because cricket is the game for gentlemen. It has style, and what do I mean by style?

"It needs long practice in the nets, it needs chaps who can be relied on not to fumble catches, who are on the alert. It needs to have a team proud of themselves by being well turned-out, it needs instant obedience to the captain and it needs sticking to the rules. It needs a sense of fair play and, if a chap gets out with a duck, you clap him just the same."

Burbridge faltered. He was running out of ideas. He glared at them. "Bravington, construe."

In chapel, they sang with a cracked lustiness. "And did those feet in ancient time?" Whose feet, and what were they doing with arrows of desire in dark, satanic mills? Was that something to do with cupid throwing Mills bombs, getting messed up with someone's feet? It was all very confusing.

The headmaster had served in India. His favourite theme for prayers was admonishment for those who maltreated animals. Davis thought it was directed at Ferrers who collected butterflies and accidentally tore their wings off sometimes when he mounted them.

The headmaster was in the middle of one of his perorations. He had seen a yobbo, an undesirable, beating his horse as he was delivering milk. The headmaster had felt obliged to intervene by pointing out that, if the man had been in the army, he would have realised that the horse always came first.

No self-respecting man, officer or other-rank, would think of eating or sleeping at the end of a march without seeing his horse properly groomed, fed and watered. They all had a duty to their dumb friends, coming next in line to their team, their school and their country, in that order.

Sometimes the headmaster spoke about parents, or guardians who had made such sacrifices for them and who they would be "letting down" if they did not work hard and play hard at Fairlight. Never, as far as Davis could remember, had there been any reference to when they grew up and got married, or about their future duty to their wives and children.

It was a very long time before Davis found out that girls played cricket. Fairlight was a cricketing school. He learned that cricket was "character-building" for boys and men.

By holding a straight bat, bearing the pain of a crack on the thigh, or a sting in the hand without "snivelling," they became, in some way, more worthy, showing Roman fortitude. Indeed, display of feelings of any kind except enthusiasm for school, or team was offensive. To show outwardly love, hate, affection, or compassion was bad form.

Girls did this. How then, could they play cricket? Unless, in some secret way, they were like men. In which case, they could legitimately become the objects of snigger.

God had made girls from men. Not from the spare rib, of course. That was nonsense. But Davis' teachers informed him that Genesis was a book of "great, hidden truths" and there was no doubt that God had made males first in his own image and, as an afterthought, brought about females for helpmates, destined to become either mums or tarts.

The college

Sports days were those rare occasions when mums, fathers, aunts, but not tarts, could come to Fairlight. Burbridge wore a straw hat and a Fairlight tie on that day and glowed with genial hypocrisy, patting the heads of the boys of his house as he moved around in the grand manner, offering tea and cucumber sandwiches to fawning parents.

Davis ran in the 440 yards. Mr. James lined them up on the track in staggered intervals.

"On your marks." They crouched like young panthers. Davis was wearing spiked shoes for the first time and could feel the little points biting into the ground.

Mr. James held the starting pistol aloft. It was always kept in the headmaster's study as "a dangerous weapon" to be fired only on sports day, with blank ammunition carefully checked and counted.

This, at last, was the real thing. Far off, round the curve of the track, was the finishing tape and a hassle of assorted masters with tickets for them all, right down to No.5 who would still get one point for his house just for trying. They knew who that would be before they started, the miserable Ferrers, forced to run.

They would all be waiting for him painfully to finish, and then they would clap him for a jolly good effort while some of them sniggered at the ludicrous spectacle of Ferrers hobbling home.

"Get set." They tightened their slender legs and Davis looked down momentarily. His number, on thin card in house colours, was pinned conspicuously, but slightly askew, to his vest. He could feel the summer breeze pulling his thin shorts.

The pistol cracked. He put all he had, was ever likely to have, for always, until death did him part, into his legs. He was on the inner lane and most of the others were in front of him at first. He liked it that way. It seemed a bigger challenge. "Always do the bad things first," aunt Grace had said. "Keep the good thing until last."

He did not remember passing Watson and Bream. Ferrers did not count. But Canning House had Scott, a terrier of a boy with short legs shifting him like a hare. All the odds were on Scott as they came up to the straight. Davis's short, slender legs were more suitable for the mile.

Time vanished for him. All thoughts of the parents, masters, the tea tent, the school, the tape itself disappeared from his mind. Only Scott remained. Davis felt he would burst. He did not know he had won until afterwards when old Brace, one of the decent masters, handed him the No.1 ticket.

"Well done, old chap. You've put Abbey House in the lead." He never forgot it.

With this and his cricket, Davis had redeemed himself. He had overcome the limitations of his background, forcing them to admit there were, as the headmaster put it, "some jewels in the muck heap": that not all who came from that part of the town were yobbos, loafers, arsonists and horse-beaters, but, given a decent education, some might serve.

"Of course," as he later confided to Burbridge, "if one only knew the facts, one would probably find an ancestor of noble blood who had sowed a wild oat or two that had ripened unexpectedly generations later."

chapter 3

The school

For McManus, education had been just as inadequate, but in a different way. His school had been a big, brick, three-decker one with gloomy stairways and rubber-covered treads like black mosaic, mounting, twelve at a time, until they reached a bleak landing before turning for another flight.

He knew there were twelve steps, because he used to count them like a religious ritual, one by one, while the prefects, stationed at each turn, ensured silence as the kids trudged up in single file from the playground below.

Whistles were blown to marshal them. It was one blast for a dead stop with frozen statues, mummified gestures in the middle of play. He enjoyed that.

Then, two blasts meant "walk". "Yes, walk and I don't mean run to your lines," the teachers used to shout. Three was to make your line straight, with arms extended. It was like soldiers, it was like Russia. It gave the teachers an easier time and invested them with the authority of block wardens.

There must have been 60 children in each class, or "standards" as they were called. Unless you obtained the required standard, you stayed in the same class.

Every week he had changed his desk, going up or down the grinning hierarchy, its pecking order freshly displayed. At the bottom of the class, until he left in a year's time, was a big lad who stuttered and made incomprehensible sounds. He was about 13 years old, while the rest were mostly three years younger.

McManus detested "sums". They were a nightmare to him. Every morning there were "tables" followed by coloured arithmetic cards. If he got them wrong – and this happened with regular frequency – he had to do "corrections" on Friday afternoons when the successful ones were rewarded with a story. He never heard the story in that class.

Large, high and dirty windows looked out across the smoking chimneys of innumerable rooftops that stretched as far as he could see, except on a clear day after a rain shower perhaps. It was then, miles away, he could just detect the vision of a small, green hill. If it wasn't the same one as that in Mrs. Alexander's hymn, "without a city wall," it deserved to be.

Shooters Hill, they called it, but it was as remote to him as Cathay.

Many of the teachers were "emergency-trained." They were men from the army, or navy with a year's course behind them so they could fill the gaps of war in the board schools. Ninety-eight per cent of the kids left at 14 for menial work. The few who gained apprenticeships had the status of doctors of science in other educational establishments.

Everyone feared one teacher among a fearsome lot. He had laid the foundation of his reputation years before. McManus had another nightmare when he heard that this teacher would be in charge of them.

Small, dapper, with clipped moustache, nothing pleased Mr. Lipman more than to sit on the teacher's table, his little legs dangling above the floor, cleaning his finger nails without bothering to look up, or making passes with his cane in broad sweeps, while 60 boys in platformed rows scratched with scrubby pen-nibs on their measured pieces of paper.

Every day with Mr. Lipman was the same, except on those blessed Friday afternoons when they could bring their own picture books to school.

War books were the most popular. There were artist impressions of French soldiers charging over the top killing Germans and showing something called their "élan," which nobody, including Mr. Lipman, quite understood.

It might have been their little peaked caps. Jack Sweet swore he knew what they were and drew them in on the picture, big and unmistakeable, in the right places, when noone was looking.

Then there was a picture of the English attack on Loos, showing tiny star-flashes of gunfire above the soldiers' heads, as the Germans, clutching their chests, fell in their death agonies.

These works were in great demand and were passed round with eager anticipation. Even Mr. Lipman, taking time off from his manicure to walk up and down between the desks, stopped and deigned to look. They knew they had the advantage then, his Achilles heel all exposed.

If only they could get him onto the war: not just on Friday book-times, but any time, even arithmetic time. At mental arithmetic time, he was vulnerable to the war.

Then he would digress and become recognisably human, as he dilated on the way "the Ities" had run at Caporetto and the English had to be sought to rescue them and how he, Mr. Lipman, had played this vital part in stopping the Boche, or Austrians, or someone, from "breaking through."

Once a week in summer time, when the black asphalt in the yard turned soft and gleamed in the harsh light, when there was a smell of dust on the plane trees and the glue-works became more noisome than usual, they were taken down for cricket.

They were marched downstairs through the girls' floor – mysteries, indeed – through the infants and out into the sun. A wicket was drawn in chalk on one wall, old bats and a sorbo ball were produced, and they were stationed, mute but alert, in fielding positions.

God help them if they missed a catch, or allowed the ball to pass between their legs. At those times, Mr. Lipman was pleased to show them, "How it should be done," by taking the bat, facing up to Jack Sweet, the best bowler in the class – like he had done to the Germans, McManus supposed.

Sloshing the ball far out of the yard, he grinned wolfishly at his own inveterate mastery of ball, bat and boy.

Because McManus was a slow sort, Lipman despised him while not being above taking the credit when, to everyone's astonishment, he passed the exam to go to the higher elementary school and became entitled to leave at 15. In fact, Lipman had taught him nothing.

It would be untrue, however, to say that the school had taught him nothing at all. Three occasions of learning he remembered, their impact matched by their rarity.

One was when Lipman was ill. The kids were overjoyed. They prayed he would never come back. As week followed week and he was still away, they thought he might even die.

Guardedly, they asked the headmaster how he was progressing, showing nice concern, and then they secretly rejoiced when given yet another week of reprieve.

It went on so long, another teacher had to be found, an old drudge of a chap, old Muffins, they called him.

He did not seem to be aware of the cankered remains of meals, half-consumed long before, that patterned the front of his black suit. There was a musty smell about him as if he slept in his clothes. In the afternoons, stranger smells still pervaded his presence, akin to those that came from the off licence shop down Harold Road. But he read to them.

He read Dickens' "Oliver Twist." And all alive it was. He altered his voice for the characters, Oliver and Bumble and Charlie Bates. They loved it. Old Muffins would come in again and again and try to teach them arithmetic and they would call out – an unheard of liberty – "Please, Sir, can we have more Oliver Twist," and he would look secretly pleased and, with some show of reluctance, take the tattered volume from his high-stooled desk and read on and on, while they listened to him entranced.

Mr. Cole, the headmaster, taught McManus the second thing. Mr. Cole was obviously a nice man. He had his big desk in the hall, with the classrooms all round from Standard I to Standard VII, Roman numbers.

Mr. Cole was stern, mind, but just. Boys were lined up and caned each morning and afternoon for lateness. There was no excuse. There were the first bell and the second bell that tolled across the town, and then – panic.

The school

McManus knew he would never make it on time, heart straining as he ran and ran, puffed to the wide. It must have been late for there was no-one about.

Then came the deadly silence as the bell stopped, its last clangour dying away into the dusty corners of the streets as he rushed past Mrs. Knight tottering out of the off-licence shop with her jug of brown ale and quite oblivious of an event that, to McManus, was comparable to the sinking of the Titanic.

He stormed up the flights of stairs, round each landing to the very top, broke though the swinging door of the hall, there to see the late boys already lining up.

Too late. No mercy was given or expected. It was hand up, bravely, for the stinging cut, but not, with Mr Cole, on the wrist or finger tips, because he was nice. With him, it was always straight across the centre of the palm, one for each time late, morning or afternoon, in that week.

Some, by Friday, taking their punishment like fairground automata, right hand, left hand, right, left, right, to the bitter end, not blanching one bit, were like our boys going over the top from the trenches in France in the war book pictures.

But Mr. Cole was a nice man and just. At 4 o'clock bell, he was off with his umbrella and spats to walk briskly down Harold Road to the railway station for the train that would take him to his home far away, to green grass and trees and the sea.

He must, they thought, have a fairy castle there. They knew he had a garden because he was always telling them about it. They had to learn his piece of poetry, which he taught to all the classes he took when a teacher was away.

>"A garden is a lovesome thing, God wot
>Rose plot, fringed pool, ferned grotte,
>And yet the fool contend that God is not,
>Not God, in gardens, when the eve is cool?
>
>Nay, but I have a sign,
>'Tis sure God walks in mine."

This piece of metrical junk had been embedded deep in McManus' brain ever since, like shrapnel from the bursting shells in the war books. It would take a hefty bit of leucotomy to remove it now.

He was taught one thing more. No doubt, there had been many other contributory causes. This was a love of history. On one occasion, McManus remembered, someone had actually prepared a lesson.

A student it was, though McManus did not know at the time. To him the new teacher was just a well-built and rather earnest young man. This man spent the time when they were at play and the other teachers were drinking tea in the staff room, drawing on their one blackboard, a coat of mail, a Norman helmet and a battle axe.

Visuals! An incredible innovation. The young man told them the story of Hastings, watched disdainfully by Mr. Lipman and a mysterious, elderly stranger who asked them questions afterwards. It was all a little solemn, but he had not forgotten it. It fed his imagination.

McManus, as an only child, lived in a world of this imagination. At the centre, he tried to pattern its fortuitousness. God was looking at him rather specially too. Each night on his knees he prayed for his mother, father, uncles and aunts, the neighbours, his few friends and himself.

God looked into his every deed and the times he sinned became seared into his soul like brand marks. Even now, he blushed to think of the time he wrestled with the devil in an empty classroom knowing that, in Tom Thorn's jacket, lying on the back of a desk, lay the one cigarette card he needed to complete the set of "English cricketers" – Wyatt, the batsman ready at the wicket to strike. And there it was, he knew, lying at the bottom of Tom Thorn's pocket in amongst dirty bits of string, stained marbles and a "milky" screw.

Dare he creep along the lines of empty desks and "nick it"? The rest of them at games would not be back for half an hour. It took him 15 minutes to make up his mind.

The big classroom clock ticked loudly and the leaves from the plane tree sadly scraped the window outside. His hand searched the pocket and found the card, the card that would complete the set, the card he had expected for weeks from Uncle George's packet of fags that he bought for him daily at the corner shop.

But the eye of the Great Jehovah was upon him and he was condemned for life never to forget.

In retrospect, though, there were for McManus some sun-drenched times of happiness when he scored for the cricket team. He had never made the first eleven, only rarely being called on as eleventh man when someone else was away, but he was useful to them as an interested and reliable scorer and followed the team to neighbouring schools in nearby streets.

Once, the school side had reached the final. At 4 o'clock, they were marched in twos by Mr. Rosser along the granite pavements, past terraced villas, down Belton Road where his grandparents lived, a long way, fully a mile, to the scrubby playing field near auntie Edie's corner shop.

Broken palings bordered the field, smelling of creosote and pirates. The field itself consisted of a patch of infertile gravel supporting tufts of coarse grass and thick bunches of camomile. It was the nearest open space to the school and most unsuitable for cricket, but the coconut matting was securely pegged down and the stumps shakily knocked in.

The teams were noisy and excited as they established their bases. Boys hid their fears by much bragging and little displays of mock prowess as they practised in the corner of the field like young soldiers before a battle.

The sun shone in the late afternoon as McManus lay down close to the tiny flowers of the camomile and the dust of the gravel and the smell of hot deserts as he wrote the names of the team in the score book.

"What's your team? Whose first in? Brooks and Stanley?"

"No, it's got an 'E' on the end of it – Brookes". He turned to a scruffy kid from their rivals, "And who's your bowlers – Wright and Thumper? Thumper? How do you spell it?"

"He's reel fast – got all Stock Street out for 15 last week." The miracle-worker looked as if he had been chiselled out of dirty ragstone, a chimney-sweep boy in another age. They were a tough side, no doubt about that. We would have our work cut out. What a comfort that he, McManus, would not have to measure up to the Thumper.

The captains tossed up and his side fielded first. Mr. Rosser placed the boys carefully. They did not know the positions by name, but had to be waved, or called into place. Once there, they stood like sentinels guarding a palace, each determined never to let an enemy ball past.

There was a silence like the minute before the whistles blew and their fathers had clambered over the top on the Somme.

McManus forgot who won on that great day. The match went on for a long time. In those days there were no limits on the number of overs, or the time it had to stop. He remembered they had battled on until the great gold sun dipped behind the forlorn elm by auntie Edie's shop.

But Mr. Rosser had come and stood by him when the match was finished and had looked at his score book. "How neatly done," he said. "And you've even worked out the bowling averages."

McManus had made no sign he was pleased. Teachers' praise, like teachers' canes, must always be ignored. But it was something he would not forget, that and the scent of the camomile in flower in high summer.

chapter 4

The Test

The two men in the car were silent as the cricket commentary rambled on. McManus continued:

"I think I was more protected than you were when we grew up. Not that we had more money, the reverse. But we lived in a very shut-in world, the world of the street. Streets in the East End of London were warm, comfortable places. There were street parties, like those for George V's jubilee.

"The street was like a village and the next street was a foreign country. After mum and dad, we loved the other kids in the street. They formed a tribe that you joined once you were let out to play at about the age of six and your membership lasted until you got to work at 14.

"We formed our own football and cricket teams and we felt looked after and cared for by the older kids. To us, the street became a mirror of what we conceived as the big world outside."

The voice on the car radio became animated. "How z'at – yes, he's been given out – no doubt about that decision."

Strange, thought McManus, how no man can be out unless there is an appeal. It was the green-painted lamp-post that came to his mind and a different Test match.

"How z'at?"

"It went above it."

"No it didn't. It just caught the top."

The Reunion

They were all clamouring and the clamour was part of the game. Every time the batsman missed it and the wicket-keeper missed it and the mangy tennis ball went on down the gutter, they argued about it.

Screwy took his batman's chance and ran to the cracked kerb that served as the bowling crease and then back to the lamp-post wicket as fast as he could go, counting the runs. He tapped the bat with deliberate determination at both ends, otherwise, they would argue it was a no-run.

"31, 32, 33 . . ."

He might just make one more while the dispute went on. Only little Springall – "Spring Onions", or straight "Onions" for short – was doing his best to chase it.

England was in a strong position. They only had 15 to make before the light failed. No umpire would call a halt to the match, but Mrs. Harris at No 24 would be first to come to the gate and she could have stopped armies in their tracks.

It would be, "Harry! I want you."

"All right, mum. I'm coming."

"Not later – now!" And Harry would be the first to retire to the "pavilion," but as the gas lighter came round, propped his ladder against the chamfered iron pillars, climbed up and lit the lamps with his long taper, one by one, along the street, the others would be summoned to duties equally pressing.

"Bob, granddad wants 'is paper and get some fags – ten Capstan."

"Ivy. Do an errand, there's a good girl. You can keep the change."

The change was a farthing for which she would get a strip of shiny, black, striped liquorice, or a hard, round, red "gob-stopper," neither to be despised.

Ivy, like little Onions, or big, goofy Ern, was always one of the last to be chosen by the English and Australian captains. Girls couldn't catch, handled the bat like a tennis racket and threw the ball quite unpredictably. In fact, they could well have done without Ivy altogether, but they were fed-up with seeing her watching disconsolately night after night.

The matches took place between teatime and nightfall, when the street became the Oval, Headingly, or Lords. You could take your pick. In summer, the boundary was marked by the lines of privet hedges, trimmed and neat, their small white flowers garlanding the medieval lances of iron railings.

At this time the Indian toffee man came to sell his sticky lumps to those whose mothers had not warned them of the dangers of eating the stuff. He gave them the toffee with thin, brown fingers, the nails startlingly white, and grinned conspiratorially as if he knew about the plagues, sores and spots he would transmit if you bought it. The risk was well worth taking.

With chalk, they marked the wicket on the lamp-post, picked their teams, tossed the penny and the die was cast.

"We'll bat first," said Tich Malloy. They all sought instant gratification and to "have a go" with the bat their chief delight.

That bat was something special. Only John McManus possessed one. He wasn't much good at the game, but he had the bat, and it conferred monopoly powers. Like a totem, the bat was worshipped by all. Genuine it was, with three springs. You could see them on the top in the cane handle, all miraculously part of the inlaid splice.

It was signed by the great Wilfred Rhodes just below. McManus' dad had mended it. 2/4d it had cost, a fabulous sum, but the splintered shoulder had been repaired with loving care. You could feel its spring when you faced up to the bowler, unlike the cheap replicas in the 6d stores, and it could actually hit a hard ball and not shatter.

"You'll look after it? And don't use it to bash the stumps in, except upside down with the handle. And don't throw it up in the air for tossing up," dad said, and McManus took dad at his word as he scraped off the old varnish with sandpaper and drenched it with linseed oil while carefully circumventing the splice. To him it gradually changed from an old brown veteran to a new shining musketeer.

It presented a problem though. It was too heavy for Ivy and little Onions to lift in time for the balls, especially when body-line Ginger showed off and ran 15 paces up to the cracked kerbstone before delivering one of his wild ones. Then, the ball might land in Mrs. Nancarrow's front garden where it was all swanky with flower pots above the porch.

This house had a name, not just a number like all the others. It said "Le Bonheur" on a little hanging plate that no-one understood but, somehow, did not seem to fit the occupier who sat behind her lace curtains in the front room, waiting to pounce.

When the worst happened, only the bravest dared to get the ball. After careful reconnaissance, he would dart through the wrought-iron gate, up the little path of crazy pavement and retrieve it from behind the privet before Mrs. Nancarrow caught him.

Sometimes the ball embedded itself in the hedge and was as elusive as any bird's nest to find. On these occasions, McManus was reminded of dad's stories when brave soldiers in the trenches threw back the grenade to the Germans before it exploded.

"One was blown to bits trying to do this and not a piece of him was left afterwards," dad had said.

"34, 35, 36 . . . .." England won that night. Screwy made the 48 runs and would have gone on and on, but Mrs. Harris and the other mums made their higher fealties very plain.

At home, inside, it was the nine o'clock news. The wireless was cracking up: not permanently, it needed a new valve, but it would be a week or two before dad could save the money. In the meantime, it grew weaker day by day like some pale consumptive as it caught and gave deceptive signs of improvement when first switched on.

McManus was disappointed. Henry Hall's dance band had finished and all that was left was the news. Big Ben struck. They counted all nine strokes. All that talk of Hitler and Mussolini did not count.

Would the wireless hold out until the big time? The fifth and last Test at the real Oval.

The Test

England were in trouble, certainly, right in the rut. Australia 475 for 2 wickets: Ponsford not out 206, Bradman out for a mammoth 244, bowled Bowles, caught Ames. All Test records had been smashed in a colossal stand by Bradman and Ponsford.

Dad groaned. "And it's no good, that body-line bowling, not fair," he commented as he put his ear close to the set. "They should bowl at the wicket, not at the man. First class cricket's getting just a matter of gate money, childish strife and back chat," he went on, "not like the old days."

McManus did not follow this too well and, anyway, he was thinking of other things.

"Dad, Squidger's dad has got a real leather ball. He says he'll lend us it for a game. We're wondering if we could go over the flats with it."

Pictures of Mrs. Nancarrow came to mind as he contemplated the possibility of a real leather ball in her garden. So catastrophic was this contingency, he promptly rejected it.

"What do you think, mum?" Dad always referred these matters to mum.

"Well, I don't know about that. I don't like him going all that way with some of them in the street." The flats were half-an-hour on the tram. There was a park nearer, but hard balls were not permitted there. It wasn't just the journey.

She could see some sore shins and broken fingers.

"Aw, come on mum. Squidger's all right and we can always pop in and see auntie Sue." He knew mum liked auntie Sue and she might even buy him the biggest luxury of all time, an ice cream in lemonade.

"All right, I suppose so. But it'll have to be Saturday afternoon and you must pay your own fare out of your pocket money." She sounded reluctant, but it would give her a chance to go with dad and get the glass mirror she needed for the room they were converting into a bathroom.

It rained right up to Saturday morning. The big day was almost called off. When the little group of ten – all that was left of the 20 or so who had promised to come –

The Reunion

got off the tram, the gravel flats were covered with countless puddles reflecting the ever-changing skies. Blots of inky cloud moved steadily above them like squadrons in formation for battle.

Far to the West, across stretches of tufted grass, a ray of misty sunlight slanted to the heath below from some half-obliterated heaven.

Squidgy had the ball, Screwy had the stumps, Ginger the bails, John McManus the bat. They had no eyes for the sky as they surged across the road from the tram stop. The unbelievable space gave speed to their legs and joy to their hearts.

The first task was to find a place in this waste where they could play. Twenty-two yards of hard, bleached soil, free from tufts, was difficult enough, but to reach agreement about it was well-nigh impossible. At length, by majority verdict, they settled for a piece of ground near one of the desolate copses.

The stumps were hard to fix and the bails continually fell off in the wind. "Oh, leave them off. Let's get started," shouted Squidgy. As he owned the ball and McManus owned the bat, they became uncontested captains.

They tossed up twice. The first result elevated McManus to lead England, the second gave the decision to bat first to Squidgy.

"Do you want a game?," enquired Harry from three scruffy kids who had drifted up and were looking on at all these preliminaries. After all, five a side were hardly enough to get anyone to field when they had sorted out the bowler, the wicketkeeper and, most vital of all, the man at long stop.

"We don't play first-class cricket," they jeered as they saw the hard, red ball and the springed bat.

"Please yourself."

Australia batted first and did well. Onions at long stop was much in demand. Bob ran back and forth through the puddle halfway down the pitch, piling on the runs, and did not seem to mind the hard ball at all. Ivy dropped a beautiful little catch as everyone groaned. The hard ball beat her long before it got anywhere near her tentative hands.

"41. Aren't you going to declare?" England were getting anxious and more than a little tired. "Give us a chance for a knock, we've got to be back for tea."

"What's the time, mister?" This to a grown-up passing by, who might just as well have been a visitor from Mars. "4 o'clock."

"We've only got half-an-hour," shouted England.

Oh, all right. We declare." They had reached 52 and it seemed safe enough.

"Well, hurry up then. Who's going in first? Onions, you go, then Ivy, then Harry, then me."

McManus left himself last. He felt more secure that way. It was a shame for Ivy and little Onions. All that way and not even to hit the ball, but Harry was a hard nut with plenty of grit. He was actually in the school team, second eleven, and played real cricket on coconut matting on the pressed cinders of the gas works ground.

Harry quickly assumed control. Not even the wild delivery of Ginger could daunt him and Bob, behind the wicket, let more and more through.

"Six byes," they roared as Harry religiously ran them out. "How many are we?"

"48." McManus had faithfully been keeping count.

"50 . . . 51," shouted Harry, triumphantly sending Squidgy's uncertain ball straight across the ditch into the copse.

"Lost ball," they yelled as there was a halt to the proceedings and Bob hunted around. When this happened, you crossed your fingers like "feign-its" and the war ceased for a time, like a truce to collect the wounded.

Squidgy took his time on the next one. Things were looking serious. He measured his steps carefully. He was just beginning to understand what his dad had told him about pitching the ball just in front of the bat – a good length, they called it.

He grasped the ball between thumb and forefinger. He was beginning to bowl well. The ball swerved in the wind as Harry confidently made his strike. It could not be. No. Yes, it was, right into Harry's off stump. 51 and England only needing two runs to win.

They would be all right though, with two batsmen still to go. But one was goofy Ern, who now took his place at the wicket like boy Cornwall at his gun at Jutland.

"Give us centre," he called, holding his bat sideways.

Squidgy waved his hand this way and that with imperious impatience.

"That'll do you. Play!"

The next one was really deceitful, a "Yorker," they said. "A full toss," they meant, that anyone could have sent to kingdom come. Trust Ern, though, to knock it right above the wicket from where it settled, slowly, comfortably, finally and without doubt into Bob's welcoming hands.

"'zat!" screamed Australia.

"Last man in," they shouted, as John McManus took the wonder bat from Ern at the crease. A hard ball and Harry were a fearful combination. He would play as dad told him. "A straight bat for all the straight ones and only hit the ones that are off the wicket, but hit them hard."

Yes, he could risk this one. It came down fast, but it was definitely too much on the off side. He hit it with a satisfying, hollow smack, good and hard, straight past Harry, on past Ginger, on and on to the tufts far, far away. And he ran 1, 2, 3, 4 . . .

"OK, lost ball." Australia were in despair.

"We won," roared England. "We won."

The Test

Dad and mum did not seem very interested when John McManus got back. They had not bought the mirror for the bathroom, it was too expensive. Mum's feet were killing her and her back was playing her up again.

On the wireless, the news was really bad. Hammond, with 43 for England, was the best and at 5.45pm precisely, Clark, the last of the English batsmen, had been clean bowled. Australia had won by an astronomical 580 runs and England had collapsed.

It was altogether a very poor show and dad was quite despondent, but McManus did not seem to mind. As the news announcer told them that Hitler had made another speech protesting he only wanted peace, dad got up and switched him off.

chapter 5

The unholy garden

"What you implied about the emotional coldness of boarding school is true, certainly it was for me. We had a matron who was efficient enough, but about as touchable as a leg of lamb from the freezer," Geoffrey Davis observed as they pushed on through a small country town.

It reminded him of his college, just off the High Street in a similar community of old coaching inns and a market square on the other side of London.

"Fairlight was a monastic place, as well as being a competitive one." As he said it, the yellow smell of stale cabbage and congealed grease, impregnated into the tables and walls, come back to him, arousing more disturbing memories.

"We had an exeat once a month in the sixth and, if we were careful, we could get to the big cinema at the other end of the town without being seen. In the darkness, there was a wonderful sense of sin for the price of 1/9d."

He paused and added, "Friendships sometimes became rather intense: to compensate, I suppose." He relapsed into silence.

It was the cherubic face that had first attracted him. Van den Heyden was a self-contained and imperturbable boy, and had rosy cheeks and blue eyes to go with it. These qualities combined together were unusual among a group of boys embarrassed by their misfeatured adolescence.

Davis had been some time in making the first tentative approach. "Did you see the Roland Colman picture at the Colosseum?," he ventured.

"What was it?"

"Something called, 'The Unholy Garden,' I think." He added the last, uncertainly, to show he did not place much importance on it.

"No, I don't go much. What was it like?"

"Oh, all right, I suppose, but it was rotten acting. All that swank. The turns were sensational last week though. There was Lew Stone with a bigger band, a magician and a high spirited act in the style of Elsie and Doris Waters. The turns went on for an hour between the pictures. There's a new organist as well!"

The English master, who connived at these visits, was encouraging them to criticise the shows and Davis rather fancied his hand at it. "Better not to go at the last performance though. It finishes too late to get back in time and the queue stretches right down the High Street, so you can easily get spotted."

He thought of the warmth and the subdued golden lights as the organ ascended slowly from some place of mystery below the orchestra pit, carrying up the dapper little man in evening suit sitting on its body like the driver of a monstrous elephant gradually getting to its feet. The glorious resurrection was accompanied by a signature tune that surged through the palace and wrapped everyone in the security of its familiarity.

"No, I don't go much. Not much time, really, what with games and loads of prep." Van den Heyden had looked away and lost interest.

With that puzzling name, Van den Heyden was undeniably different from the others. It intrigued Davis that he came from the same part of the town as the small group of yobs, all scholarship boys, who were frightening in their uninhibited rejection of the school when they were alone with the others.

The yobs wore the uniform after a fashion, because not to do so would be to be chucked back to the state school where they belonged. But even they had the wit to realise that, if this happened, their chances of a guaranteed, risk-proof, pensionable clerical job would vanish.

Their dropped consonants, slurped vowels and enviable proclivity for girls and fags and beer and jazz marked them off as being yob, and that was that.

He could not understand why they never seemed to take the thing seriously at all. They did not bother to wangle their chemistry results to get the equivalent weight of mercury by working it backwards, or struggle to swot up their irregular French verbs.

Even so, they were penetratingly observant and quickly saw through the small insincerities and deceptions of the others. It was as if, years before, they had concluded that the whole business of education was irrelevant, but had the wit to conceal it from the masters.

"What's he doing with 'is 'and in 'is pocket?," they'd say. "Playing balls, pocket billiards – wanker – we know." They were right as it happened and his blush had told them so.

Sometimes alone, or with one friend, on a Saturday evening, he risked a walk and bus ride towards the East End of London. It was as he imagined a Turkish souk to be.

In summer it was the smell that was strange and obtrusive. It consisted, in his mind, of a combination of sweat, dust, meat faggots, fried fish and chips with vinegar, contained in an unseen, but all-pervasive envelope of the stench of burning bones from the glue works, or boiling sugar from the sweet factory: smells that were already being identified in the posh papers as "offensive odours."

It hummed with people. Shuffling old women in shawls ambled between the "off-licence" and the attic with jugs of frothy, brown ale.

The unemployed collected in groups outside the betting shops, chatting about the latest runners. One or two read "The New Leader" and waited for the pubs to open. Chalked words were scrawled on the flagstones proclaiming the message, "Slaves in peace, cannon-fodder in war."

The pubs indeed were the centres of fun, with fights, organ-grinders with monkeys, alarming displays of juggling and fire-eating and sometimes the mournful howls of bagpipes with rattling drums played by blokes in dilapidated kilts and khaki jackets from the Great War.

There were small fairgrounds and cockshies and roundabouts that thumped, jangled and let off roars of steam as the painted concourse of horses, dragons and mermaids circled round unsteadily. It was only 2d a ride, but they often went round unmounted.

Strangers were the objects of suspicion. Women and kids stood at their doors, which were rarely shut, so that there was a constant interflow of aunts, grandmas and neighbours with their kids.

Davis always looked straight ahead as he heard the jeers from behind. He tried not to show how startled he was by the ragged and barefooted children who followed him, picking their noses, or gnawing slabs of bread and jam.

He would never ask Van den Heyden to go with him on one of these trips. Van den Heyden would despise him for going. But Van den Heyden came into his dreams. They were strange, ill-defined dreams associated with an itch of longing for Philip, the name he used as both boys gradually got to know each other more.

If Philip was not interested in the pictures on a Saturday, what did he do on Sundays?

"What about taking a tram to the Highwoods and having a walk in the gardens. Have you seen the glade. There are little hills in the woods there. They must have been made when they dug out the lake for the big house."

Hardly daring to expect an affirmative, Davis could feel an unexplained excitement. A lot seemed to depend on the answer.

"Could do, I suppose."

"How about next Sunday, then?"

"Can't come then. Corps in the morning and church in the afternoon."

"Well, what about the evening?"

"I'll see."

Philip came at six o'clock. It was expensive to Highwoods. 4d single, 6d return. There was a measured formality in boarding the tram. It was a kind of landship with the pilot in front, legs astride, steering and controlling the thing with polished grip handles. It swayed as it descended hills and then ground, protestingly, as it prepared to grapple with the long haul up the other side.

They paid down below "to save the conductor's legs" and climbed to the top before swaying and staggering to the front. Up in the forward fo'c's'le, where the seats were hard slats and the dried spit had become engrained in the grooves of the wooden floor, they could feel the breeze fresh in their faces.

The journey took half an hour. Davis had done it before, but it was still an adventure. He counted the stops and noted the road names. There was Connaught Road, South Esk Road and Windsor Road. As a young boy, he had written down their names, identifying them with the real places in Ireland, Scotland and where the king had a castle.

Then there were the pubs where the tram stopped: pubs with romantic names like the "King of Prussia," the "Eagle and Child," or the "Ship and Shovel". The "Princess Alice," be-starred and ribboned, showed herself proudly on her newly painted sign.

All the stops had their names printed on little rectangles of coloured paper, cleverly punched by the conductor exactly in the right place where you got on and off.

When they got off at the Highwoods, they walked on to gravel and pebbles stretching a mile to houses on the far horizon. A big notice, covered with innumerable prohibitions, told them the land belonged to the Lord Mayor of the City of London. It was hard to reconcile their image of this moneyed gentlemen in golden chains and ermine fur with the forlorn "flats" as the space was called.

The flats were slowly becoming a well of darkness as the light began to fade. It was deserted and this was appropriate. The houses of its perimeter were marked by a row of equidistant lamps and the tiny lake had become a dead pearl.

They walked in silence. There was only the pebbly crunch of their footsteps. An embarrassed awkwardness came between them. Did Philip feel a longing for him? If he could only touch his sleeve: if only they could be together for always, not just on the flats, but on some great voyage of discovery to the far steppes of Russia perhaps.

But nothing could be explicit. They rounded the hills and walked by the lake in the garden. In summer time, especially on bank holidays, crowds of people went there, with military bands and little boats to hire on the lake.

At night it became an unholy garden for couples who lay in the ditches surrounding patches of copse. Out of sight, below the flat levels, boys and girls made love. Exactly how, neither Geoffrey Davis nor Philip Van den Heyden were sure.

They got back on the tram, returning through a market where the night flares of Jewish vendors revealed knock-down prices at the end of Sunday trading. Had not Hitler classed them with gypsies, lunatics and homosexuals as scum to be eliminated from healthy society?

"You're late. Where have you been?" The senior prefect eyed them suspiciously.

"Only for a walk. We went to the Highwoods garden."

"Don't know what you want to go there for. A lot more places should be put out of bounds. Anyway, glad you're back. Just in time for supper."

Davis hated the cocoa and bread and cheese.

It was years later when they had met again. Philip Van den Heyden was married with kids. He had done well in the world, made mayor, not of London, but a goodly-sized suburban town, Conservative, of course. Another war had intervened.

Philip, as a young infantry officer, had caught it in the back on patrol, the second night in action in Algeria. But he was all right now – fine! There was a vision of Philip in his mayoral robes with nice, warm fur and the never-revealed longing of the walk in the garden. The guilt had gone years ago.

There came a comical thought of rolling around with Philip on the carpet of the mayor's parlour warmly enmeshed in that fur, but only for an instant.

"The whole country's gone to pot in more ways than one," Philip was saying.

"People are having it off – swinging, they call it round here – like so many rabbits.

And as for those homosexuals, why do they call them 'gay?' In my time it meant something different, proper meaning of the word then.

"I've got no time for them. Poncing about, dramatising themselves. Bloody revolting, if you ask me. I'd let them have it hard, where it hurts most, right in the goolies, if one of them came near me."

chapter 6

Wealth is life

McManus broke the silence between them: "I hope you don't think I was starry-eyed about war like a leftover from the days of Rupert Brooke. The first war was too close to us for that. We had seen films about the Somme and had listened to men who had gone through it and somehow survived. Some of us were approaching political maturity and had begun to give up the simplicities of Communism and Fascism by the time it all happened."

They had got on their way much too early and McManus was talking over a cup of tea. They were savouring the time together away from home.

"I can pinpoint the period when I began to understand a little of what it seemed to me to be all about. Leaving school at 15, I was denied the chance of forming my ideas systematically."

"Once you start, you'll have to go on." John McManus had been hearing that sort of advice as long as he could remember. It was the counsel for inaction. This time it was about shaving.

"The hairs will thicken and, instead of once a week, it will have to be once a day." McManus thought of uncle Ned where it was every twelve hours to keep himself smooth for the girls. "Well, if you must, you'd better use the safety I bought from Boots. I can't get used to it."

Dad had tried, but nothing compared with the shiny concave blade he stropped daily on a leather hanging from its big hook in the new bathroom. Selecting judiciously one of the two blades snugged in their velvet case, he would stroke it ten times up and down, no more and no less, with a swan-like movement of the wrist every day, except Sundays, at precisely the same time.

The Reunion

He would lather his face with the soft ivory brush, screw himself round the light and poise for the first, artistic, incisive cut and the satisfaction of a good clean shave.

Routines like this assured him of the purpose of life.

"And don't touch your blackheads. Leave them alone."

McManus looked at the face staring back at him in the mirror, and poked his tongue at it just to make sure the image did likewise. Those unseemly dribbles of hair on the upper lip and the revolting pimples disfiguring his nose would have to go no matter what Dad said.

It was 7.00am and autumn time. The mist outside had crept into the bathroom where new pale-grey lino made it colder still.

Dad was downstairs reading the Daily Herald and eating his third and last slice of bread and jam. He always prepared his breakfast the night before: teapot with two spoonfuls, three cut slices of bread, the jam preferably blackcurrant. It was the same every day, except Sunday.

He left the house at 7.50 to catch the last train of the day to attract a cheap, workman's fare.

John McManus never had much time for him. He seemed so obtuse. He read that ghastly paper and was sitting, as predicted, watching the clock when John got downstairs.

"Take your mother a cup of tea after I've gone and think carefully before you give up that job at Johnsons."

"But I've got this job at Bartletts and it's better than Johnsons."

"So you say, but always consider very carefully before turning any job down, or changing it." To have one job and then be offered another was almost beyond his comprehension.

"I can't have two jobs."

"Don't give me cheek. I'm just saying weigh it up carefully. I must go."

He looked at the clock again. It ticked away inexorably to 7.50 and it was right. He always checked it with the nine o'clock news the night before. "And, keep the fire in before your mother gets up."

The front door slammed as McManus poured a cup of tea and glanced at the headlines. "Italians revenge Adowa. Haile Selassie withdraws." Uncle Edward, in tin on the stock market and with a posh house on the London outskirts, had no time for the blacks.

"I heard the other day what they do to Italian prisoners," he told dad when they had gone to see him the previous Saturday. He was careful to ensure that mum and aunt Sue could not hear.

"They cut off the genitals and hang them up before the prisoners' eyes before putting them to death, the hideous barbarians. The Italians are only getting their own back and they've brought law and order to the place for the first time. We could do with Mussolini here at times."

John McManus agreed. Hard work, regular discipline, sound military government would restore order to the wild tribes and allow decent economic development. There was a lot to put right here too. He and David, a friend from Johnsons, had gone for fun to a political meeting at the Public Hall, a red brick Victorian monstrosity, its stained steps dingily lit by low-volt bulbs.

Outside two stalwarts of the opposing parties vied for attention. "Action 2p" from the Blackshirt was echoed by "Fascists Plot" from the Daily Worker.

It was a meeting of the Independent Labour Party. A graceless troupe of comrades had taken their places behind folding tables and red posters, utopian and splenetic. "Food for the Workers. A Fair Wage for Fair Work." David sneered.

"Work? They don't know what it means."

The chairman silenced the chat and scraping chairs. "The proceedings will begin with an address by comrade Grierson." Comrade Grierson stooped to his feet, his brown suit and red tie stained with grease, his hair flop giving his hands a useful gesture to aid the rhetorical pause.

It was a soft, stroking voice that asked them to consider the evils of capitalism. The argument was forceful and sustained.

It was a prelude to comrade Hertz who stood after the applause and poured out passion and spleen. "There are two classes," he shrieked, "the working class and the ruling class. Take the rifles handed to you and make yourselves acquainted with their use, for it is necessary that, from the capitalist war of imperialism," – he lingered on the word and tortured it – "shall come the civil war against the bourgeoisie."

The audience remained unruffled. It was barren soil for raising class-consciousness.

A lowering "cap and muffler" looked around disdainfully and left the speaker to his raving. He made an irreverent gesture at the door. The others stayed inside apathetic and unmoved. It was warmer there and Friday night had mopped up the spare cash for drink.

McManus despised the speaker and all he stood for. He searched for a man of vision with the will to lead, someone like the great heroes when Britain was respected in the world, like Drake, or Nelson, or Scott, a British Mussolini to inspire the will to work for a cause and not to count the cost.

He hated the workers who did not work and the intellectuals driven by envy. The way ahead seemed simple and direct.

He was an office boy at Johnsons. "It's steady. As long as you behave yourself, you've got a job there for life with a good pension at the end of it. Well paid too." Dad approved of it.

The pay was £100 a year. It worked out to about £1.11s a week and did not compensate overmuch for the times he left at 8.00pm to despatch the post when there was a lordly extra of 1/6d for tea. You could wear a sports coat on Saturdays though and leave at 12 midday on alternate weeks instead of 1.00pm.

He took messages, wrote out the envelopes in his best handwriting, stuck on the stamps, writing each address in the big postage book with the cost of each one – 1d for letters, 1/2d for postcards, all to be balanced at the end of the week.

The postcards said, "Dear Sir, I acknowledge receipt of your letter of the 12th ultimo which will receive our attention." Copies of these went to the pending tray of the under-manager and stayed there for a very long time, McManus thought.

He also turned the big copying machine, rather like mother's mangle. All letters and orders went through it and their copies had to be filed and indexed in the big red binders the next day, a task that never ceased, like painting the Forth Bridge.

But of all these tasks, the most important was undoubtedly the making of tea.

There was a tea book with 20 names, 6d a week from each subscriber. By care and adding a few pence of his own, he could be well thought of by the others if he gave them a milk cracker and an extra cup from the slender profits.

On Sundays, he stayed in bed like everyone else and read. Mother had the Boots 2d lending library for the endless novels she consumed. McManus used the public library. Great tomes there were, all mixed up and half digestible. "Shelley and the Romantics," "A New Background to Science," "Ancient Man In Britain."

Later in the day, he might put Wagner on the wireless at full blast and struggle with Einstein's theory of relativity at the same time.

No wonder mum complained when you thought of it. "Turn that thing off. You can't really like it. It goes right through your head."

Things were always going through Mum's head. If it wasn't Wagner, it was Mrs Hopkins next door, or the coal man tipping sack after sack of shiny nuggets into the huge cellar under the house like the avalanche of a black volcano.

"David and I are going up to Toynbee Hall tonight to hear a talk."

"What's it about?"

"He says there's a man call Tawney giving a talk about philosophy. It's all free."

The Reunion

"Just the two of you?" Mum was always suspicious. "No girls going with you?"

"No, honestly. Not interested." They were interested, of course, but hardly dared reveal their secret thoughts, the one to the other, let alone tell mum.

"It's a long way. You'll have to change trams twice."

"I've been up that far before."

"Mind you're back by 10 at the latest. Promise? I worry about you. It's right near Limehouse and the Chinese gangs. Goodness knows what they get up to, taking people off the streets and into opium dens."

The 2d novels thrived on it. "All right, then." She pecked him on the cheek to confirm her possession.

From the top of the tram you could see the serried lines of grey plumes from terraced chimney stacks. The evening pall thickened as the coal stocks from each cellar were expended. Near the river the fog was thicker. Ships passed like grey ghosts on their way to the spume and rain of the North Sea and the high tide sucked at damp piers.

"Workers Education Association," it said on the pamphlet when they got there. The words were anathema to McManus. The audience was depressing too. More unemployed "caps and mufflers," some clerks and shop assistants, a few artists from the club upstairs. No more than 30 all told, they sat whispering among themselves.

John McManus and David moved into the back for a quick escape if necessary. The noises of the street could be heard through the grubby fanlight. A big man, middle-aged, untidy in dress, but ordered in mind, appeared before them. Professor Tawney had come from Oxford to speak.

"Have you read his book, 'Religion and the Rise of Capitalism'?"
whispered David, who had just borrowed it from the library and found it hard going. McManus shook his head.

The voice had a persuasive and compassionate warmth. There were confident sweeps of history with telling illustrations. Some of it was autobiographical, about life as a sergeant in the trenches in the war. The man's grace and humility shone through. McManus was fascinated and reconciled.

"Capitalism is that whole system of appetites and values with its deification of the life of snatching to hoard and hoarding to snatch, which seems sometimes to leave a taste as of ashes on the lips of a civilisation that has brought a conquest of its material resources unknown in earlier years, but that has not yet learned to master itself. There is no wealth, but life."

The last phrase stuck. They sat for a long time in silence looking out from the rain-slashed windows of the tram on their way back home, past the cobbled streets, the pubs, caverns of throbbing light bursting with energy, the gas lamps flaring from the Jewish market.

"Adam is going to the Fascist rally next week at the public hall. You going?" David seemed uncertain about it himself.

"No. I don't think so."

chapter 7

Job vacancy

Davis had been listening with some surprise at his friend's account. "I got around more than you did. I was 18 when I went into my first job, an articled clerk in the Town Hall as aunt could no longer afford the fees at school. I was soon involved, strange as it may seem, in air raid precautions.

"This was regarded as a new and unwelcome intrusion into local government at the time and treated disdainfully at first. However, it gradually assumed more and more importance until it came to swallow up most other aspects of work once the war really got going.

"It was a time when I became aware of the tribal feelings of a nation rather than that of a street. Nowadays they call it racism, though it wasn't the blacks they focused on then as scapegoats."

"How do you mean?"

"It came up when there was a vacancy in the office once. It is hard to convey the slow pace of the time and the incredibly stilted language, a sort of tranquillising legalese designed to keep things ticking over gently with the minimum of change.

"In my mind comes the picture of a large, black cat, everyone's pet in the office. It roamed everywhere and symbolised the sleepy, gentle, quietness of the place.

"One day, it found its way, for the second time that day, into the council chamber. It had been summarily ejected once, but Mr. Love, bustling in with more files, opened the polished oak door and back came the cat. It leapt with an eager spring onto the mayor's table where it proceeded to play disdainfully with the fire chief's papers – a clear case of 'lèse-majesté'."

"Mr. McGregor, the chief fire officer, was a big teddy-bear of a man, as slow and comforting in speech as he was in movement. He tolerated the cat, liked it even, and the cat obviously got on with him as it clambered on his neck. He let it nestle his ear before propriety insisted he put it gently back on the table. There it finally stretched itself, tugged lazily at the chairman's coat, curled up and went to sleep.

"Only a corner of the council chamber was needed on Wednesday afternoons. It was always generously heated in winter and the cat's rhythmic purr was a fitting accompaniment as the fire chief took his pipe from his mouth with pensive deliberation and began.

"'In accordance with your Committee's instructions dated the 10th January, 1939'. He started to use the officialese designed to be one stage more carefully non-committal than the Home Office memorandum that had instructed them to instruct him two years before.

"The air raid precautions committee could only muster five members in the afternoon, the rest were at work. Two unemployed men and two housewives were there and Councillor Cook, the chairman, had managed to escape from his wife and his small shop for a few hours. He was the only one who took the proceedings seriously.

"Labour had held an unbreakable majority for as long as could be remembered and many members were pacifist at heart opposed to giving time to Anderson shelters, sand-bags, gas masks and the like when big problems of slum-clearance and the unemployed were facing them daily.

"It was lucky in a way that Councillor Cook of the minority party was willing, not to say eager, to be chairman of air raid precautions. He had been a major in the Service Corps in 1918, supplying the troops with sardines, so it was rumoured.

"Miss Salmon, who minuted the proceedings, whispered to the town clerk as the fire chief droned on.

"'Do you want me to put all this down?'

"The town clerk shook his head slightly. 'No need.' He knew they would pass the report without much discussion while congratulating Mr. McGregor who had been with them for a long time. It would not cost them much money and what they did spend could be nearly all recovered from the Home Office. They might even get away for tea. 'But just get rid of that confounded cat. Put it right outside and see it doesn't come back again.'

"The town clerk agreed one could not take the whole matter of air raid precautions very seriously. What had Chamberlain said? It was horrible – fantastic – incredible that we should be digging trenches and trying on gas-masks because of a quarrel in a far-away country between people of whom we knew nothing, and certainly impossible that a quarrel that had been settled in principle should be the subject of war.

"However much we might have sympathised with a small nation confronted by a big and powerful neighbour, we could not in all circumstances undertake to involve the whole British empire in war simply on her account. If we had to fight it had to be on larger issues than that.

"Chamberlain's umbrella, the crest of peace and island security, had become the new watchword of the year to rival Gracie Fields and Shirley Temple. It was the butt of comedians and cartoonists. A museum in Italy wanted it to go on display with its Roman statuary. By it, peace was promised 'in our time' and the umbrella was a much more sane and sensible a symbol of the future than any bundle of Fascisti rods.

"The town clerk left the meeting to Miss Salmon with the excuse that he had so much to do. The members nodded their approval sympathetically. They did not know of the custom he had, just before Christmas each year, of looking through the pile of files on his desk accumulated over the year. It had reached nearly a foot high last time.

"'That one can go down to the vaults,' he would say to the deputy. 'It's settled itself. This, we'll have to keep alive for the time being, but they'll give up if we stall for another two months.'

"Like many a good lawyer, he was a firm believer in delay until pushed up against the wall and, for years, the policy had undeniably been vindicated, time and time again. His retirement was due in a year or so. His digestion had already suffered, badly affected by the gross impatience of some of the younger members and, to add to it all, there was this ridiculous business of air raid precautions. Like Chamberlain, he found the dark, irrational heart of man disturbing and unbelievable.

The Reunion

"'We shall have to complete the High Street widening next year though,' responded the deputy. 'Traffic densities are increasing out of all proportion in spite of the effect of driving tests!'

"It was just about as humorous, he reckoned, as the town clerk could bear. He was anxious to succeed when the old man left, had allied himself with the awkward, thrusting group on the council without going too far.

"The council always rewarded loyalty. 'Oh, by the way, I've taken on a new shorthand-typist. The committee have agreed. This ARP stuff is growing and the Home Office are expecting another huge return on fire precautions. McGregor 'phoned me last week saying the Minister was pressing. There are only 30 authorities who have still to send in their proposals and he's produced something at last.'

"'I'll leave that to you. Who is she?'

"'A little Jewess, as a matter of fact, mildly crippled, which helps us on the disabled thing, but highly qualified. She's got our equivalent of Higher Schools, as well as good shorthand.'

"'You're sure she'll fit in?' The town clerk was not really bothered, but had registered a slight tic of surprise. He belonged to the golf club, which would not let them in at any price.

"'Oh yes, I think so, she's an unobtrusive little thing.' The deputy was patronising as well as being progressive. Only that week he had run a meeting of the town's cinema managers. Now, there was a Jewish lot. He had been trying to get them to run an ARP week. They had explained the difficulties. Had he remembered Baldwin's fund week when they had lost ten per cent of their takings to help German refugees?

"The thought of disturbing audiences with ARP displays was daunting. It would mean chaps lumbering about in the auditorium dressed up in oily, yellow capes, grinning inanely through gas masks looking like some monastic order from Mars. Some of the managers had felt it necessary to go on the platform before the 'turns' to explain that subscriptions were meant for all refugees, gentiles as well as Jews. Outside, the Fascists proclaimed with placards that they were against helping the Jews.

"Any spare money around should go to help our own unemployed. There was no doubt that this message was popular.

"Helen Katz, the new typist, started the following Monday. Office hours began at 9.00, but she was there waiting a good half an hour before. It was a bad start. Miss Salmon always took some time in the cloakroom before she sat down at her typewriter to wait for Mr. Love's double buzz and the daily dictation.

"The cloakroom was where she met Miss Cooper who liked the chance for a cosy chat before work with someone of her own age. It made such a change from her elderly mother at home.

"'I hear she's Jewish.'

"'Katz is the name. It can't be anything else.'

"'I don't mind, but they can be so thrusting.'

"'Fancy getting here as early as that. The post isn't opened till ten and Mr. Love never starts dictating before half-past.'

"'I'll have to tell her about it.'

"Miss Katz was about as demure as they came. Small, dark, with eyes full of poetry, she was so eager to help. If you watched her closely, you noticed her handicap. Her keenness to move, help and learn was hindered by just the hint of delay as one foot left the ground. She tackled the work with a speed that left the others standing and, as well as that, she could spell difficult words like 'incident' and 'emergency.'

"'We shouldn't have to type all these things about the public baths,' exclaimed Miss Salmon. 'Do you know what it says here?' She interrupted Miss Cooper who was still looking at the displaced wisp of hair in her mirror.

"'They reckon, within the first ten minutes of an air raid warning, they'll be dropping bombs and gas and there'll be hundreds of dead people, so that they'll have to use the baths as mortuaries so as to wash the bodies down.'

"'Disgusting,' agreed Miss Cooper. 'I don't like all this ARP work. It was much better when I worked for the mayor. He actually asked me to do a lot of the work on the reception myself.

"'I got the flowers for the mayoress at Jacks, you know them? They do marvellous bouquets as well as funeral offerings.'

"Not only was Miss Katz first in the office, she was often the last to leave – 6.00, 7.00, 8.00 at night. The others could not reconcile their sense of duty with such bizarre behaviour.

"'I don't mind staying for Mr. Love for half an hour after five,' Miss Salmon put the point clearly. 'And I don't think we should claim overtime for helping to give out gas-masks. After all, Mr. Chamberlain said it was a national emergency. It might even stop them using it. But, she shouldn't be staying all that time. It's not as if it can't wait. Who's going to thank you for it anyway.'

"The office staff mostly agreed. 'Do you think she likes dramatics?' posed Miss Cooper, who was rehearsing the lead in a performance of A.A. Milne by the office dramatic society. They had not yet found a replacement for Miss Platt who had been doing the maid and was certainly keen, but could never get the ginger wig to stay on straight when the hero's cue, 'Dash it all, old man, she's not that sort,' brought her on stage and it flopped over her left eye, distracting to Miss Platt and to the audience. When it said 'tripped,' she thumped across the boards and when she ran, she toppled.

"They both considered this carefully before rejecting it. It would save them feeling guilty about Miss Katz doing all that extra work, but with her slight limp she would have more problems than Miss Platt and, besides, there was that Jewish/German accent.

"The next day some of them heard Roosevelt on the wireless. It was the speech to Congress, relayed on the BBC. The applause came over in distorted waves of sound. There was a mild fade-out as he spoke of the need to help the European democracies against the totalitarian regimes, but the loudest clapping came when he reached the bit about the need of economy in the administration.

"Darkness came early at that time of year. Outside, it had turned sharply cold again and more snow flakes drifted in from the east, settling silently on the brown mush splattered by the High Street traffic.

"In the side streets the snow was hard packed and glinted with tiny spangles in the lamplight. It was 4.30, the first of the letters had gone through to the town clerk for signing and the office boy was serving tea. He was bringing round those nice new Bourbon biscuits. They loved the crispy chocolate with the cream centres.

"Suddenly, there was a fracas of noise and the sound of raised voices. The door marked 'Enquiries' was thrust open. Twelve unemployed benefitmen, as they were called at the time, erupted into the small anteroom of the main office. Most of them looked sheepish and ill-at-ease, but their spokesman banged his fist on the counter.

"'We want to see the town clerk.'

"Miss Salmon and Miss Cooper were aghast.

"'You can't see him, he's busy,' said the hall porter. 'What's the trouble?' The UB men had brought a crude reality into the room. Some were stamping their feet with the cold and had not yet accustomed themselves to the warmth of the office.

"'We want to see the bastard,' they exploded.

"'Wait here. I'll find out if he can spare the time to see you. The hall porter knew he wouldn't, but some pretence had to be made in the face of such language before ladies. 'Would you mind waiting while I see if he is free?' He was polite. There were twelve of them. He went to the inner office.

"'What appears to be the trouble?,' inquired the chief clerk.

"'I understand they were used to clear the snow this morning, Sir, and, now the snow has given out in the High Street, they've been paid off.'

"'Well, what do they expect? They get a better dole now.'

"'If we weren't lumbered with all these Jews, there'd be less of all this and more jobs for the rest of us. There's nothing I can do about it. The rules are perfectly plain. The town clerk certainly can't see them.'

"'Would you come and see them then, Sir?' The hall porter was anxious. A stone had been thrown outside.

"'No, tell them the town clerk is in committee and they must put their case to the ward councillor. If they don't leave quietly, you'll have to threaten them with the police.' He bent his head down to the file on cinema licences.

"I was astonished they left so quietly, muttering to themselves. They were so docile. Perhaps the wait in such unfamiliar surroundings had made them apprehensive. The office had returned to normal and began to get ready to go, but the office boy would make a fresh cup of tea for those who wanted it.

"Miss Katz had been standing outside the glass partition that guarded the chief clerk's office. It could be embarrassing sometimes when you could so easily be overheard, when, for instance, Mr. Love got angry on the telephone expostulating over the scheme for new road names. Councillor Hudson had made it quite clear he wanted 'Hudsons Road' and not 'Park Rise' which was the borough engineer's preference.

"At 10.30 the next day, Miss Katz still had not arrived.

"'Can't understand it, she's usually so early,' exclaimed Miss Cooper who had just been given even more ARP typing to do. 'At least she might have rung.'

"We were not to see Miss Katz at 10.00, 11.30, or ever again. Nobody on this earth would see her a year later.

"Enquiries at the hostel where she lived revealed she thought she ought to go back to her parents in Germany. All efforts to dissuade her had failed. She seemed to be under the illusion that she was not wanted. 'So funny,' they said, 'when we told her she was doing such important work.

"In any event there was another vacancy for a shorthand-typist."

chapter 8

The birthday party

The M4 opened before them. From now on it would be an easy run to the west. There had been silence between them for some time. They remembered their innocence and how the war had brought it abruptly to an end.

Each generation is haunted by fear of the future when it begins adulthood. Sometimes these anxieties are so acute that they dare not be expressed and remain beneath agitated distractions like sex, or drugs, or fierce efforts to keep fit. Others turn to yoga, or meditation for induced tranquillity. God knows, this generation had something to worry about.

It seemed to John McManus that the sun became obscured as he spoke. "The shadow of what was to come was with us for a long time, from when I was about 15, I should say. Being an only child, I read a great deal, listened to radio talks, clung to the hope that it could never happen again, not after the First War."

"We had the two minutes' silence when everything stopped," responded Geoff Davis. "It was always in the middle of the service in chapel at school. We looked up and saw the names of the fallen on the roll of honour. It was made clear to us that we could not possibly ever be as fine, brave and noble as the chivalrous knights who had scrawled their names on our desks and later had 'laid down their lives' for us like Jesus Christ.

"That had been the war to end war. Nobody would be insane enough to start another one, unless they wanted to profit from armament sales, or made some kind of horrible miscalculation. Nobody conceived of the idea that there were people who could actually enjoy killing."

"Yes, there were certainly some like that, psychopathic snipers, I remember," agreed McManus. "They came into their own in war. But going back to what we mentioned

The Reunion

earlier, I don't think we grasped the idea that, before it all began, in some inescapable way, we shared the common guilt. Our innocence and ignorance colluded with the events to come.

"Even when I was 21, I was about as socially advanced as an American eight-year old today. I can distinctly remember my 21st birthday party, a comment on innocence if ever there was one. Mother had spent days before preparing for it.

"Auntie Edie was the first to arrive. It was hot that summer and she suffered from asthma.

"Anyway, that was the excuse for coming in the afternoon and leaving early, but everyone knew that she did not want to meet the other side of the family. They were 'too stuck-up' for her. She gave me three handkerchiefs and it must have cost her two days of her widow's pension.

"'Who's coming?', she wheezed.

"'Well, there's his aunt Ethel and uncle Harold, aunt Maisie and uncle Ernie. They want to come and join the young ones. Harold thinks he is good at table-tennis and can knock spots off John's friends,' mum replied hurriedly, wanting to get on with the final preparations.

"She was all in a flurry. They had cleared the back room that opened onto the tiny enclosed garden, but there was still all the sandwiches to cut for the tinned salmon, not to mention the peaches and cream for 'afters'."

"It was a fine summer. The grass in the garden had just been cut by dad's push-and-pull mower that needed sharpening. It had left a lot of bents standing, whispy silver straws in the evening light.

"The cut grass had fallen in places on the little concrete path, carefully segmented to make it look like the crazy paving that everyone admired. Only the newly dug Anderson bomb shelter, freshly implanted by the wall at the end of the path, broke its symmetry. Winged insects darted about, hopping up and settling down. Sometimes they hit the path with inaudible bumps like tiny aircraft out of control. When they landed, they rolled lazily on one side and pawed at the sun with their hair-like legs.

The birthday party

"The presents consisted of half-a-crown from granddad who was looking forward to seeing the girls, and a Royal Artillery tie from mum to proclaim that I was in 'The Terriers.' They all admired the zig-zag pattern as really flashy!

"The combined clock and lamp in serpentine stone came from uncle Ernie. Good art-deco it was called, years later, in the junk shop. The best gift was Beethoven's Seventh Symphony, the latest HMV on six sides with Toscanini frenetically conducting. Dad could not stand it when it played and thought my enjoyment was a load of 'swank'.

"When it got to the fifth side, he insisted it was turned off.

"At 7 o'clock the young people began to arrive. There were embarrassed silences as they were introduced to the adults. Babs came with a flimsy veil from her hat, half concealing eyes deceptively coy. Clem, a fellow 'Terrier', showed his vigour by sporting a pipe and making his eyes flash when meeting mum.

"Violet was shy and secretive and not very forthcoming about her new good job as typist. Bob and Daisy came together, already like a long-married couple having met at school. They would be together for ever and ever and share the same grave. Their exclusiveness was sealed by a dozen glances and small gestures by which they declared their arcane knowledge of mysteries beyond our ken.

"Jean came in a saxe-blue frock with large, inviting metal buttons on the breasts. Her eyes were so radiant, she must have used make-up, mum noted.

"Last of all and someone special entered: Pauline, perky, lively, straight-from-the-shoulder Pauline, already thinking of joining the WAAF. She had her hair tied in a small silk bow at the back and frizzed out in an impertinent little coxcomb in front. When she laughed, she screwed her face into an even smaller circumference and became button-mouthed and dimple nosed.

"Bert came with her. He listened to the others and did not say much himself – ever, a good bet for any girl. He had reacted so, I've no doubt, when he was spinning down over Mannheim as a rear gunner in those last few seconds of consciousness two years' later.

"'What have we got to drink?'

"'Dad's got some cider.' There was a chorus of naughty laughter.

"'And we've fixed up the dartboard.' Safer ground this and mum and dad had spent a lot of time arranging it to stop the darts going into the wallpaper. 'And there's the gramophone. I know you young people want to be on your own, so we will go into the other room. But don't make too much noise, because old Mr. Butler is next door and he can hear everything through these walls.'

"The adults went at last, though granddad seemed reluctant to leave them. The young acknowledged this bounty with deference and politeness. Not to have done so would have appeared ungrateful and appearances were what you were judged by – clothes, speech, clean fingernails, polished shoes, creamed hair, how you said 'please' and 'thank you', all these and much more besides mattered a great deal for getting on in the world.

"Bob and Daisy were together, of course, in the same team for darts. He was an apprentice lighterman with some practice in the dockside pubs and they won easily.

"'How about forfeits?'

"'I never know how to do that.'

"'It's ever so simple,' said Vi, who was gaining confidence with the cider. 'If you lose, you have to pay a forfeit.'

"They all joined sitting in a ring and passed the bundle. Each time the gramophone stopped, the unlucky one paid his forfeit. The game had not changed since the parties they all remembered as young children when they played ring-a-ring-a-roses, or oranges and lemons. Just the prizes had changed.

"By the time Pauline had collected the forfeits, they had tired of the game. She was the last one and would go into the big, dark clothes' cupboard outside the room and, by touch alone, would guess the boys who came to claim them back. No-one could stay long because the others would wait their turn outside.

The birthday party

"I knew I would touch her for one precious moment. I would kiss the button mouth and dimple nose, feel her small white shoulders in the dark and maybe fondle the dear, small breasts made of skin so softly flawless that no pores could possibly exist.

"In the darkness I groped and found her. She was surprisingly responsive as I kissed her clumsily and without knowledge. I could feel her small hands gently on my neck. Her powder smelt a little of sweat.

"'Can you come out with me one evening?,' I whispered hoarsely. 'Love to. Which evening?'

"'What about next Friday, outside the Odeon?'

"'What time?'

"'Er'm, half past six all right?'

"'I'll be there.'

"The others were making cooing noises now. I reluctantly and gently left her and adopted my sophisticated and knowing look when I got outside.

"By ten o'clock they had all gone. It was late and there was the clearing-up to do. Tomorrow was Sunday and dad, needing his 'lie-in', did not want to face it then. As they went up to bed, he turned to me with the magic pronouncement, 'You can have the key of the house now.'

"I was 21, a grown-up at last.

"With the key came something more daunting on Monday morning. It was a pale-blue official foolscap envelope baldly addressed to 'J. McManus. On His Majesty's Service.' In the top left-hand corner were the words, 'Urgent. Mobilisation.'

"Inside, a printed message called upon J. McManus to attend the drill hall on Friday. The same McManus would be 'liable to be proceeded against if he did not present himself.'

"On the outside, it said, 'In the event of non-delivery, return to the officer in charge.'

"It had landed on the mat with an audible bump and with evident determination as if the postman felt it was his patriotic duty."

chapter 9

The camp

"I joined the Territorials with a friend." Geoffrey Davis was much more matter of fact. "We didn't go to political meetings, but instead to the drill hall for rifle practice and running around a dummy gun. Call-up came as no shock for me. It coincided with summer camp.

"My political knowledge was infantile, but I had grasped one conviction like most other people. When the Communists made friends with the Fascists and the Russians made a pact with the Germans for the carve-up of Poland, war was inevitable. Political ideology is the stuff of fools. What matters is sheer national self-interest, not any 'ism', political or religious, whether democracy, or tyranny."

"I would not say that always applied. Think of the rise of Islam, or what is happening in Iran now, but I certainly agree that we could no longer be satisfied with cries of, 'The War to save Democracy', or 'The War to end War' of the previous generation," said McManus.

Davis struggled to define his ideas. "While we were in camp, we used to talk about it, some of us, in our tents at night. There were six of us in a bell tent, clerks, a teacher, a trainee accountant, specialists, they called us, sorted out as people with some basic knowledge of maths to help in gunnery calculations.

"'War is about national survival,' said someone. Somebody else talked about Clausewitz, whoever he was, and stated that war was merely the extension of diplomacy in that struggle."

"Depends what you mean by 'the nation'", McManus contended. "It conceals what everyone sees as his own procurement. Samuel Johnson's remark that 'Patriotism is the last resort of the scoundrel' applies. There is a delusion about the so-called national interest when it would be more honest to say it was more in the interest of maintaining the advantages of age, or wealth, or class or, for us at the time, the young, keeping our personal esteem in the eyes of others."

"Talking of Dr. Johnson though," Davis paused, "the prospect of death certainly served to concentrate the mind like nothing else.

"Small rivalries, career prospects, home ties, love affairs, they were all cut down to size. I can remember going off to camp with a friend, Bill was his name. He came to collect me at midday, right on time. He was like that, a reliable, painstaking lad of 19 who took himself rather too seriously, but never let you down. That is, of course, except when it was a question of rivalry in love. Then, like everyone else, he could not be trusted.

"It was not that Joan was much of a catch, being small and podgy with a slight cast in one eye, but it was a lively eye for all that. She had made it plain to Bill and me that 'the more necking there was,' as she put it, 'the less likelihood of an interesting friendship.' That in itself was not a promising start, but both of us were very shy and we were prepared to go on taking her out on different nights, hoping for more positive signs of affection, but not daring to push our luck too far.

"Bill's punctuality was customary. What was unexpected was the clatter of his boots. I heard him stumble over the step by the gate and pound uncertainly up the path before the bell rang. I had got into the king's uniform an hour before for the first time except for the boots. They were two sizes too large, although the smallest in the stores, and would have made me look like Pop-Eye in the cartoon.

"'Ready? We're on parade at 13.35.' Bill was already using the 24-hour clock.

"'All ready. Just got to say good-bye.'

"We looked at each other in scarcely concealed astonishment. Bill had his pipe for reassurance, but removed it deliberately, gulped and gave an affected laugh.

"'Is this what they call battle-dress? Look at this collar. It hangs three inches below my chin. I feel like a pregnant woman.'

"I supported him. 'My trousers are much too long. Aunt has had to take a tuck in

The camp

them.' I looked down at my stiff, chlorinated, khaki trousers, pressed sharp as boards, with a little metal eyelet in the bottom. What that was for no-one knew. Getting fitted out had been quite outside our previous experience when, a week before, we had lined up in the drill hall in preparation for camp.

"This was quite unlike the one night a week in sports coat and flannels that had gone on for nine months as a freakish diversion. The thick grey socks, the absurd rolls of puttees, the shapeless, coarse green shirt with its clumsy metal disc at the throat, the forage cap which never stayed on, they were all an unbelievable joke, but we accepted them without demur.

"'We're off, aunt.' I took the suitcase that she had packed with my pyjamas, handkerchiefs, tooth-brush and the safety-razor, which as yet I hardly needed, and moved off, calling back, 'It's only a fortnight and I'll write.'

"Aunt Mary was getting anxious, although uncle had confidently echoed the headline of the Daily Express when it said, 'There Aint Gonna Be No War.'

"Where were we going? The New Forest? Aunt and uncle had never been there, but didn't cousin George live somewhere near Bournemouth and wasn't that quite close? It shouldn't be too bad then.

"'Don't forget your aunt will be worrying about you, so wrap up well at night – plenty underneath you, and let's have a line.' Uncle remembered his own mobilisation in 1916. They all agreed it had been so much worse.

"On our way to the drill hall, we kept up a running fire of chat to divert us from the embarrassment of being the object of attention. Bill put his pipe back in his mouth and I smoked fags continually as a sign of our unshakeable self-confidence.

"An advert we passed proclaimed, 'Don't be afraid of Hitler. Book your holidays now.' A much greater animation and sense of camaraderie than was usual greeted us when we arrived. From the sergeants downwards all the blokes were mingling together flushed by beer and excitement. Those with stripes freshly sewn by mums, wives or girl-friends, sub-consciously turned their arms as they walked so that everyone could see their new distinction.

The Reunion

"'You'll have to get that done a bloody-sight better than that,' exclaimed Sergeant O'Loughlin to his newly-created bombardier. 'Who put that on, the battery equipment repairer?' Bombardier Hawksworth's stripes were wildly askew and uncertainly secured. As a 40-year old, the sergeant was undeniably an old sweat and was the only man present to have his First War medals to prove it.

"His knowledge of range-finding was sketchy and antiquated, but he had a compassion for the new squaddies and appreciated his nickname of 'Pop.' In spite of all this, the social gap between the men and the officers seemed to have widened.

"Some of the junior subalterns were fancying themselves no end, swaggering about, canes under arm, with assumed nonchalance. Second Lieutenant Crichton-Brown (Inter BSc, Sydney University) was very proud of his new hat, crushed down on both ears, as if he had been through the Somme, quite unlike the straight cheese-cutters bought last week from the Army and Navy stores.

"'On parade,' screamed the sergeant-major. The noise stopped. Bill and I formed up with our own little group of 'surveyors' shepherded by Sergeant O'Loughlin.

"'Battery, attention!' The mixture of the veterans and the callow became awkwardly still. Uniform inspection began.

"'Why brown shoes and no puttees,' asked Crichton-Brown.

"'No size to fit me in the stores, Sir.'

"'That's right, Sir,' chipped in Sergeant O'Loughlin. 'He'll have to wear his own till they come through.'

"'Well, put in another chitty to the QM.' Crichton-Brown was testy. Brown shoes were an exclusive privilege for an officer and my shoes were a silent insult.

"'And,' continued Sergeant O'Loughlin as if he had not heard, 'he can put in a claim for extra pay for the use of his own shoes for camp.'

"The inspection was over. There were no guns to examine, only men. Four guns were waiting for us down at the camp for firing, two 18-pounders and two 4.5 howitzers

The camp

from the last war, lent by the regulars to the Territorials to play with. The guns would be fired only once for the camp, as there was no ammunition to waste and safety precautions ensured that this would be one round of blank.

"Major Milton, the battery commander, stood before us. He was a gentle, slow-thinking man who had said goodbye to his wife, children and dental surgery earlier that morning.

"'I want to congratulate you on your turnout, men. For many of you it will be your first camp and I hope you will spend your time profitably and with pleasure.' The sergeants grinned knowingly at this. 'I hope you won't grumble too much if you find conditions not quite as you might expect them to be, but we shall do all we can to help put them right. Carry on, sergeant major.'

"He turned uncertainly towards his tower of strength from the regulars and acknowledged the latter's immaculate salute with a touch of his cap.

"'Battery . . . .dismiss. Parade for move in half-an-hour.'

"Bill and I went to the pub across the road. You could hardly get to the bar for half-a-pint amid the clamour and jovial pushing.

"'At least, the weather's better.' Bill was struggling back, spilling a lot on the way. 'Did you read in the Telegraph that the last lot were rained out. They had to pack it in after a week.'

"'I saw the picture, floods weren't there?'

"'Should be drained off by now.' We were already showing good morale.

"Nearby was the train, a special one, going all the way without stops to a station six miles from the camp. The weather was behaving itself in these last days of August as English summers rarely did.

"When we arrived, we formed up again in the station yard. It was to be the first of many, many parades. First, it was for PT, then for breakfast, for marching drill, for gun drill, for dinner, tea, guard and supper. To us it seemed as if they were afraid we might discover some kind of truth behind the appearances and decide to clear off. To prevent this, they constantly checked your presence like being in prison.

"As we marched to the lorries, a band struck up. It was there for all the new arrivals. 'Roll out the barrel', 'South of the border, down Mexico way.'

"The familiar tunes had an unfamiliar dead rhythm. They did not seem to engender much military pride. The officers' attempts at singing seemed to make matters worse. We clambered awkwardly into the backs of lorries, all, except me, weighed down by heavy boots.

"'Fucking laugh,' pronounced Gunner Cook, 'that fucking band. Can't fucking-well play fuck-all.' He had been to camp for some years.

"It was worth it. You got 14/- a week pay, free food, cheap beer and, now, the firm paid your usual wages as well. A regular snip, it was. But he had never had a band before, that was new. 'If we're not fucking-well put on fucking guard, we'll fuck-off to the pub. What's it called? The New-fucking-Inn or something, in' it?'

"We jerked and swayed across the wide heath. Outside was sweetness and summer scents. The bog of Beaulieu was drying out. At last, the camp came into sight. It was a great circus of brown tents like the encampment of a Mongol horde. The sun slowly declined over the plain, the ground purpled to indigo and the tents were tipped with crimson.

"They even looked a bit like Mongols round the cookhouse, where a collection of soya stoves bubbled and smoked and were stirred from time to time by attendants in greasy sacking hung about with knives and big metal ladles. In the meal tent that night, the forms and long wooden tables rested uneasily on the ground. Inside it smelt of men's feet and stale sauce.

"With Bill and me in our sleeping tent were Peter, a big-boned dark youth, quiet-voiced and steady-eyed, two Scottish lads, Ginger and Alec, and Bombardier Hawksworth who was in charge. We were all under the watchful eye of Sergeant O'Loughlin who came along before 'lights-out' almost as if he wanted to tuck us up in bed before he went off to the sergeants' tent.

"'You boys all right? Got enough blankets? Don't forget to bring your mess-tins, knives, forks and spoons for first parade.'

"'OK, sarge.'

"It was growing rapidly dark and some were assiduously polishing their boots before light failed altogether. Alec was spitting on them, just a little, to make them really shine.

"'Good-night, lads.'

"'Good-night, sarge.'

"It was lights-out, except in the sergeants' tent where, inside, the candle light flickered, distorting men's reflections, making them grotesque hunchbacks and giants in turn. Even the voices of the sergeants were now subdued.

"I found the ground hard and damp and it quickly got very cold. Hawksworth made a piggish sound, but not rhythmical, not sleep-making. The others stirred and grunted but, as Hawksworth was the bombardier, they would not dare to disturb him."

chapter 10

War games

"There were no fewer than four parades by 7.00am the next day. As it paled slightly in the eastern sky, 'reveille' came first. We tumbled outside to long washing troughs and shaved by the light of torches in front of precariously balanced pieces of glass." Davis held to his theme, his memory stirred.

"Then it was PT when the ill-arranged company of angular young men flapped their arms and twisted their heads like an assortment of ragged crows. Next was the parade for breakfast, two hard-boiled eggs rolling about in a mess tin, bread and margarine and a mug of chlorinated char.

"'Dig your irons into the ground, that'll clean them,' advised Sergeant O'Loughlin to our bemused smiles.

"Whistles blew for parade number four and for the first exercise in military tactics. I had never seen the dawn before. The sky was cloudless and the great plain prickled with colour and light. Pockets of mist dispersed and the larks ascended singing the glories of a new day.

"We were expectant and eager, and good it was to be alive.

"The four guns with light trucks lent by the regulars were there for the taking. We set out across the heath. By 11.00am, the major had lost his way, three trucks had broken down and the guns were bogged down in soft black peat.

"Help was summoned, but it soon became plain that the wireless would not function as well. Silence descended once more on the plain except for the larks who obviously had better things to do. The exercise would have to be abandoned.

"Three red-capped officers, deft hands with their shooting-sticks, appeared from nowhere and made it laconically plain to the major that better things would be expected next day. He was obviously a little out of his depth away from the dentist's chair.

"Bill and I came back hanging with fatigue. Bill's boots were like a pair of medieval foot-crushers.

"'Only twelve days to go,' I tried to console him.

"'Have you heard the wireless?'

"'That lot all broke down.'

"'No, not that, you clot, the main news.'

"'Has he attacked Poland, yet?'

"'Not as far as they know, but there are reports of German movements on to the Danzig Corridor.' Bill always kept up with the international news. 'It's all very well taking about twelve days, but suppose we're mobilised and never go home again.'

"'They're not likely to do that, are they? They're bound to give us leave before anything happens, surely.' Neither of us were very clear about the future. Nobody was.

"By day five, everyone was getting more used to it all. By then there had been three more field exercises. According to the major, the last one was quite a success. The guns were fired for the first and last time. The blank shot made a loud report and there was a lot of dressy white smoke. Everyone was very elated.

"'We could have made it pretty hot for the crowd of enemy infantry moving en masse on the horizon – scuppered 'em,' he reported. The men looked at him dumbly and, as if embarrassed by their lack of response, the major continued uncertainly.

"'That's what we're here for, after all, you know.' He would become quite a knowledgeable officer, his dentistry long forgotten, when he and most of the others would be killed, or captured at Mount Cassel whilst covering the rearguard to Calais and Dunkirk, less than a year later.

"By four o'clock, the exercise was over. Bill, Peter and I, in shirt-sleeve order, were as brown as young Greek gods and eating like mammoths. We lay in the heather, drowsy with physical ease, and watched the rabbits whisking about, each movement a tiny jerk, white tails perked up on every hop.

"The prospect of the pub once more that night with the aimless stamping, boozing, singing and whistling up the solitary girl behind the bar was beginning to pall.

"'Seven days to go.' I was thinking once more of the secure comforts of home and then there was Joan. She had pleaded a tennis party last time she put me off and I knew she had been going out with Bill.

"'Hawksworth, Alec and Ginger say they are going to make Bournemouth to chase prostitutes. Don't fancy it myself.' Bill and Peter agreed. It was a horrifying prospect quite outside their ken.

"Another field exercise had been planned for the next day, but we were astonished to awake and find the guns had gone. Rumour had it that a party from the battery had been ordered to take them back to Woolwich during the night.

"'I hear that the first line is being embodied,' revealed Sergeant O'Loughlin to his brood. 'We're having battery sports instead and there's to be a concert tonight in the YMCA tent. But these events did little to assuage the sense of disquiet in the camp. No-one seemed to have his heart in the sports, although the officers showed their spirit by taking part in all the events.

"'Silly cunt, that Brown,' pronounced Gunner Cook as Crichton-B appeared in the shiny black running vest with shorts to match, gallantly chevroned with yellow stripes specially donned for the occasion. He gave up, panting, half-way.

"The concert was also a half-hearted affair and the YMCA tent was more dimly lit than usual and stank of stale beer and male sweat. Its earth floor was trodden hard, littered with fag ends and scraps of paper. Along the sides the tawdry little Union Jacks decorating the wooden tables hung dejectedly on their stands.

"The individual performances were unremarkable. There was an accordionist and two friends with mouth organs. A little tap-dancer brought some applause. 'Give it 'em, Dodger,' they shouted, adding 'Send 'im off,' when he persisted on the stage after another act had started.

"Once again, the officers took part, burlesquing gunners from different nations. There was a lazy Spaniard, an expostulating Frenchman, a volatile Italian, a jingoist German (great boos) and, at the end, one of Britain's own, Union Jack and all (exaggerated cheers).

"The beer was making them forget and soon the singing began. 'Our sergeant major's got a crown upon his arm, when he ought to have an anchor up his arse.'

"When it got to the one about the Queen of Spain, the officers prudently withdrew.

"It came to the ninth day, the day of reckoning.

"'CO and kit inspection,' announced Sergeant O'Loughlin authoritatively. 'Get your kit buzzed up, 'ard. It's a real duff parade, blankets, scrubbed mess tins, knives, forks, spoons, spare boots, the lot.'

"And, to rub in the misery, 'church parade afterwards.'

"'Stand by your kit,' came the order later. They had been standing by for half an hour before the little bevy of officers and sergeants appeared round the side of the tent, its canvas bottom rolled up neatly and the ground swept clean inside.

"'What's them?' blurted the sergeant major, aghast, as he spotted my shoes.

"'There's no boots for my size in the stores, Sir.' I must have explained it a dozen times.

"'Sergeant major, not Sir.'

"'Sorry, sergeant major.'

"'What's this all about, sergeant?'

"'Quite right, sergeant major. This man has no boots of the correct size and 'as special permission to wear his own shoes.' He repeated the confirmation like a litany. And portentously, 'He's allowed to put in a claim for the use of 'em when the boots are issued.' The sergeant major swallowed visibly. Time before church parade was pressing. He looked straight through my head.

"'Grease,' he exploded.

"I looked blank.

"'Grease,' he repeated. 'Vamoos, disappear, make yourself scarce, scram. Report to me at 13.00 hours.'

"'Yes, Sir, sergeant major.'

"I slipped away as the others marched off and went down to the village to buy a paper. The headlines were worse than I feared. 'Russo-German Pact,' they announced. 'Molotov and Ribbentrop sign Non-Aggression Treaty. Chamberlain summons Parliament. A State of Emergency Declared.'

"So it would come, the war, after all. Hitler would make his lightning stroke at any time. The announcement was almost a relief. I told myself I was not afraid, while knowing it was self-deceit. When I got back to camp, the news was everywhere.

"'There's nothing to alarm you,' said the major on parade. 'Certain precautions will have to be taken and embodiment will be carried out quickly.'

"The battery was subdued. Some made specious jokes. Some would get drunk on their five pounds embodiment fee, they said. Some would get married instead. Some laughed nervously, the sun glistening on their tanned faces, their eyes squinting in its brilliance. Some were silent.

"That evening I went with Peter and Bill to the small church in the village. We were late for the service, the singing had begun and the voices emerged in strange whispers on the wind.

"We went inside and knelt down on the hard knee rests. Slanting rays of a dying sun caught the columns and dimmed the radiance of a small red light on the altar. The rector beamed round. There was a silence broken only by the faint noise of a dog barking in the far distance, as we found the next hymn.

"The ragged singing of the small congregation, led by the strident voice of the rector, was sadly out of tune.

"'Let us pray.'

"Two women whispered in front before all was still. When the others got up, Peter and Bill were still there, their hands covering their faces.

"'Let it end soon and may we be safe,' I breathed to myself. The camp had already become for me a comforting haven as I contemplated the horrors ahead. I wished I could stay there forever.

"There was little sign that war was imminent when the train bringing us back drew into Woolwich. A few groups of Territorials were guarding the power station, that was all.

"I telephoned Joan before Bill could get to the box. Joan's mum answered.

"'She's not in – gone out with Jim, I think.'

"'Oh, never mind. Tell her we're off on Tuesday, both Bill and I.'

"Joan did not seem to matter any more and our last rivalry had ceased. We had served our short apprenticeship and would soon be qualified in the craft of war."

chapter 11

L'amour d'enfance

"The town was founded on profits from the wool of Cotswold sheep, but had been in decline for centuries. Boulter Mills had ceased production before the war began and they had been replaced for some time by the ammunition factory as the principal source of work for unskilled girls." A mental image formed in McManus's mind as he continued.

"But there had been no point in blowing-up the Mills. No-one wanted to build another factory there and, although it was a prime site, dwelling houses for artisans, as they were called, were not in demand.

"So there the Mills stayed, right in the centre of the little town, with their tall, brick chimneys, poky yards, vast three-storeyed weaving shops denuded of machinery and with their big wooden gates glumly boarded-up.

"That is, until we came. Then they were rapidly changed from being a factory for wool to a factory for men. All it needed was a military mind to see that, with six hundred wooden trestles, with straw bags for men to sleep head to tail, a dozen large pails for night soil, one for 50 men, some soya stoves in the boiler house, the scrubby office as regimental headquarters, a line or two of metal sluices and some duckboards for washing and latrines, above all a nice new red and blue sign with a cannon and the noble words, 'Ubique quo fas et gloria ducunt' (variously interpreted with more or less obscenity by those who passed to and fro under its stern injunction) and voilà, Bob's your uncle as you might say, you had a regimental billet for a territorial gunner regiment.

"We de-trained at Berkeley Road Station and marched the four miles through a gap in the hills to the valley below the scarp and had no idea that Boulter Mills would be our home for six months, through one of the coldest winters that century, until the time would come for us to go to France.

The Reunion

"'Roll out the barrel' – we swung our arms high, felt proud, spirited and together.

"'Eyes right,' to the colonel, a barrister of the Inns of Court three months before, and an ex public school boxing blue. 'Eyes front,' to the backside of the baggy battle-dress of the man in front and the hard scrape of unrelenting army boots, leather-new, brushing aside the beech leaves that littered the lane.

"It was a 1914 repeat, except we had the silly 'cunt' caps and ankle gaiters instead of cheese-cutters and puttees.

"As we filed steadily into the town, it seemed that most of the population had turned out to greet us. They were not waving flags, but were just curious. We were the first soldiery in the town since the Royalists in the Civil War and nobody remembered them, but civilians and soldiers shared a sense of gallantry and generosity and expressed their feelings with innumerable cups of cocoa and tea and buns and cakes in the manner of the West country which has always been for the king.

"When we saw our quarters in the mill, a lot of the excitement wore off and, by the first morning on parade for HQ troop in the street of back-to-backs behind the mill, with the rising sun shafting through gaps in the forest screen high on Stinchcombe Ridge, I was not feeling very elated.

"It was a bleached, cloudless sky as we waited for colonel's inspection, silent and apprehensive, listening to the church bell strike nine o'clock and following it with a cheerful little carillon.

"I was thinking of the previous night. I had been awarded one stripe a few weeks before and found myself in charge of 30 men, some of whom had crawled back roaring drunk.

"'Oh bollocks, what a shit-house', as they had crawled fully clothed under the blankets, or, 'The piss pot is full, what do we do, piss in the corner?'

"Or that breakfast, lining up with our mess tins in the boiler house in darkness as men stamped and swore and banged their 'irons.' 'What's happened to the fucking cooks, fuckin' well boiled theirselves in the fuckin' porridge, what the fuckin' 'ell?'

"As Bill Staley put it later, 'The cooks must have had a right bollocking for holding up the colonel's parade for one whole hour.'

"We were supposed to be in training for the expeditionary force in France, but, with only four old 18-pounders from the First War in a gunpark farmyard outside the town, our exercises were called TEWTS – Tactical Exercises Without Troops.

"This consisted of marching about, imagining where the enemy was, setting up notional command-posts, firing fictitious guns, and achieving chimerical victories.

"For me life consisted of 'skiving.' In the words of the sergeant of transport, 'Always be seen to be moving, but keep just out of earshot.'

"The best place for this was down at the Forge Cafe in the little High Street for coffee and rolls at 10.00am until the sergeant major discovered our hide-out.

"I was among half a dozen favoured beings still being paid a wage from our civilian job, or subsidies from wealthy parents, and we quickly discovered a secret long acquired by our less-privileged comrades, that the army could be one long, big 'skive!'

"Guard duties you could not skive. Your name came round regularly on battery orders and woe betide anyone not on this particular parade. The penalties were dire: loss of leave, loss of pay, detention, extra drill under the sergeant major, at worst, the glass-house.

"And with one stripe as a lance bombardier, it was not too onerous. Lance bombardiers were 'marching reliefs.' This meant that they marched one poor miserable gunner replacement from the guard house to his post every two hours and the half-frozen unhappy gunner replaced, back to the guard house. It was as simple as that.

"The gunners were outside for two hours at a stretch, the lance bombardiers for five minutes. As for the sergeant guard commanders, they never went out. That is, of course, until the guard was 'turned out.'

"We were guarding the four guns, against whom nobody dared ask. They were in the farmyard, we were in the barn.

The Reunion

"After a week, the smell of dung and straw had been flavoured by a permanent mixture of acrid smoke from the coke brazier, a sweet scent of mould from the piles of uneaten bread in the corner, the sharp essence of pilchards in tomato sauce and the foetid stench of sweaty socks.

"But it was warm. You ate Mars and Cadbury choc. bars, drank the cocoa, and pitched the ration of bread and tinned pilchards to rot in the corner.

"You dozed, you played pontoon, you pulled-through your rifle, you polished and cleaned your boots and equipment until it shone, you squared and unsquared your kit, laying it out meticulously to a mystic formula probably instituted by Wellington, and you dreamed of home.

"In the afternoons, as the children came home from school, two little boys, David and John, used to come and talk to the guard, ask them about their rifles, what they had to eat, what the cap badge meant. It was obvious that, to them, we were a race apart. We were estranged from them.

"It was as if we talked across a great distance and that, maybe, we should never return to a life of families and games and childrens' toys, or, for that matter, have any children of our own.

"Our reveries were disturbed once every 24 hours and usually at one God-forsaken one, of the unholy ritual of 'turn out the guard.' A convenient time for the orderly officer was after the last gin about midnight before turning in.

"Then there was the scramble for helmet and rifle, greatcoats shuffled on, gaiters fastened and, falling outside into the darkness, you hobbled to attention, eyes to the front, watching the beam of the officer's torch, and you waited for the bollocking that it was the duty of every good orderly officer to administer, the bastard!

"It was not so much the physical discomfort that came so hard, however, as the invasion of privacy and personal dignity.

"Looking back on it now, I can see how good it was for me. I remember I had a wet dream the first night in the factory 'dormitory,' which must have been accompanied by some appropriate sleep talk as I became the subject of amused and benevolent comment the next morning.

"'What were you up to last night, bomb.? A bit of all right, eh? Alf 'ere 'as no need of that, do you Alf – 'ad it right up her arse, last Wednesday, didn't you Alf.' And Alf went on proudly and gleefully to dissect and embroider his experience as they sat around, their minds focused on an experience that seemed almost as routine as mounting guard, or polishing brass.

"It was the monotony of repeated low expectations, of the sensation of being ground into a mould of uncomplaining, automatic response to words of command, of a process of brutalisation that I found even harder to take.

"I was not alone and the six of us who had the money to spend gave ourselves the illusion of freedom when we could, by our clandestine meetings at the Forge Cafe, or by a drink at night in the saloon bar of 'The Bell' -that is, until the sergeant major discovered the one and the officers informed the landlord of the other and that it was unseemly to have us in the same room as themselves.

"It was the loss of two escape routes that accidentally led me to find a freedom I had never known before and was to serve me for a lifetime.

"In love, they say, is perfect freedom.

"By early December, the blackout obliterated the few Christmas decorations in shop fronts and parlours still to be seen in the late afternoon. The townspeople hurried home before dark.

"That day we had been on the top of Stinchcombe Ridge, our greatcoats buttoned up to the neck, braving a blast from the east that scoured the grass of dead leaves.

"A small group of us had been trying to survey the land, measuring angles from the Wye to Gloucester. Far below, a miniature smoke trail indicated the push- and-pull from Berkeley Road station, too far away for sound.

"We were feeling clean, but shivery from our weekly shower in the stables behind The Bell. Twenty men in our party had raced down the street from Boulter Mills in

The Reunion

'shirt-order, braces and slippers, towel and soap', naked bodies standing in a swill of grey lather, hair streaming, bottoms rubbing, covering up our shame by horse-play.

"There had followed a 'short-arm inspection', dressing and back to barracks for dinner.

"'Coming down to the Post Office?' asked Bill Staley. 'I've got a parcel to send home for Christmas.'

"With nothing better to do, I agreed. A nice enough bloke, Bill, but little in common with me. Yet I recognised he was ahead of me in girl knowledge. He claimed to know such mysteries of why they said 'no' when they meant 'yes' and, more important still, how to get them to say 'yes.'

"It was indeed he who spotted the girl in the telephone box. She was gesticulating with delightful, but unnecessary animation to her caller. He was missing a lot.

"'She's got some life, that one,' pronounced Bill, marking her down for prey as she pushed the door into the blackness outside.

"'Did he get the message, love?'

"'What do you mean, him.'

"'I mean', Bill was insistent, 'have you got rid of him and can I take his place?'

"'Cheeky.'

"'Why cheeky? If not tonight, how about Monday?'

"I could not see her in the dark, but sensed her pleasure at being picked up. There was a short pause before she replied.

"'What do you propose. I can't come tonight.'

"The accent was soft Gloucestershire, but the 'propose' made it unlikely she worked in the ammunition factory.

L'amour d'enfance

"'What about coming to the pictures on Monday then?' It was the old, familiar stand-by and there was an Odeon just outside the town.

"'OK. See you here at 7 o'clock.'

"'Fine.'

"I had been standing by meekly all this time, amazed at the ease with which Bill had justified his claims. I interrupted hesitantly.

"'Fine for Bill, but have you a friend?'

"'Sorry, I'm Bill – this is John.'

"'I'm Mary.'

"'How d'you do.'

"'How d'you do.'

"Yes, she was definitely a cut above the ammunition girls. 'My friend is in the car as a matter of fact.' She might have been smiling if we could have seen her. We certainly were, for here was the most remarkable statement of all – a car!

"With petrol rationed to a few miles a week and the black-out, the few private cars on the roads had been reduced still further. For two girls to have a car was not a status symbol, but a practical place for post-picture petting. She was a find indeed. Bill had done well.

"I was just able to make out the little girl in the back seat, but was excited by her low voice, BBC-cultivated, obscuring the Gloucestershire. I blundered on.

"'They're going to the pictures next Monday. Can you come too?'

"'Are you, Mary?' Mary had returned to the car. 'Do you two know one another?'

"Mary nodded. She did not need much knowing.

The Reunion

"'All right, fine. Yes, I'll come.'

"The first of the winter gales blew hard that Monday. In the morning we struggled up the slippery path to the top of Stinchcombe through the beech woods torn of their last tatters of leaves. Sheep sheltered miserably behind stone walls and it was all we could do to peer out of streaming eyes through the theodolite director lenses across the stretches of brown bracken to the top of Peaked Down.

"Bloodless finger stumps from army-issue mittens faltered as they scrawled the angle on army issue pad No. 54. 'Angle to the clump on top of Cam Long Down 85 14.'

"'85 14,' I repeated, but my mind was on the meeting, the warmth of the cinema with seats at the back, the hugger-mugger and the dreams.

"I remember I had seen the film months before in London. 'The Plainsmen' was a Western about as far removed from life in the Cotswold town as a Japanese 'No' play, but that was the whole point of cinema going. The film was just a subterfuge for experiencing the closeness of a girl, holding her hands, sensing the perfume of her hair, of having affection reciprocated.

"For three hours of dreams, I would forget the darkness, cold, war and death outside. It was as if I had temporarily thawed back into someone sentient, a person not a number, after the army had done its best in a few short months to annihilate all thoughts of home.

"Forget home and obey commands was what we were taught, but now there was to be a brief, self-indulgent respite.

"Mary and Bill put us down outside her 'digs' in Cam village and there we kissed and hugged and kissed again under the cold, clear stars until, by running hard all the way, I could just make it back to the Mill by 23.59 hours. It must have been a mile, but I did it in ten minutes flat.

"It was the first of many meetings. I had many visits to a small front room with a roaring coal fire where an understanding landlady left us alone.

"I used to go in the evenings and find my love marking children's attempts at the alphabet in little grey-covered lined exercise books, which she would put on one side and lay her head in my lap while I stroked her hair and loved her more than I had ever loved anyone, or anything before.

"Early in the spring, the regiment left for France still untrained. It was to be decimated on the heights of Mount Cassel, protecting the rout of an army fleeing to Calais-Dunkirk.

"I had been posted to Scotland. I left her too, full of pride and secret delight and tenderness. The thought that anything might harm her was unbearable. I would have gone to the end of the earth for her. I was badly, blindly, irrevocably and irresponsibly in love. I was rendered unfit for war and, at heart, the antithesis of a good soldier.

> "To live again, within the heightened vision
> Of life as they saw it in the hour of battle
> When the worn and beautiful faces of the half-forgotten
> Come softly round them with the holy power
> To raise the wounded and dying succour
> Making complete all that was misbegotten
> Or clumsily abused or left neglected."
> — Alun Lewis

chapter 12

Les Miserables

"There were many reasons why we grew up quickly after a very slow start." McManus pursued the subject. "We travelled around the country from camp to camp, met people from all walks of life, lived rough, ate wholesome food often badly prepared, got cold, wet and tired, suffered sleep loss and knew what it was to go without a bath, or shave for weeks on end.

"We had not yet experienced fear intensely, or pain. That was to come in battle. As for sexual education, opportunities were there for the taking. I was not so callow as some, but considering we were anything from 18 to 23, we were unbelievably inexperienced compared with our sons and daughters of this age.

"It all led to a great feeling of comradeship lasting our lives. Close fellow-feeling is one of the few benefits of war. It forms an exclusive club and divides people into two fundamental groups: those who have been in combat and those who have not, those who have had a heightened life sense in the presence of death at a comparatively early age and those who have not.

"Talking of joining the brotherhood, I remember we went to Scotland early in the war. It was a foreign place to us, undeniably different, though, in a way, since my great grandfather came from the Borders, it was for me like going home after a long absence.

"At first, you don't notice the change. There is nothing to mark the frontier except the River Esk which gushes wildly under the road like any other mountain stream.

"Now there is a proud lion on the verge nearby to proclaim a revived Scottish consciousness. Then there was only a scruffy little cottage at Gretna Green for eloping couples escaping irate fathers.

"At Hawick, however, there is no mistaking the difference. There is a verdigrised statue at the entrance to the town, less than life size, to commemorate a little victory over a little band of Sassenach louts by a little gang of Scottish louts after Scotland's biggest defeat in all history.

"After the body-blow of Flodden, this must have been small compensation.

"You stop and listen to the people speak. If they come from outside the town, from remote homesteads where the snow still lingered in late March, it was no knowing what they meant. Close listening for a week might reveal that, 'Oh aie, hei's sawf in th' heid', is a comment on someone's rationality.

"In spite of this disability, they showed a remarkable disparity from the English.

"They were so open-handed. This was a surprise to us. We had become accustomed to music-hall jokes that put the Jews and the Scots together as the most penny-pinching, parsimonious bunch of profit-takers in the world, a right bare-boned miserly lot.

"Far from it. When we were on any of those infernal army exercises and stopped at a two-roomed cabin, reminiscent of the times of Bobby Burns, there would come forth such a generous share of provender and potions, we, the English, were dumb-founded.

"Bright-eyed bairns, lying on a bed in the one living room, would kneel up to watch us, the soldiery, scoffing porridge, home-made bread, bacon freshly cured from the rafters, bramble jam, and tea from the family's scarce store, while we were moved to mumble our inarticulate thanks.

"They were generous in other ways, as we shall see. To some extent it was explained by the fact that we were the first soldiers who had come that way since the Bonny Prince had been chased back by Cumberland's redcoats.

"Hawick is a mill town, more prosperous then than now. A Beecham rail-cut has left it a dingy shadow of its former self.

"At that time, it was thriving. It could scarcely keep up with the demand for army blankets, greatcoats, battle-dress tunics, woolly long-johns and long-armed vests.

"The broad main street was busy with people until late at night, except on Sundays. Then it was largely empty until evening when young and old queued outside the town hall, a great grey-stone, Norman-French, Scottish-baronial bastion of a place, which offered the only entertainment for miles around.

"After a long wait, we could clump up the narrow stairs in our hideous boots, swarm into the gallery, pack ourselves tightly on the wooden benches and look down on the townspeople below.

"There we would be regaled with a passionate, but tedious sermon on our licentious and lustful sins and the pure, divine, heaven-be-praised looks of the female choir who rendered the hymn. But then came the prize. A group of lassies tripped on stage and danced to an accordion with all the zip and flourish of the rosy-cheeked spirit we expected from the Scots.

"The price paid for a bit of warmth and pulchritude on Sundays was worth the sermon, hymn and every minute of the cold wait outside.

"Hard drinking, all male with McEwan Tartan bitter and gushes of more incomprehensible language were all that was on offer in the pubs – but not on Sundays. That is, unless we went to the officers' billets in the inn at the end of town just short of the Tweed Bridge. This was what we would delicately describe today as up-market.

"Here, by signing a lie in the hotel register to say we had walked three miles, we could get a mild ale, or glass of shandy, which was about the limit of our drinking at that time.

"Women could be seen in this pub too – elegant ones, mill-owners' and bailiffs' wives, in for Sunday lunch. And there they would eat with discrimination good Scotch fare of roast lamb and spring vegetables and crisp, baked potatoes, and leave a lot on their plates, while we thought about the boiled spuds and cold gravy awaiting us in the church-hall barracks at the other end of town.

"There were five of us and we came from different parts of England – the north, midlands and south, but we were unprepared for Hawick, for the grim black stone of its mills, houses and shops built to last forever.

"Nothing short of a blast from God Himself could ever destroy so impermeable a town, every block a fortress, with cramped alleys down to the Tweed, and decaying wooden doors to garrets, storehouses, stills and bawdies high above.

"Except for Ron Hubbard, we formed a group of young men who thought we were different from the others. Intellectuals, insufferable prigs, we searched for occasions to talk together about music, politics, art, or literature, rather than families and football.

"One of us was reading Victor Hugo at the time and we called ourselves, facetiously, 'Les Miserables.' We were all misfits. That is, all except Ron. We admired and respected Ron. He was a tough old talker from Vauxhall's in Luton who listened in on these elevated matters, but who could contribute two topics of his masterly own.

"Trucks and girls! With trucks he had a kind of sixth sense. Some have green fingers, Ron had fingers like sparking plugs, mechanical power emanated from them. With a hammer, a screwdriver, a gobbet of gum and these fingers, he could get anything back on the road from a jeep to a tank.

"Even this, however, did not excel his knowledge of girls. He was a practised expert and amatory opportunist combined. The 'gala performance,' as he termed it, with his young Luton wife on the last night of leave, merely added to the zest he employed for every passing 'stray' on road, field, village, or town who happened to catch his ever-roving eye.

"Ron was tough, but good. He had gusto for other things as well from time to time: home-made bread and bramble jam, for instance, or a dram of pure blend.

"Even scenery caught his eye. I remember the splendid desolation of the Scottish hills, etched in snow, once evoked a staggering response in Ron. 'Gor fuck me – ain't it pretty!' But he kept mostly his expressions of delight for girls.

"As we drove across country, collecting provisions, or surveying a gun site, through wild valleys, or by empty lochs, even after dark, he might see a light wagging on the empty road ahead. 'A tart,' Ron would exclaim, as he passed the light and brought the truck to a startling halt. 'What's she doing out at this time of night?'

"'Hallo, love,' he'd say. 'Going places? Want a lift?' He would let no opportunity slip by, but, for all that, he was always a gent., never objectionable to press his attentions beyond the limit, even although the limit seemed infinitely extendable.

"Of the other three, George Hope and Frank Deedes were a complementary couple. Both came from the north of England, which put them in a race apart from the start. Both had rejected the ethos of their public schools. Both suffered, from time to time, fits of the deepest gloom.

"Frank had gone from Durham to schoolmastering in a prep. school. He had registered as a conscientious objector when the war started, but, after serious reflection, had changed his mind and joined up.

"Whatever moral integrity this action had displayed, it had certainly marked him for good as a perpetual gunner, private, unpaid, unforgiven common soldier for the rest of his army career until death did them part.

"The army had no time for this kind of intellectual arrogance, even later on, when he was humping sleepers on the Thailand railway as a Jap prisoner of war.

"He was a serious youth with fair, wavy hair and a slight stoop. With a slow, deliberate way of speaking, he appeared to think carefully of the fitting and judicious word before he uttered it long after the conversation had moved to other topics and sometimes with quite bizarre effect.

"It was the same when he read. Impassively donning his spectacles, he put himself in the right gear, as it were, found the appropriate passage and then delivered it with the authority of a judge.

"Frank was a lazy soldier, utterly disinterested in the business of war, but refreshingly egotistical without a trace of self conceit. He was not at all good for George.

"George needed someone with a quick humour and spark to keep him from ever sinking into long, unproductive silences of deep despond. He was the son of a mill owner, a tall lad who affected a pipe, read D.H. Lawrence and missed his home.

"It was a big disappointment he had never been recommended for a commission. His strong Lancashire accent, which Rossall had done its best to erase, was almost as much of a stigma as Frank's lapsed pacifism. The two of them would sit at nights in the little tea cafe in the town that served as our club and refuge, silently facing each other, both trying to say something wise, portentous, or cynical and utterly failing to do so.

"Stephen Benedict used to say they looked as if they might compose a Russian play between them, but it would never get on the boards.

"I have left Stephen until last because he was a real braw of a boy. Only nine months out of Greshams, he represented for me all the effortless superiority and insouciance of the best products of the English public school and I thought about him with more than a tinge of envy.

"He was tall and slim, with slightly protruding teeth that went with a certain equine set of features and the fact that he came from the hunting shires.

"He was always cheerful and inconsequential, not caring to reveal his good knowledge of history and literature. He had some penetrating views on Lawrence and was well acquainted with the premiership of David Lloyd George. Whereas his father may not actually have known that gentleman, we gathered he had had a life-style befitting such an intimacy.

"There was a country estate, a connection of long-standing with the army and fox-hunting and cock fighting were habitual pursuits. Stephen had been born with a golden spoon from a charming mother. She came to see us once and treated us with the solicitude, generosity and gentle calm that comes from a respectable income and an assured place in society.

"He dubbed me 'the eagle' from watching me peer from my balaclava on icy mornings, all avarine with a pinched beak of a nose. He told me bluntly I was unfit to be an officer for my aloofness, poor physique and a mind more fit for methodical planning than for coping with the unexpected.

"'A good lecturer and fair administrator,' he predicted for me. It was a judgement I have not had cause to alter.

"Patriotic to an unbelievable degree, Stephen always stood to rigid attention for 'God Save the King' even when we were sitting in the cafe and it came over the radio. Nothing pleased him more than talking about his school, the school that had, so it seemed, given him so much: his unbounded self-confidence, his ease in 'handling men', above all the ability to laugh at the privileges of his background.

"'All because my father's a brigadier,' he said when told he would leave us in a month's time for officer training in India, which was partially, if not entirely true.

"I liked him a lot, loved him at times, but there was one thing his school, his mum or his dad had not given him. And that was what to do about girls. At 19, girls are bound, one way or another, to intervene in one's life and it was in this crucial area that Ron and I had an indispensable part to play."

chapter 13

The initiation

"With Sergeant Ron Hubbard in charge, all five of us, Les Miserables, were despatched one day across country to reconnoitre a new position. It was a desolate place in middle March with vast, uninhabited, upland fells supporting a few hardy sheep.

"We took enough petrol for two days, haversack rations for the night and off we set, Ron at the wheel, huddled against the hard sides of the truck, dumbly anticipating six hours of frozen ache in our feet.

"The roads were snow-covered. The snow deepened hour by hour, drifting against banks and hedgerows and driving horizontally across the road and into the back of the open truck.

"Firs covering the hillsides swayed in the blast. No-one spoke, not even Stephen Benedict. Frosted eyes, screwed up tight, we scowled beneath our balaclavas and our breath condensed on muffled scarves. We lived up to our name. It was bloody miserable.

"We got to Moffat in the late afternoon. The wind had dropped leaving a frozen stillness. We disencumbered ourselves from the truck and got down like arthritic old men.

"'This barn will do us for the night,' said Ron. 'Brew up first.' Even he had lost some of his usual garrulity.

"Frozen fingers unloaded the petrol burner, fiddled with the pump and eventually got the wretched thing going. It was always 'a right sod,' as Stephen put it.

"Before long, however, the tea, like benison, was thawing the ice of our minds.

The Reunion

"'Cheer up. We're here for the night. Might as well make the best of it.' Ron was already feeling more himself and while George and Frank were still like refrigerated crows, Stephen was jumping about, legs astride and arms stretched.

"'There's a village hop tonight,' Ron went on. 'Saw a notice in the shop. Could do with some spare myself. What about it?'

"The intellectuals looked doubtful. Stephen was out of his depth. 'Let's get the stuff down and get bedded in first. We'll think about it when we've got something inside us.'

"By seven that night, that is precisely what we had done. Mrs. McAdam, next door, had offered her downstairs room and a couple of sofas. Mrs. McAuliffe at the grocer's had given us some bangers off-ration and Ron was frying the chips.

"Outside it was still like the Iceland floes, but it was becoming more bearable every minute.

"'Well, what about it?' asked Ron again.

"'About what?'

"'The hop, the jive, the dance, of course.'

"There was no response. Ron looked up from the chips, sizzling and sodden with fat. 'Well, I'm going.'

"'Is there a bar?' Drinking was allowable, girls more doubtful.

"'Bound to be.' Ron seemed to want our support.

"'OK then, we're on.'

"'Fine. No good getting there till 9.00 though. No action till then.' Ron knew all the mysteries.

"And he was right. By 9.00 everything was warming up. The snow outside had melted

The initiation

and left muddy pools by the door, or dripped from dun-coloured coats in the dingy lobby. There was no lack of drink and, much to Ron's satisfaction, plenty of 'spare' too.

"There was a pianist who showed misplaced confidence unbridled by competition and an accordionist who more often than not struck the right notes.

"The couples on the little floor were up to all sorts of tricks. Some just jigged about, others attempted Scottish reels. Two girls danced together in the corner, mutually mesmerized. Children danced with dads and mums and all round, backs against the walls. Watching and approving were granddads, aunts, nieces and neighbours, and lots and lots of spare!

"They were mill girls, mostly, 18 to 20-year olds, with a few elderly, ravaged looking ones approaching 30, with husbands away in the wars.

"Ron did not hesitate. A quick survey, with the appraising eye of a competent farm bailiff, led him to the most attractive girl in the hall. They danced together with an eagerness that demonstrated it was just a prelude.

"I stood and watched them, observed the tatty flags from the rafters, took in the smell of beer and cigarettes and rancid sweat. It was enough to daunt any hero but, Ron in the lead, I braved the enemy.

"'Will you?' I stood awkwardly before the girl. She had thick lipstick slightly smudged, and she had put the rouge on in bad light. Her eye make-up was like Cleopatra's and she had a fresh shampoo and set. She got up languidly, too self-conscious to look at my face. We started clumsily to dance.

"'Have you lived in Moffat all your life?'

"'Noh.'

"'Where then? Glasgow?' It was one of the few other towns I knew in Scotland.

"'Nearby in . . . .' The name sounded like Beelzebub, then a long silence as we edged painfully round, avoiding the pressing couples.

"I tried again. 'Excuse my boots, they've got iron tips and they slide. But there's too many people here, anyway, to dance properly.'

"She made no attempt to ease my awkwardness. Speech counted little for communication. There were other signs, more reliable ones.

"I took time to look around once more, half my mind on the steps of the dance. Ron and his partner were going great guns. Frank and George had not ventured from the bar and were unlikely to from what I could see. But, what was this? Stephen was trying his best to dance, looking rather shame-faced about it all. And his companion was one of the experienced ones too, a real breast-pusher, as Ron would say, whose generous gifts were hardly contained by the low-scooped jumper. Amiable, she looked, dancing as if she fancied him, but perhaps more like a mother for a son.

"The dance stopped. The accordionist mopped his head and the man on the piano knocked back a pint from the three standing gleaming on the top.

"'Can't I get you a drink?' I led her gently to her seat.

"'I'll have a gin and orange.' She spoke with the harsh, cracked voice of a woman of 40, but she could not have been half that age. It was a message I could interpret. We could progress.

"'Shan't be long – keep a seat for me.'

"It turned out her name was Lilian and she worked in a mill. Dad had left home and had worked on the railway. Mum was also at the mill, but staying at home to look after the other kids.

"'What's that you're wearing?' I pointed to the heart hanging from a tiny chain round her neck.

"'Me dad gaive 't me. He said it's for luck!'

"I fondled the heart, a small piece of red coral gripped by a cheap clasp. She hadn't got too bad a pair of breasts either, I thought, but her eyes were without softness.

The initiation

"We had two more dances and three more gins. She said little more to me, but more was expected.

"'Can I see you home?' She nodded. 'You'll wait. Aye mus poderr mae nohse,' she giggled.

"It was not far up the street: a small cottage, two up and two down, and all as quiet as the grave. She had the key.

"I went in without asking and she made no protest. It was all expected. She put a finger to her lips and looked up to the ceiling. Mum and the kids were upstairs.

"She slipped off her coat and sat on the sofa. Not a word was said as she lay back and gentled my hand under her jumper and under her bra.

"'Wait a minute.' She got up without fuss and took off the jumper and bra. Her breasts were hard and conical and magnificent. She moaned softly as I caressed them.

"Her little gesture of rejection was quite ineffective and not meant to be otherwise as I tore down her skirt and, all too quickly, reached an aching climax.

"'How did you get on?' Ron was all for an early start and was already stirring the brew.

"'Didn't think much of it, though I noticed the buzzard was well away.' George looked superior.

"'How about you, Steve?'

"Steve had said nothing. He was not his usual self. The schoolboy nonchalance had gone.

"'All right.' His sadness belied his words.

"'Did she rape you, Steve?' Ron was not really jeering, he was too nice a bloke.

"'Not exactly, no.' Stephen looked away. No-one felt inclined to press him further.

"It was weeks before I discovered what had really happened. I was sitting in the cafe with him just before he was due to go. Once more the little shop had become our refuge from the brutalities of the day. The other three were still to arrive.

"He wanted to tell me something. I could tell.

"'Don't say anything to the others,' he finally broached it. 'But I've just been through a hell of a time!'

"'What is it, Stevie, old lad?'

"'That was a terrible balls-up that night in Moffat.'

"'I thought you were doing well. Quite a genius for picking them up.'

"'Well, quite honestly, I've been worried stiff since then. Had a pain you know where, in the old JT – decided I ought to go and see the MO.'

"I was shocked. Poor old Steve. It was all too horrifying. 'What did he say?'

"'He asked me what I'd done. And I told him.'

"'Christ. And then what?'

"'He said I'd got nothing to worry about, laughed like a drain and said I was still a virgin.'

"He did not have to watch me too closely to see I was immensely interested. He went on, 'You see, at Greshams, we were not told about girls much, but it was dinned into us that sort of thing was bound to happen if we mucked about with them.'

"'Stephen,' I said, 'You'll always be as pure as the driven snow. You'll never muck about with them as long as you live.'

"I never knew whether he lived long enough. He was killed the next year and there's more spare in one Scottish village than in all the jungles of Assam."

chapter 14

Temporary gentlemen

Back in the hotel, it was nearly time to go to the bar. From Newcastle to Exeter they would be collecting there now. Davis would be on the top table among the ex-officers, McManus among those below the salt.

Casualties among gunner officers in the desert were becoming serious by 1941 and it was seen to be time to train the second line of potential subalterns. Davis had been posted to Catterick in Yorkshire.

"Before we start on the beer, I wanted to tell you about Catterick," Davis began. "It was at the time I began to appreciate how some could regard the army as a career. I actually began to like guns and the technical know-how associated with them: how to position them, shoot them effectively, unravel the mathematics of a barrage, understand weather corrections, calculate what sort of ammunition to use and study signals and communications. It was a sort of practical military university, providing something I had missed.

"We were imbued with pride in the standard of our drill, of being part of a human machine reacting automatically to a set pattern of predictable events. Our concepts of respect, loyalty and obedience to a certain hierarchy were reinforced. Political responsibility for what was happening was taken from us. This was handled by 'the politicians' whom we scorned.

"Although a few of us discussed our hopes for the future over late night NAAFI cocoa, it became more and more just a job to be done, for the Germans and Japs to be beaten even if some of the rules had to be broken. At the same time, we were being processed for our future role as temporary gentlemen, just as if we were being prepared for a closed military order, like knights and squires of the Middle Ages, with our behaviour dictated down to the smallest detail by the mores of the landowning class.

The Reunion

"We marched past the Union Jack on Saturday morning ceremonial parade and our boots shone like glass.

"'Eyes right, eyes front.' All of us reacted like automata to the sergeant-major's instructions slammed into our heads by countless repetition.

"'You keep your arms by your sides and count to yourself by numbers.' The robot ballet would remain with us for life.

"As one man, we swung past and our heads jerked round sightlessly. You could almost hear the click of our necks as the officer in front gave his salute the full treatment: longest way up, shortest way down.

"The colonel, beneath the flag on his tiny rostrum, responded like a marionette.

"For some days, he had been deliberating on a problem. After all, it was not just the quartermaster's complaints, but the principle of the thing. Mind made up, he decided to appeal to the cadets in the only way he knew. He would appeal to their reason and their natural good sense.

"Marching into the canteen, we clambered on to forms behind the folding tables.

"'Battery – attention!' Everyone was up stiffly with a clatter. One form fell to the floor in our enthusiasm.

"The stage being set, the colonel appeared. 'Stand at ease, stand easy.' Then, as a concession to informality, 'Gentlemen, you may sit.' He was slightly flustered by the sergeant-major's efficiency, but the way was freed for a human appeal, straight to the heart.

"'Gentlemen,' he paused, doubtfully assuming a common inheritance with the cadets in his charge. 'The object of your presence here is to fit you to become officers of the Royal Regiment of Artillery and, while you are here, to treat you as if you were at "the shop" at Woolwich.'

"He hesitated again, searching for words, and then proceeded querulously. 'I expect you to behave here as you would behave in your own homes. I refuse to believe that some of you act here in accordance with the standard of your own homes.'

"What was coming? VD with the local ATS girls on the 'passion field' at the back of the barracks? Piss-ups in our rooms, defeatist talk, treason?

"The awful truth came out. 'I find this morning, not from that side,' pointing to the orderlies' canteen, where ate the gunners of the permanent staff, 'but from this side.' Another shocked pause. 'This enormous mass of uneaten, buttered bread. How any one of you could butter a whole slice of bread at once is incomprehensible to me in any case. Surely, in your own homes, as in the officers' mess, you only butter your bread as you require it. Why should your standards drop here?'

"He went on to elaborate the crime of waste and on to the dreadful losses in the Atlantic, but it was the buttering iniquity that outraged him.

"Silk purses and sows' ears were often referred to among the officers in the seclusion of the mess. There was some pretty unpromising material being sent up for a commission these days: solicitors, estate agents, prep. school masters, bank clerks, even regular army sergeants, some as old as 33.

"He would maintain good standards though and insisted on returning half of them back to their units after a month or two. But five months for processing gentlemen was much too short.

"Pressures were on him to pass through more. The war was hardly going well. Dunkirk had made some frightful inroads into officer strength and the German tanks in the Western Desert were killing many more.

"The course had to be shortened and intensified still more. It was reveille at 6.30, main parade 8.00, half an hour for lunch, lectures until 8.30, prep till 10.00, lights out 10.30.

"It would not allow much time to eat, or excrete, but it served to weed out the undesirables."

Geoffrey Davis was drinking NAAFI tea that night discussing it with Neville Scorer.

"Who were those creeps asking the old boy those stupid questions? Does he see through them, do you think?"

"I doubt it."

"You've got to appear to be so bloody aggressive and arrogant," said Scorer. "I haven't got over the horse yet." He was a thoughtful young man who had forsaken his practice as a solicitor to run a boys' club in the East End before the war. He was not robust, but more than made up for it with his quiet determination.

At first a pacifist before the war started, he had wrestled with his conscience until finally convinced that Hitler had to be put down by force like a mad dog.

The gym horse ordeal bothered him. It was common knowledge that those who failed the physical test of jumping it unscathed would be 'RTU'd' (Returned To Unit).

In desperation, Scorer had joined the voluntary practice squad after prep for half an hour each night. With him was Fatty Martin and poor old Parry, a 32-year-old and married!

Time and time again they thumped their way down the shiny floor to the springboard, only to land excruciatingly astride the confounded thing at its far end.

Davis had made it first time.

"And that bloody lecture on unarmed combat was a farce," Scorer continued.

"When the infantry major said 'the only good German I have known was one who had been on the wire for a week'", he meant it. He mimicked the cold arrogance of the man. "And what about those clowns demonstrating?"

Davis remembered how poor Scorer, his glasses removed, had fumbled with his opponent. "Knee him and go for his eyes," the PT sergeant had cried and then, to show them the way, demonstrated on a little, puppet-like bloke who bounced back like a grinning rubber ball after each dreadful experience.

"You, there," he had pointed to Scorer. "Stop! What do you think you're playing at, girls' ballet? What do you do after kneeing 'im?"

"Push his eyes out, sergeant."

"Push his eyes out? Gouge 'em out!"

Poor old Scorer had done his meek best, but the sergeant had shaken his head in disgust.

Indeed, there was a fight for personal supremacy among the cadets that impelled them all day and half the night. Natural selection was given many an extra push.

Up to lights-out and beyond, those who felt threatened by rejection were to be found polishing the floor round their bed spaces, braising their cap bridges, oiling their rifles, even shining the tiny clasps on their gas masks just in case it made the difference next day when they came glinting, creased and blankoed on parade.

By the time the major appeared, you couldn't see the place for miniature Napoleons, all vying with one another to display their military prowess.

The camp was a jungle. Humour was often out of place. There was no time for it. Those who had prepared little jokes to sweeten their "lecturettes," quailed when it came to the point of delivery.

Tension rose at lecturette time. "There's a deathly hush in the close tonight," whispered Neville weakly, as the first aspiring gentlemen was summoned to inform the others about aperture back-sights, defence in depth, infiltration, or moving to the right in column of route.

Fatty Martin misjudged the scene completely with a courageous attempt at humour about engine valves on their seatings by drawing some buttocks on thunder boxes on the blackboard.

It was pathetic, schoolboy stuff, but it deserved a laugh in any responsible institution, even one to create gentlemen killers. There was a nervous titter from the class, quickly suppressed as the major at the back, unmoved, marked him down. The major plainly shared the padre's view that "Officers would also have to be lay-preachers."

The men would look up to them to confirm their belief in God, as life was not worth living unless there was a chance of salvation and eternal life. Buttocks and thunderboxes had no part to play then.

"The best bloke, of course, is Tom Lewis," commented Scorer. "He knows it all backwards: gun drill, vehicle maintenance, tactics, organisation, law, the lot, and he never gets flustered. A sergeant he was in the regular army in peace time. Good bloke."

I nodded agreement. Tom had had eight years to learn these mysteries since he joined as a boy in Rochdale. On Saturday afternoon he helped the others to improve their gun-drill as they sweated in a sultry drizzle.

"Take post. Without dragropes, prepare to advance." Tom gave the orders to them naturally without bombast. He seemed to like it all and knew it like the proverbial back of his hand. At times like these, we flew to our positions at the gun, hared about lifting trails, or turning the little brass wheels to raise the muzzle while the gun-layer stared through the sights.

Flaying our arms, the parade ground gravel spurting in all directions, we "doubled" to other positions as Tom, an ordinary cadet with the rest of us, gave the orders and explained it all carefully afterwards.

We respected Tom and felt exhilarated when, after it was over, the ablution room rang with shouts and singing.

There were the days we went on exercises and assumed different roles like signallers, gunners, drivers, or troop officers. The chief instructor sometimes upbraided us for our laziness. When this happened he seemed to switch over to a stream of pre-digested words, grimaces and gestures from some revolting, festering sore inside him.

"Large lumps of shit," Scorer described them.

"Unless you bloody well wake up, take a greater interest in things and shake off your bloody sloth, you'll find yourselves under six foot of earth, or two if there isn't time."

It was surely a depressing thought and there was certainly no singing after that.

The nine-o'clock news was unusually grim that night. Greece, our one ally, was going down. There did not seem to be any answer to the German armoured division.

The policy of continuing the war was being questioned in the House. Churchill declared that Hitler could only win by invasion, or by closing the Atlantic. He did not say how we could win, or, if we ever did, how long it would take.

"The danger," said Scorer, "is being over-vindictive to Germany when it's all over, like it was last time."

"How optimistic can you get?" I replied. At night in the canteen, we considered these huge issues with solemn and touching innocence. I remember at one time we produced between us a sort of manifesto. Like the young of every generation, we deemed it possible to change the world in our time and words like "immediate" and "imperative" were repeated.

It went something like this.

1. In education, equality of opportunity is imperative. All children, no matter what the status of their parents, should have the same chance in life.

2. The two nations of our land must come together into one community with the abolition of all forms of privilege derived from the past.

3. The working class should have appreciably higher standards of living.

4. There should be an immediate change from the concept of the fixed boundaries and rights of small nations. Distinct tariff and custom rights are temporary expedients and must eventually disappear.

5. There must be freedom and independence for individual human beings, not of nations, or forms of government.

And so on and so on, like young men have talked for generations. But these considerations were far from the minds of those who had charge of the 426 Officer Cadet

Training Unit whose task it was, not only to process temporary gentlemen and leaders of men, but, in common with other institutions, to foster good relations with its influential neighbours.

There was, for instance, compulsory attendance at a lecture to be given by Sir George Falkirk, Bart., MC, OBE, who happened to be a nearby landowner, on the subject of India.

We all moaned. It meant we would have to make up the time from our diminished leisure periods for preparation on the insides of the internal combustion engine. But there was no dodging it.

He was a charming old man, Sir George, child-like and genial. The lecture was all about the Raj 30 years before and about as relevant to our needs as a dissertation on flower arrangements.

At the end, it deteriorated into a series of disconnected reminiscences like stories from Rudyard Kipling, charming in their way. "Are there any questions?" He beamed as the talk drifted to its close.

The colonel looked around his "lads" expectantly. Fortunately, one creep responded. Jason had a beautifully modulated voice. When he spoke, there was an implied counterpoint.

"I love my voice," it said. "It makes me feel warm. Don't you feel that too and aren't you enraptured with it as well?" But sometimes the voice spoke with fatuity in the dominant.

"What is the connection between the Aga Khan and Ibn Saud, Sir?" "Well, yes. Ehm. They're both Moslems and . . . both very rich. Can't say much more than that, I'm afraid."

There was an awkward pause. The colonel looked at Jason with approval. There was another long pause. He got up. "We are deeply grateful, Sir George, for giving up your valuable time to tell us about your most interesting experiences."

The old boy nearly wept with delight and exploded into something about the immense honour and pleasure he had in lecturing to "such an audience of future officers." Thankfully dismissed, the future officers, those who would make it, hurried back to their valve seatings.

The School of Super-Heavy Artillery was our other powerful neighbour and about as irrelevant as Sir George. The Super-Heavies consisted of a few batteries of 12" howitzers on railway mountings: huge, ungainly beasts of destruction, dinosaurs of their kind, slow moving and hard to conceal and very vulnerable to air attack.

The batteries moved by train and the school had a large, internal model railway inside a big glass case with dandy little electric switches to operate the trains.

Here "transportation problems" were solved with the solemnity of Jove by red-capped colonels and majors. They pressed the buttons and pulled the switches and the little trains sped along their miniature tracks, disappeared into tunnels and came out again past toy woods and stopped deftly on dainty spurs.

The monster guns themselves were no longer made, but some "pieces," as they were described, had been "mothballed" from last time. The sensible thing, they said, was not to scrap them, but provide men to work them until their firing life was over.

"Of course, railway mountings, ranges of 14 miles and more, and not much ammunition left to fit, meant careful conservation of target," they added.

"And added life to the men whose careers flourish on their survival," rejoined Neville, under his breath.

The red-capped major turned the tiny handle at the side of the case while the others watched with fascination. "Nothing but particularly important targets to be engaged," he explained, as the toy replica emerged from its tunnel and raised its little brutish muzzle to the sky.

"You mean a target like the Spanish Armada," muttered Tom Lewis. We never knew if he was over-heard, but, at the end of the second month, the list of those to be RTU'd. went up. These unfortunates had a week's leave to get over the shock.

"You're not on it," said Neville Scorer to me, bursting into the barrack room. "Nor am I, yet! But guess what?" He paused for effect. "Tom Lewis is RTU'd. They bought him off by promotion to sergeant-major in the Super-Heavies. And who do you think is senior cadet? Jason!"

Nobody spoke for quite half a minute.

chapter 15

An historical view

"In some ways, I share your interest in guns." McManus had been listening to the story. "But for me the greater appeal was their history, how tractors replaced horses, how breach-loaders were superior to muzzle-loaders, how guns were first deployed in battle.

"If we knew more details about what happened in the past, we could detect patterns of repetition in history. There are some people who claim to have experience of déjà vu, or to have been re-incarnated with direct experience.

"They are mostly charlatans, but I can vouch for something of this kind that happened to me in the Borders. My family came from this part, as you know, and this may have had some bearing on it.

"You will remember that when the guns were on the move for long journeys, there was always an early start. Reveille was 5.30 that morning in the east-coast town where we were stationed. The young ones said it was hardly worth going to bed the previous night.

"We, the old lads, knew better. You snatched sleep where you could, at any time. It all counted.

"Soon afterwards, tented in ankle-length greatcoats against the North-Sea wind, the men trundled from their billets to the cookhouse down the street, their mittens a poor protection from the cold metal of their mess-tins.

"A dollop of porridge went in one half of the tin, and fried spam with grease-soaked bread into the other. The grease quickly congealed and joined the layer of fat from previous meals lying at the bottom.

"During the day, the children threw snowballs at us, derisively, as we plodded about the streets in ungainly boots, but we took no notice, passing on, disconsolate and indifferent.

"Goodbyes had been said to girls in Nelson Street and at the end of Britannia Pier and now we were going, no-one knew where. The guns were waiting, hitched up to their tractors in the school yard serving as the parade ground, and light snow powdered the canvas covers.

"Rumours about destinations had been current for weeks. Wales, Kent, Greece, all had their advocates. The best to be hoped for was to be remitted to a place near home, or where kindly 'locals' would allow us to 'get our feet under the table.'

Bets had been placed. Bombardier Barnes was the favourite tipster. He worked in the office and got to see the confidential orders from Division. He was also something of a prophet and, at 33, one of the old ones. He was, of course, sworn to secrecy and had no intention of losing his soft job by thoughtless indiscretion, but he might be persuaded to drop a hint or two after two pints.

"Where's it to be, Bomb?" Gunner Baker was with him in the corner of the bar where the bustle and noise would conceal his conspiracies.

There was a pause while Barnes took his next draught. He enjoyed his power being in the office. Provided he kept the rules, he could even keep the sergeant-major at bay, like calling him Mister McNab and standing up to attention from his desk when spoken to.

"Can't really say," said Barnes. "But it's my guess, it's Scotland." Barnes, in a whisper to his friend, added, "They shove 'em up there to do their practice shoot on the ranges before issuing tropical kit and packing them off."

"What are we going to do for cunt?" Baker was always outspoken about his needs and was now looking positively lugubrious. "Bloody Scotland's miles from anywhere."

Barnes blinked at the obscenity. As an office bloke, he always mentally tripped when Baker used these expressions. "They'll have to put some more bromide in the tea."

An historical view

"Toss ourselves off more likely," responded Baker. "Remember that time in Wales on the last firing practice when sarnt-major McNab stood looking at those sheep. Just like him, they were, chewin' and looking straight at him, in the pissin' rain, recognising him, he'd been up there so many times before.

"Just like 'im, said old Lakey at the time. Bloody right. Probably 'is relations now, the living survivors of the time he was buggerin' up there in peace time."

"Scottish sheep are different from the Welsh, more puritan." Barnes tried to bring the conversation to a more abstract level, but Baker felt more gloomy still as he left to tell them on No.4 gun crew.

The town was still silent and dark as at 7.00am precisely, headed by a troop commander's carrier, we drew out of the school yard in turn, the tractor "Quads" towing the guns and limbers, a solitary red light at the tail of the muzzle.

Each one kept his authorised distance. The snow softened sound and vision. Inside each tractor, the gun crews dropped off to sleep again despite the cold. They slumped in twisted postures only moving reluctantly when a bump in the road or the sway of a heavy gun behind disturbed them.

It was a sad cortege.

For some hours we travelled until, somewhere near somewhere which might have been Kings Lynn, the pallor of dawn revealed a paralysed countryside, flat fields and sparse hedges swathed in snow. A flat foreground receded into the mist of a flat distance.

There was the smell of stale cabbages, a depressing place, but, by now, you could see that the whole division was on the move. Lorry succeeded lorry. There were carriers, tanks, bridging material, staff cars and wireless trucks.

They churned up the same dirty puddles, the water gushing back into depressions before being scattered yet again by the next vehicle keeping its same stated interval. As one road met another, a fresh tributary joined the river, all keeping time to the master movement plan as the dour procession grew larger.

The Reunion

There was more than one division. "Did you see the Oak Leaves and the Wyverns?" I asked the driver. "It looks big, this lot. Perhaps Barnes is right."

Our tracked carrier, open to the wind, ground steadily on. Our eyes were slits above our balaclava helmets, with noses well covered and breath condensing on the wet wool.

It did not help to know that the war was going badly. Greece was falling and Britain stood alone against a Nazi Europe stretching from the Channel to the Caucasus. The Japanese were attacking Malaya and sweeping south to Singapore.

Our division, moving north with measured destiny, could well be intended for the Far East as Barnes had predicted.

At fixed intervals, we stopped. The gun tractors pulled off on to the rime of the verge and waited dumbly for the order to move on. Then came a stillness that was unnatural and threatening, broken only by the sound of a farm cart scrunching on ice far away, or the sad drone of wind soughing the telephone wires.

A crow glided silently on to the road and flapped its wings searching for food. To me, it seemed like a harbinger of a fate still undefined.

The driver of the tractor behind us jumped down leaving his sleeping mates undisturbed like a mother off to the mill might, letting her children go on sleeping.

He flapped his arms like a crow's wings and the tiny red spot at his mouth from the stub of a woodbine glowed for an instant.

We dossed down the first night in a school hall just south of the Scottish border. It was when Stephens, another bombardier, spotted the book I was reading just before lights out.

"What's that you're reading, not a history book, you can't be?"

"It's about the Tudors, as a matter of fact." I remember I felt mildly embarrassed about it, but went on. "I've been checking on an event that happened near here, the battle of Flodden, 1513."

An historical view

"That was a disaster for the Scots, wasn't it?"

"It was something like the effect of Agincourt on the French. The Scottish king himself was killed and the flower of the nobility went with him."

"The word 'flower' is curious as applied to a lot of thugs, but I suppose it has something to do with seed, genetic seed. The nobles conceived themselves as having good blood, or stock like plants and animals.

"We don't hear much about the ordinary blokes they took with them. I suppose they went for the loot, the women camp followers, or just because they had to go. Yes, it was a terrible defeat for the Scots. It took them a long time to find the king's body afterwards, under a great pile of dead."

I paused to see if Stephens was still interested. It was rare to find someone to listen.

"Even those who knew the king could hardly recognise him, stripped naked by the looters, with a hideous wound from ear to ear and one hand nearly severed. As the news of what happened got back to Edinburgh, there was panic. An order was issued forbidding the women to wail in the streets and, if they were found outside, were forcibly pushed back into their hovels to prevent the panic spreading."

"What makes you want to read about it now, though?"

"We're getting near to the place tomorrow and there are some interesting parallels."

"In what way?"

"Although it is counted as the last medieval battle with knights and the conventions of chivalry, artillery played a vital part for the first time."

I paused, uncertain how to continue. "Then there were the usual omens and warnings beforehand, like the appearance of strange crows and warning soothsayers."

"You mean like Barnes?"

I smiled. "Not exactly. The king was a romantic fool. He threw his army away in a chivalrous gesture that was already out of date and really only wanted to make a demonstration across the border. Can you imagine how the English and Scots gathered their forces together beforehand and then slowly came to the rendezvous like the divisions meeting up on the roads today."

"You're not suggesting we are all going to our Flodden, are you?" Stephens snorted his contempt for these fancies.

"No, of course not. Anyway, the English and the Scots are on the same side now, but there is something else that interests me. There happened to be a McManus who fought for the Scots and escaped death in an unusual way. He was left for dead on the field, but, the next day, was carried still breathing to a nearby cottage and, after months of careful nursing, became well again. He married the daughter of the owner, produced sons who later had sons and so on. The descendants still live in the cottage today."

Stephens was asleep. He had lost interest and I could not blame him. I pulled the blanket over my head, dropped the book and passed out like a light. The dream I had was vivid, so clear I could not tell whether I was asleep or awake.

chapter 16

Flashback

For weeks it had rained intermittently. Sometimes it fell in sheets and fierce gusts, sometimes in a soft spreeth that soaked slowly into the bogs between the hills.

The mists did not clear until late afternoon and at this moment half concealed the men who were pulling cannon up a long slope. Amongst them there had been much conjecture about where they were.

Most of them agreed that they must be somewhere in England and that they must have crossed the border some time before, but the many halts had been confusing and progress painfully slow.

When the great wheel of Meg, the culverin, sank deep to the axle, McManus' crew stopped to consider what to do next. The oxen pulling her were snorting and panting, their heads drooping with effort. They shuddered to extricate their own legs from the mire, and whips could barely shift them.

The king had given special orders for the cannon to be moved to the far side of the hill where they could be lined up with the carts containing stone balls behind them.

Stone was cheaper than lead and just as murderous, but a few metal shot was kept in reserve for special use. The worrying problem for McManus was to keep the powder dry in this, the devil's own weather. It was contained in canvas bags, well-lined, but the damp still seeped in.

Meg, a bronze-cast beauty, had already been fired a few times and there was little risk of splitting now. Everyone knew that the king's own grandfather had been killed, 50 years before, when a culverin had burst, but methods of casting had improved considerably since then.

McManus had been away from home for weeks. It was hard to reckon up how long. He was part of the McClean clan which, in turn, formed a small group in the great Scottish host.

From time to time, McManus had seen the foreigners he distrusted so much. They were Frenchmen, they said, armed with pikes from Switzerland. They carried them balanced across the shoulder and the handles were far too long for comfort.

He reckoned they might do well against horses, but one of the McInnes told him they were unwieldy and hard to pull out and turn quickly once they had reached their target.

As he watched the struggling beasts, he remembered that Thomson had vanished the night before. There had been an argument. "Brother John" Thomson was a sour, thinking man.

"I see not why we should follow the king. He is made of the same mould and metal that we all be made of. Why should he have so much of the prosperity and treasure of this world and us so little. We all are the children and right inheritors to Adam as well as they. Why should they have this great honour, royal castles and manors and so much land and possessions and we but have poor tenements and cottages?"

Tom McClean took up the same theme. The other men could not stomach his preaching. "Christ bought as dearly us as them and with one manner of price which was his precious blood. Why should we do them so much honour and reverence with crouching and kneeling and they take it so high and stately on them?"

Thompson saw he had an ally in McClean. "Our souls and theirs maketh us all to be men, not like the beasts, and God created us one manner of nobleness and our souls be as precious to God as theirs. Why should they have so great authority and power to commit to prison, to punish and to judge us?"

"That is lewd talk," McManus countered. "You may be sure that the high providence of God is that you should do so, as he declared himself right plainly to his chosen people when they desired a king. Therefore, mind you not this purpose – that is, the equality of the moulds between the noble and you and not your knowledge of the pedigree from Adam."

Alan McDonnell supported him. "We must consider that God hath set in due order by grace between Himself and angels and men and between men and beasts. Even by nature only between beast and beast."

But the argument had availed nothing and Thomson had deserted in the night. Some of the others could scarcely be relied upon either.

The rain soaked them cold, glistening on beards and dripping from the rims of their wide hats. Oxen were brought from another team and harnessed with the others making eight in all. With whips and goads, they finally dragged the great gun to her place.

By now it was four in the afternoon and the mist was clearing. The English cannon and a great cohort of men from Cheshire were positioned on a lower hill opposite just within range. A great slippery morass lay between them. Orders were passed down the line to start the cannonade.

"Now we will show the English goddams our metal and mould," McManus muttered as he helped to load one of the precious lead balls and rammed it hard down Meg's throat. He watched apprehensively as Alan set a light to the fuze for the chamber.

There was a pause as the fuze took some moments to catch. Their limbs ached, the joints were swollen in places. Tom complained of a pain in his back tooth and was surprised that the liquor had not helped. The broken stub felt as big as a tree stump with his tongue.

All down the line men were shouting, oaths, catcalls, snatches of song to lift their spirits. Meg would soon give roar and the ball would lob into the English. The captain had said it could kill 60 of them if it crushed a crowd.

McManus remembered a blinding white flash and nothing more when it came back to his mind six months later in the cottage. He was not to see the explosion that split the sides of the bronze cannon with the force of lightning, thrusting a jagged lump of metal the size of a fist into his right side and sending Tom's body, like a piece of broken sacking, high in the air before it landed, poor distorted scarecrow of a thing, on to the forward slope.

The force of the explosion even uptipped the cart of stones, tumbling out the balls into a small avalanche down the hill.

All along the line on both sides, culverin, saker and serpentine were flashing through the mist, and stone and metal were crashing like deadly smoking meteors into the tense array on the other side. The battle had begun, the die was cast, but McManus would know nothing of the outcome until long afterwards.

chapter 17

Repeated echoes

"I must have been the only one who bothered to notice the stone cross marking Flodden Field the next day. Firing practice took place, tropical kit was issued and embarkation day for an unknown destination was set. And then, as luck would have it, I was posted away from the division and was never to see Barnes, Baker, Stephens, sergeant-major McNab, or any of them ever again." McManus went on while Davis was absorbed in the other man's account.

"I was overjoyed to get a few days leave before joining another unit and telephoned my girl friend straight away. 'Is that you, love? I'm still here and with two more days leave. Let's celebrate.'

"We arranged to meet at King's Cross. We would not have much time together and, in any case, the trains were not reliable. The night express was due into London the following morning.

"I remember waking in the small hours. The train had stopped and the silence of the moors filled the carriage. A wan light by the track lit up the sleeping soldiers, their collapsed faces shadowed pale blue as if they had died. I felt warm and comforted. Whatever had caused the delay, whether a troop train switched, or an air raid on some Pennine town, I was certain somehow that I would get to Kings Cross sometime in daylight and she would be waiting for me. We would meet again and it would be the old glory.

"I had not seen Jane for six months and when we parted she had insisted she would wear the same outfit next time. It was crazy. It might have been years. But images of continuity were important in those days. They had to survive a long time, be flavoured and reprinted in the mind again and again every night like a kind of spiritual exercise.

The Reunion

"I had pictured her waiting with her page-boy hair style and wearing that small round box hat with its ridiculous curl of fur along the top. She was a small, eager, self-possessed person who always seemed to be about to take off on the next flight like a migrating bird. Her brown hat would be carefully matched with a neatly fitting coat, cut decently just below the knee, with six brown buttons carefully positioned down the front just as her mother had made it.

"Jane would be waiting, small gloved hands together, with her legs trimly set off by the silk stockings I had bought for her, as precious as an extra pound of butter on the ration, or a couple of gallons of petrol without coupons. As it was cold, she would be wearing those absurdly small 'booties' with the fur lining which gave her a slightly top-heavy appearance when she walked.

"The soldiers were leaning out of the window, train doors half-open, eagerly scanning the platforms, as the train finally pulled in two hours late, coming jerkily to a stop just short of the buffers and hiccupping a cloud of steam with the effort.

"I saw her exactly as I expected. The recognition was simultaneous. The chemistry of our meeting was already working.

"'Darling.'

"'Darling.'

"And we came together, her face lifted full of the sun. Her hat was knocked out of place and her smile caused the small lines at the side of her eyes to make tiny fans hinting of irony.

"We enfolded and warmed each other. For that moment we were safe. There would be air raids and, what was worse, the slow agonizing greyness which gradually darkened to despair as the hours passed, minute by minute, inexorably, until the time I would turn away, no longer see her except in the mind's eye, and board another train. But, now, we existed, one for the other, exclusively, a reflection each in the other of our own being.

"Much later I recalled the dream. It was when I read about the fate of the East

Anglian Division months later. It was only a short column on the second page and hedged with officialese.

"It seemed they had been captured by the Japs when Singapore fell, many still on the boats. Churchill had been advised not to send them, but it was an act of chivalry on his part committing them so late.

"A few had landed and crossed to the forward line at the last moment only to be surrounded and cut down. They had been marched off to die wretchedly on the Thai railway, some of dysentery and typhoid, some from Jap sword thrusts badly mutilated.

"The news filtered through to the villages and market towns of Norfolk and Suffolk. There was nothing certain about their fate. Most of them were posted as missing, believed dead, but the women did not have to be ordered off the streets. Grief had become more silent since the days of Flodden.

"For Jane, however, the pregnancy was going well. She saw we would have to get married and somehow she was sure it would be a boy."

chapter 18

The Goat

Davis and McManus delayed going to the bar to meet the others. Some re-adjustment was necessary before encountering people not seen for a year.

"It's not quite time to go down yet, but I need some cigars. I'll be back in a minute. Just wait for me." Davis could get what he wanted before the others began to arrive and they could face their entrance together.

The bar was still empty. He pocketed the cigars and went to the foot of the stairs. From the corner of his eye he noticed one of the first arrivals. Much aged, the face was yet unmistakeable.

The thin cheeks with wisps of a beard, the watery eyes and a far-away, half-lost look proclaimed the owner to be one of the permanent losers of this world. "The Goat," they had called him, the living symbol of the human capacity to blame others for one's own faults, the easy target for the dart of personal frustration.

"My God. I've just seen someone I thought was dead," he blurted to McManus.

"Let me tell you about him. It was before you joined us. I had just come myself, a raw subaltern. 1941 it must have been."

The Jews, the gypsies and the homosexuals had been the collective counterpart of the Goat.

The front line was unusual then. Wide rivers and seas have always brought armies to a halt ever since the Greeks and Persians and no doubt long before that.

The channel was once more England's moat. The regiment formed part of what the Higher Command described as the thin crust against an imminent invasion. We were expendable after the first few days, just there to allow time for the reserves to concentrate for the counter-blow.

The calm, golden autumn persisted for days on end. Shapes and colours were vivid and precise in the long afternoons. The dying foliage, static but luminous, could have been made of porcelain. A duplicated line of white cliffs were sharply defined on the enemy side, so close that a giant could grasp them in one hand.

We took turns at the observation post to watch the calm waters and day followed day with the same unreal quality.

The war here seemed to have reluctantly petered out.

Newspapers and the wireless referred obliquely to what was obviously a Russian collapse, but it was unpatriotic and not very relevant to mention the defeat of our new, objectionable ally and some, in their hearts, were rejoicing in it.

Just to remind us what we were there for, once in a while, an aircraft, far off on patrol, broke the stillness of those dreamy afternoons while, at night, a few gun flashes like summer lightning were succeeded by the low thunder of explosions.

You counted for a minute or two before there came a strange, wobbly sound overhead as a big one passed over to land miles away in a Kent field.

The battery never replied to any of them. Our little shells would only have splashed into the water. In any case, ammunition was precious, to be reserved for the day they would come.

They had nearly ventured across one year before. The Russian collapse would make it more certain now. In the meantime, we waited and time dragged and morale was a problem. It was hard to inculcate an offensive spirit when "the Hun" was so long showing his hand.

"Lay on a fox-and-geese game, Davis, and tie it up by Monday."

"Yes Sir, but what's that, Sir?"

The Goat

"It's time you found out." The major snapped it back at me before striding off.

He was known as "steel hat" by the blokes. They feared, but respected him. "He's always bloody fair," they'd say when they were put on a charge and docked a day's pay for an uncertain shave on morning parade, or lost a week-end pass for a smudge in their rifle barrels.

When his digestion was not bothersome, he treated them with the solicitous condescension he gave to his farm workers at home. They could not expect more.

To him, they resembled horses. Exercised, fed well, kept well groomed, they would give loyal obedience and reasonable performance at the jump, or through an awkward passage in the covert.

"Oh yes, and by the way," he called back. "Make certain you're with Eames tomorrow as orderly officer. I'm having an early reveille followed by a quick five-mile run and some arms practice."

He was brisk, some called him impetuous.

"Shit, the bastard," I muttered to Eames whom, I had discovered, everyone nicknamed the Goat. "He had us up yesterday at five. What's he trying to prove?"

The other subalterns were horsing about playing rugger. Eames and I had struck up a friendship and were idly scraping paint from a gun barrel. The Goat it seemed was from a large, clergyman's family in sleepy Somerset.

He was a sad, resigned Goat and he sucked an evil-smelling pipe, the end of which he had gnawed to a black stub that fitted into a gap in his stained teeth. Some said he was getting engaged, but noone appeared to want to probe the matter further for fear they would discover something more wet and depressing about him.

Who was the girl? Who could feel passion for such a man? Surely he would be as limp in bed as the pipe that hung from his mouth.

"I hear that Gunner Harris has trouble at home. I'm going to see if the major will agree to another compassionate leave. I know Harris was home only a month ago, but he says unless he goes again she'll be off with some chap down the road. Do you think the major will wear it?"

"Worth trying," I replied doubtfully. "He can be spared. He is only on cookhouse fatigues most of the time, but the major is a stickler for regulations."

I respected the Goat's concern for his section. He was always so patient listening to the men's complaints, head on one side sadly absorbing their sad tales. Obviously some were having him on, but the Goat was patient with them all, reflecting his father perhaps in that disorderly, but affectionate menage back in Somerset.

Some of the other subalterns took concern for the men as signs of weakness. There was a thin, foxy old man of 28, Faulkner was his name, who despised them. He was lazy and supercilious and in his troop there were feelings of mutual contempt.

Some said he had been a captain in France before Dunkirk and had been demoted afterwards for something disreputable, but this was as close a secret as the Goat's engagement plans.

That evening we sprawled in our chairs after dinner. The major had gone to a local country house to spend the night and have a round of golf the next morning.

He was away and for once we were at ease. We would not miss his icy remarks, nor the watchful fear that kept us on our guard.

Occasionally, one or other of us rang the little brass bell and a mess servant brought a gin and tonic, presenting the chitty book for signature.

"I wish those damned servants would shut the bloody door when they go out and stop the bloody draught," sulked Faulkner.

"The lock does not always work," the Goat responded quietly.

"Well, for Christ sake get something done about it, you're mess secretary." The Goat looked composed as he glanced up from the letter he was writing, the only one gainfully employed.

The Goat

Faulkner eased himself upright. "I'm doing the rounds now. It's early, but I'm turning in." His job as orderly officer for the day would be done perfunctorily as the major was away.

The ante-room was still. Some had fallen into a gin-eased sleep. I waited for the Goat to finish writing and we went upstairs together.

"Another mess night, tomorrow night," confided the Goat. "I hate them."

Who's coming this time?"

"Colonel Redbridge, I think."

"A bloody bore that will be". I shared his distaste.

Mess nights, once a week, followed an unvaried ritual. Only the guest in each case was different. It was the way of maintaining good relations with neighbouring units and influential locals. They were marked by mess rags that become more vicious and unruly the more the boredom of gun and vehicle maintenance and the daily stare across the waters became unacceptable routine.

The Goat was, more often than not, the object of the rag and in some weird way seemed to enjoy it. He became the focus of their frustration, but at the same time was briefly accepted as one of the group.

Mocked and chafed constantly by the others, with collusion by the major, on mess nights, in a celebratory finish, in some twisted way, he played an indispensable role. There are takers, as well as givers.

The day of the weekly catharsis began early. Five rounds each were fired on the run and we paraded for the foxes and geese in the afternoon.

I spent most of it lying unforgivably in a hay-stack checking the posses of men as they ran, puffing and heaving, arrayed in shorts of all shapes and sizes from baggy long "colonials" to summer pants, up the long hill to the manor house where they were quartered in Nissen huts.

I gave them little pieces of paper with new clues for the fox. They took their indignities in good part, I thought, preferring this to killing Germans, though both were equally insane.

In a field nearby, some gypsies who had dodged the call-up were idly picking potatoes. Lucky for them the stars had drawn Hitler to the East.

Something of the former style of the manor house still remained. For the officers, there were still some of the cheaper casual chairs and furnishings, but the owners had advisedly removed everything else except the walnut Jacobean panelling.

It was large enough in the dining room to seat a dozen officers and still leave room for the mess waiters, attired for the occasion in white coats, to pass behind the chairs.

The major sat at the head of table. In descending order of rank and seniority, came the captains, lieutenants and second lieutenants. I was at the bottom.

The conversation, I remember, was stereotyped and very limited. Women, politics and religion were debarred as topics too controversial. Of art, music, or drama, there was none.

"How're your horses, Davidson?," enquired the major from an elderly subaltern. He always led the talking and the others toadied along. "Do they get enough feed?"

Davidson ran a racing stable, still in business, although the war had entered its third year.

"Yes, Sir. Still bearing up. We've lost a few grooms called up, but we can still scrounge enough hay from the locals."

"I've had to give up my hunter. Had him put down, poor beast. Time for it anyway." He was an ex-cavalry man and never forgot it, determined to maintain good morale in his new, undistinguished command. He shared the regret of many of the others in the passing of horses in the regiment and their replacement by motor transport some years before.

There was silence as the meal dragged on. The port was passed round. Captains and above were allowed three glasses, subalterns no more than two, a wise precaution for many.

"Gentlemen, the king and Colonel Redbridge." Upstanding, we echoed, a little uncertainly, "The king and Colonel Redbridge."

"Gentlemen, you may now smoke."

The tension relaxed. It was not long before someone suggested we should "break-up" the mess. It was a sign that subalterns could leave and change from service dress into something more suitable. Mess dress had been dispensed with, in itself a craven concession to the European war in the major's eyes.

"We meet in ten minutes to debag the Goat," came the cry.

The Goat smirked. His time was approaching. He was recognised, mentioned by name, account had been taken of his place in the game. Some came in rugby shirts, some in the hated battle-dress.

"Canada," a volunteer from the colonies, had sunk half a bottle of rye in the ten minutes, was stripped to the waist and already a bit unsteady.

The major withdrew satisfied that his charges were properly employed, no unhealthy intellectual conversation, not with women, not too drunk to react to an alarm. They could safely be left to their games.

The games began with "submarine" as beer was poured down a coat sleeve on to the face of a prostrate innocent lying on the floor. Piggy-back teams charged and fumbled at one another across the bare boards. The scrum of the previous afternoon was repeated without the rules among the shards of the casual chairs.

High cock-a-lorum came next. The high point was still to come.

They nearly forgot and the Goat was about to remind them when they saw him in the corner, half-grinning with the expectation of a randy girl. "The Goat," they all roared as they tore the shirt from his back, pulling his trousers from beneath him while he gave the expected wriggles and moues of protest.

The Reunion

"In the cupboard with him," they shouted. "Water, water!," as the bucket was brought.

"All over him," was the chorus as the Goat was doused, his pipe still hanging limply from his mouth.

The cupboard door was shut. The drenched Goat, with the heavenward look of the martyred Sebastian mysteriously rejoicing, relaxed and fulfilled, was clapped in his cell and closed to view.

The mix of beer, wine, rye and rum took hold. Most managed their camp-beds unaided. Only "Canada," like a stuffed yellow doll, would have to be dressed and propped into his carrier the next morning.

It was while we were having coffee and the servants clearing up the mess, after morning parade, that the stunning news got round about the Goat. He had been drafted to India.

Colonel Redbridge had asked for volunteers, but none had come forward. "I've always been in Field, not going into Heavies."

"No chance of a crack at the Hun out there," they said. But Redbridge had no choice. War Office insisted and someone had to go. The Goat was the most useless officer he had. How could he know the show had lost its punchinello, breaking a symbiosis as necessary as the hippo and the egret.

It was a sorry blow. Who could take his place? They looked at me, but decided against it. "What about the new one, the little one. What's his name, Buchanan?"

But better watch out. Might be the major's favourite. Didn't someone overhear him telling the old man he'd coxed for Jesus? That would not do. Goats were hard to find, but found they would be.

chapter 19

The visitation

They usually went down to the bar about seven. Davis judged the attendance by the number of cars outside. At one time, it had dropped to 25, but, as the years had passed, as they had grown old, become retired, or gained more leisure, it averaged a respectable 75. It was an Indian summer before the lights went out and it became a funerary rite.

In some ways, the association itself had started rather like that, with young men, glad to be alive, celebrating their extraordinary luck. Had it been something about them personally, their way of life, their loves or hates, whether they prayed or not, that had caused the stars to shine on them, peculiarly on them, while Joe, Fred, or Bert had bought it?

They had no means of telling, so they came to celebrate and congratulate each other and recall the past and recount the stories repeated year by year, trimmed or embroidered, magnified or diminished each time in the telling like a children's game until the tables settled into comfortable grooves of cliche reincarnating the pale thin ghosts of young men.

They were all dead, those young men, but the bones of those who came to the reunion had still some time to become arthritic before entropy.

McManus went straight to a small group of men the army at one time had called "specialists." The word inferred that some distance existed between them and the rest of His Majesty's Royal Regiment of Artillery.

Before the war and since, they had been a suspect group: ex-teachers, clerks, civil servants. "A bolshie lot," Davis described them, only one remove from the mess-servants and batmen who occasionally showed suspicious signs of a bisexuality, understandable enough in the senior service, but not to be tolerated on land.

McManus felt more at home among the specialists. There was Sergeant Latham, for instance, with his half-a-pint meditating quietly in the far corner. He had his own bookshop in Frome now.

McManus remembered the nights they had spent together under the rigged tarpaulin that formed the troop headquarters during interminable exercises in Kent and Sussex before the invasion of Normandy.

"How's things?" They took up their friendship from last year almost without pause.

"Fine. And you?"

"So-so. I've come down with Davis. We're staying the night here. Must watch the drink and drive."

"I stick to halves. Know my limit. Two and a half pints." Latham paused, took a careful sip before continuing. "How do you get on with Davis?"

"Quite well. We've shared a lot of interests in the past few years. Of course, he looks at things differently, but the war gives us a lot to discuss. I was talking to him just now of some historical aspects of it and telling him of a strange experience I had once when we went to Scotland for practice camp.

"I had a curious feeling it had all happened before. I don't know whether you have experienced it, a sort of consciousness different from the here and now, different from the commonplace."

Latham considered this for some time before replying. "I know what you mean. It doesn't come to all of us though. It may be something completely subjective like a change in the brain chemistry perhaps. But there is a function of war where an almost tangible evil seems to emerge, a horror from the underworld in palpable form.

"It's not often you meet anyone who has a glimmer of what you mean and even fewer who can vouch for what they say as first hand experience, but when I was on one of those Kent exercises once, I encountered something out of the ordinary which I wrote down soon after the war ended. I have not told many people about it and I should have been turned over to the psychiatrist if I had revealed it at the time."

The visitation

"I'd like to read it. Send it to me when you get back. It's no good telling me here. The atmosphere is hardly congenial. Promise?"

Latham was secretly flattered. A week later McManus got it in the post. He opened it. On an army signals book, in longhand and pencil becoming faint with age, he read what Latham had written in a precise hand nearly 50 years before.

> "It is not often that ghosts get mixed up with war. Usually these deviations from rationality are mutually exclusive. For one thing, ghosts only seem to materialise when there is ample leisure, time for reading novels, or playing golf, for instance.
>
> Ghosts seem to appear to those with plenty of time on their hands, time to consider the colour of a necktie for an occasion, or whether or not to serve terrine-de-grive for supper. When people have more pressing concerns, ghosts, with Loch Ness monsters, UFOs and other psycho-somas, tend to be banished to the nether world of the subconscious from which they probably arise in the first place.
>
> I have never given them much credence myself, ever since my grandfather did a remarkably good likeness of himself in crayon, smoking a pipe with a look of the utmost amiability, and hung it above the bookcase to look down on me.
>
> We were exceptionally close, as much as it is possible for a man of 64 and a boy of eleven to be so, and I could not conceive it possible that the friendship would ever end.
>
> 'When you're dead, granddad, will you do your best to come and see me afterwards?'
>
> 'If it's humanly possible, I promise to do so every year at 7.30 pm on my birthday,' he replied, giving me a determined look.
>
> I had forgotten the qualification of his promise when, three years later, he passed on. I had other pressing things on my mind then like exams and girls and football, but I went to my room to await the second coming.
>
> The time came and went, nothing happened and I felt badly let down. Wherever it was granddad had passed on to, he had evidently found it too hard to re-cross

The Reunion

the Lethe, break the time warp, or re-emerge from a black hole, to bother to keep his promise.

I think this finally convinced me that the super-natural world does not exist, or if it did, it was irretrievably cut off from us, for granddad could always be relied upon to keep promises and be punctual.

Everything that has happened to me since has confirmed this conclusion in spite of, on the face of it, some telling evidence like the happenings at Borley rectory. But it has since became clear that, whatever it was that haunted the rectory, had more to do with the engineering tricks of Harry Price than with the medieval nun who was supposed to take a midnight glide about the garden on summer nights.

Everything, that is, except one experience and that is far from proof, one way or another. It was because this happened during war-time, when I was preoccupied with many demands on my time, that I had just the hint of a doubt that I might be wrong after all.

I was 23 at the time, full of vigour, healthy and well fed and not predisposed, therefore, to experience the para-normal. We were on an exercise. This meant careering round remote parts of Great Britain with guns, carriers, tractors and lorries, playing soldiers.

It was mid-December and in Kent. The night, I remember, was ice-cut. We had got the guns into a ploughed field under the myriads of stars and everyone was dog tired. We lay down under our gun-sheets on the hard ground and were soon inert in spite of the cold.

The wretched drivers groaned as they were shaken awake every two hours to clamber into tractors and start up reluctant engines to prevent the blocks from freezing. This done, they would crawl back numbly to their blankets under the hedge.

Moonlight cast great tree shadows. As the night passed with aching tedium, the Little Bear declined imperceptibly on its rear legs and Sirius, the dog star, sank to the horizon.

The only one of us really awake, apart from the sentry on guard in the lane, was

The visitation

the duty signaller in the wireless truck. Shut behind the canvas flap in the back in a cone of torchlight, hunched in misery, poor Watson was only half-conscious of the static on the radio.

It was my second night without sleep. I kept dozing away until the numb ache in my hands and feet pulled me to. I had just come round when I became aware of Watson's torch flashing from the back of the truck.

'Damn, what's up now,' I muttered to myself. Wearily, I got out from under the muddy blanket where I had been lying fully dressed.

'What is it, Watson?' My breath made the question almost visible.

'Don't get this, Sarge? What do you make of it?'

The silence was as profound as the ocean depth. The static had stopped.

'Has it gone dis?' The expression was ubiquitous. Everything in the army all the time was going dis.

'No, she's still on power. Wait a minute'. Watson's mittened hand adjusted the dial very slightly. 'The static's gone, but, just a moment ago, I got something. Never known it before.'

I waited. Hell, what did he want me for unless it was fresh orders from HQ. I was about to go back to the blankets when I heard it.

I find it hard to describe. The noise did not last long. But out of the silence came something like the screech of a peacock, or perhaps it was the cry of a fox, and yet, perhaps, it was the half human cry of a mutated child.

It was certainly coming through on the wireless receiver and not from outside. Evil had been done to it and, whatever it was, it was about to do evil in return.

'You're sure you're on the right net?'

Watson nodded, fascinated and frightened. He pointed to the dial that showed clearly we were on the regimental frequency.

And then it stopped as unpredictably as it had begun and the radio started to mutter the jargon of army communication.

'Bloody odd. It must have been some new kind of static,' I said.

'Hello 15. Are you receiving me?', came the voice of the regimental signaller from HQ.

'Hallo 43, 15 receiving you.'

'43, Roger out.' That was as reassuring as ever.

I looked at my watch. It was 3.35am. 'OK Watson. You're off at 04.00. Palmer takes over then. I'm going to try to get some kip, but wake me up again if anything happens. It's still bloody cold.'

I stumbled back to the command post.

About 08.00 that morning, after a mug of hot sweet, my blood began to circulate. A freshening wind wiped away the yellow sweat of sleep and the night was forgotten. There were urgent things to do.

We were due to reach our new headquarters at 09.00 and they were 20 miles away. The exercise was over.

Sharsted Court was to be a permanent billet for some weeks. It was situated a good mile from the nearest country lane. The ground beneath the dilapidated gateway, with two inches of frozen mud, indicated that no traffic had gone through there for years.

Just inside the gate, we parked our dozen vehicles and from this point a neglected drive led to the house, one of the finest brick and timber-framed of its kind in Kent.

Eric Rankin joined the Territorials at age 21 in March 1939 after the invasion of Czechoslovakia when it became apparent that there would be a war. His first officer posting was as a junior subaltern to the 112th Field Regiment – an artillery regiment – in the autumn of 1941. He remained in England through the early war years and was part of the 'thin crust' guarding the Kent coast. Then on D-Day plus six in June 1944, he landed in Normandy. The Normandy campaign was followed by the campaigns of the crossing of the Seine at Vernon (August 1944), Operation Market Garden to relieve the paratroops at Arnhem (autumn 1944), the forests of Groesbeek, South East of Nymegen on the German frontier (winter 1944), the Reichwald and the crossing of the Rhine (spring 1945) and north into the Cuxhaven peninsula where the war ended for Rankin in May 1945. By this time, he had been awarded a Military Cross for his part in a campaign to straighten a German salient before the Rhine crossing, when he was wounded by a mortar hit in the face, and was shortly afterwards promoted to the rank of major.

Eric Rankin, then a Captain, taken at Eastbourne on the South Coast in 1944 just before D-Day.

The first London reunion of the 112th Field Regiment in 1949. Eric Rankin (third from right) is now Chairman of the regiment's Old Comrades Association which continues to meet annually at the Goddard Arms, Swindon.

A Bren gunner takes up position at the foot of an undamaged village calvary to watch for enemy snipers. 'He crossed the great slope into the shattered village like a spread-out rubbish tip and noted the Christ figure still intact.'

A medium 4.5 gun firing in support of infantry advancing on Tilly sur Seulles.

Infantrymen in the Arnhem-Nymegen area flooded by the Germans with water from the Rhine. 'Water a wet November and war on land was an unnatural mix.'

The Normandy campaign:

Photos: Crown Copyright The Imperial War Museum

The Winter war and the German frontier:

Men of the 7th Bn. Hampshire Regiment, 'in hooded snow suits like white monks', advancing through minefields to the village of Putt.

...erman prisoners, all winners of the Iron Cross in Russia ...d wounded three times, captured in the fighting at Maltot. ...e could afford to feel admiration for the Germans...a hotch ...otch of convalescents, beardless youths, over fifties, held ...gether by the hard core of a few Russian-hardened tank men and ...e Tigers.'

...he battered village of ...hristot taken in the ...dvance on Tilly sur ...ulles: 'the rubbish of ...ttle'.

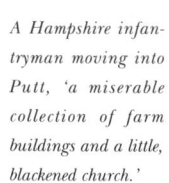

A Hampshire infantryman moving into Putt, 'a miserable collection of farm buildings and a little, blackened church.'

The Cuxhaven peninsula:

*The 112th Field Regiment march past Field Marshal Montgomery in a victory parade –
'a march of the conquerors without slaves'.*

The visitation

The sun was not yet strong enough to disperse a mist that hung in shrouds round the beech trees that bordered the drive.

Captain Chantrey, my troop commander, was a sad man who rarely spoke. I knew nothing of his personal life although he had been with us for three months.

Efficiency was his watchword. Scrupulously polite to those he met, he nonetheless often criticised them behind their backs as fools or incompetents. For this reason, I was always careful what I said to him and always felt constrained in his company.

He opened up that night for the first time. We were in the Nissen hut that served as our combined quarters, officers and senior NCO's together, an arrangement very unusual and only permissible because of the shortage of huts, the big house notwithstanding.

There were four of us: Ned, the young troop sergeant-major now in his shirt-sleeves, braces and gaitered boots; David Essex, troop officer, younger still, occupied with infinite industry on endless games of patience; Chantrey and myself.

The ancient iron stove smoked and even the pin-ups, left by the last lot, were curling brown on the dingy walls. Outside was the frozen, apathetic world of winter.

Chantrey, still in gumboots from doing the rounds, was reading an Edgar Wallace paper-back filched from one of the men.

'Who owns the house, Sir?' I felt bound to break the monotony. Chantrey did not look up from his book, but deigned to reply. 'A man called Faunce de Warenne.'

'Faunce de what, Sir?'

'De Warenne.'

'Strange name, Sir.'

'A bit odd, yes. Direct line from someone with the Conqueror. Still here. You come across them sometimes.'

The Reunion

Chantrey put the book down and looked at me coldly. 'Just himself and a couple of lads. The rest of them on the estate have been called-up. Still got his peacocks, though. What's left of them. At the back.'

It looked as if he was relieved to talk for a change. 'He wanted Lieutenant Essex and me to stay in the big house, but I declined. The place gave me the shivers and it wasn't just the cold. Every now and then I have the impression I've been there before. I walk to the corner of a wood, or the end of a wall and I know what I shall see when I turn the corner. I know without question I've experienced it all before, in a dream perhaps.'

Something must have upset him badly to open up like this especially in front of his senior NCOs.

Essex spoke for the first time without looking up from his cards. 'We all have the experience: it's common to most people, some trick of the brain.'

Chantrey was not to be rallied. He got up and wandered over to the bleary window of the hut and gazed into the darkness. 'Bloody awful war! Did I ever tell you I've given everything up?'

'How do you mean, Sir?' I was curious at this unusual glimpse of the real man and fascinated he should confide in me, one of the other ranks.

'What I say. I've given it all up. Had quite a flourishing law practice. But when the war came, gave it all up. Volunteered. Knew I'd never go back once I'd left. Didn't tell Jo that. She doesn't know. Ever seen her? Here.'

He came across to me, opened his cigarette case and showed me the picture inside. A young girl, smiling wanly, held a baby in her arms.

'Never see them again. Know it. Given them up too. Now there's nothing, but this stinking war.'

I felt drawn to the man and anxious to chase him from his gloom. 'Rubbish, Sir. You can't really mean it. Of course, you'll make it. She looks super, the wife. What's the baby's name?'

The visitation

He did not offer a reply to this and returned to his dejected inner thoughts. Some minutes later, he left the hut to check the guards. I thought it was strange he should do that again as he had already made the rounds.

'Strange bloke, Chantrey,' I ventured to Ned. 'Looks as if he's in some kind of depression.' Essex was too engrossed in his cards to hear.

'Good troop commander, though. He'll get over it. Depressing place altogether.' Ned went back to the sports page and conversation died.

Was it that night I heard it again? I can't remember all that well. I know I had been dreaming about a slow descent into some deep pit. We were going slowly downwards, all four of us, Chantrey in the lead, round the edge of the pit by means of a narrow spiral stair.

It was like a Blake print of Dante's Inferno. I awoke. Something had disturbed me. All was silent except for Chantrey's soft breathing.

The place was like a dank tomb. The stove had gone out.

And then it came again, the same sound I had heard on the set, but somehow more human. Could it be the peacocks? It resembled their cry, malevolent and seeking pity and revenge, but this time on the verge of intelligence, something nearly comprehensible.

'Shrieking Christ,' it was saying, long, drawn-out and high-pitched and then, as if the struggle to coherence had been too much, it stopped.

I scarcely dared to move, waiting apprehensively for another cry, but whatever it was, it had gone.

In the morning there was a powder of snow outside covered with innumerable bird tracks like tiny barbs.

Stumbling out of the hut half asleep, I failed to notice at first a track quite unlike the others. It was not unlike that of a fox with heart-shaped pads, two inches across and about three feet apart.

But when I observed more closely, I saw they were no fox tracks. A fox goes in a line, one foot behind the other. These were of another animal which left footmarks side by side, spaced at intervals as if it had moved in bounds. Even more curious, was a barb-like print across the pad like the claw of a creature, half mammal, half bird.

I kept the knowledge to myself. Neither Ned, nor David would be interested and Chantrey seemed to be too abstracted to care.

We saw the peacocks on our way to visit Faunce a week later. Noblesse oblige extended on his part to an invitation to the four of us to tea. The three survivors of the colony strutted and ruffled themselves lugubriously on the bleak lawn, the left-overs of another age. Otherwise they looked innocent enough.

They shared this antique quality with their owner. Faunce de Warenne looked as if he were a descendant from the Conqueror's dwarf. In profile, there was an unmistakeable squareness to his Norman head and with it went a quizzical eye.

A certain subdued fierceness carried overtones of hawks as well as peacocks. He could not have been much more than five feet high.

Tea was served by one of the two remaining menservants. He had dressed himself in an ill-fitting coat and tails specially donned for the occasion. His clothes needed a good brush, as did the cups and saucers.

Along the wall above Faunce were arrayed portraits of his ancestors. The genetic likeness was astounding. The whole occasion in 1942 was unbelievably baroque.

It soon became clear that his peacocks were his joy and he was keen to know what we thought of them. 'I had a fine flock at one time, but they are hard to feed with just two servants . . . .' His voice trailed away.

'They make strange cries,' I ventured. 'I thought at one time it must have been a fox I heard the other night.'

'That was no fox and no peacock either.'

The visitation

I was fascinated by his eyes which suddenly focused on me as if the pleasantries had ceased and, for the first time that day, he had found something that engaged his interest.

We waited, but he seemed reluctant to continue.

'What was it then, Sir?'

'Nobody knows. I have my own ideas. I've heard it before, not many times, I admit, but I've never seen it.'

He pointed to one of the portraits. 'My ancestor, Sir Gilbert there, in the 1730s, said he saw it. He wrote a memoir about it. People laughed at the time and talked about a brainstorm.'

He grinned like an old fox himself. It was all a big leg-pull, that was obvious.

'You mean, the same thing I heard the other night?'

'The selfsame.' He seemed quite matter-of-fact about it. Gilbert had some idea the creature had spored itself from a kind of extra-terrestrial visitation centuries before. As Gilbert was consigned to Bridewell as incurably insane by one of his nephews to get the inheritance, Gilbert's theories were never taken seriously.

'Hardly surprising considering their extraordinary claims. Indeed, it all became muddled up with the usual tales of death warnings, headless riders, monastery tunnels and other fancies common in the Gothic tales of the eighteenth century and always associated with any good English country house.'

'You don't honestly believe it, yourself, Sir?' Somebody obviously as percipient as he was must be spoofing.

'Of course, I believe it.' He treated me to another of his grins. 'Like most emanations of evil, it has a habit of fastening itself to the weak, the inadequate, the ones already lost. Like some animals and children, it smells fear, takes power in the scent and revels in the deprivation and the kill.'

He paused. His eyes had lost their focus. 'But now, gentlemen, it is usually the time I attend to my bird collection and I must ask you to excuse me. I hope the hut is not too impossible. If there is anything I can do to help to make life a little more bearable, don't hesitate to let me know.'

He was looking at Chantrey now. 'But my resources are limited these days. I would ask you to keep the men away from the peacocks. They are special to me.'

We rose and expressed our thanks for the tea as he rang the handbell for the servant to show us out. I was not sure whether it was 1942, 1742, or the time of the Domesday survey.

Soon afterwards we moved from Sharsted and well away from Kent.

A year went by and preparations were in hand for starting the second front with the invasion of Europe. Firing practices became more frequent, live ammunition more plentiful.

We used the ranges in Wales, all mist and sheep and wet and little else besides. In spite of the emptiness of the place – the range being well away from occupied farms, or villages and the imaginary targets lone clumps of bush, or oddly shaped rocks on far, deserted hillsides – great precautions were taken about safety.

An officer was detailed to check the guns before they fired to prevent human error. Grave were the consequences to that officer if he erred, human or not.

Chantrey was still with us and had recovered from his depression of a year before. Sharsted, in fact, had long been forgotten. Our minds were full of much more practical considerations.

As usual, Chantrey as troop commander would conduct the shoot and move forward from the guns to the observation post (OP for short) which was about a thousand yards from the target itself.

For a change, it was a lovely summer morning and the sun was up with the larks. It was only spoilt by the occasional crack of gun fire.

The visitation

At the observation post, they saw the first flash, heard the gun fire and then observed the small plume of smoke curling up on the hillside in front where the shell hit the ground. Later still came the rumble of impact.

I was back at the gun position at the time and we had been firing on targets well to the right when it came to Chantrey's turn. The muzzles swung round to my shouted orders received from the wireless signaller, who in turn got them from Chantrey at the OP.

'Regimental target high explosive 117, charge 3, zero 14 degrees, angle of sight 2 degrees.' Chantrey's muffled voice came through on the wireless set as I passed them to the guns.

The range always came just before the order to fire. There was a pause. The set suddenly went silent. And then it came. 'Five thousand one hundred yards,' oddly high-pitched, followed by a kind of distorted shriek, but quite intelligible.

'One round gunfire. Fire!' It did not sound like Chantrey, but it must have been him.

The gunners were quick and well-trained. The safety officer checked them rapidly with his compass. They were all proud of their accuracy.

The four guns fired simultaneously, their barrels slightly smoking. Twenty others in the regiment flashed at the same time. We heard the dull explosions a minute or so later and waited for the next order.

We waited in vain. It was plain something was wrong.

The set had gone dead.

'Hallo 15. Can you hear me? Hallo 15. Are you receiving me?'

There was nothing but the faint static. The wireless itself was not dead.

'Get on to regiment,' Essex ordered the signaller. 'Tell them we can't hear from Chantrey. Stop all guns from firing.'

The Reunion

It was a long search, but we found him in the afternoon. He was nowhere near the OP where he should have been. He was alone. Must have left his carrier at the OP and gone forward, trailing the remote control cable from his wireless set with him.

He was in a shallow ditch, dusty, his right arm torn off, a bloody stump for a head.

The colonel was aghast. 'Christ, he must have brought the lot down on top of him. Five thousand one hundred, you say? What was he doing right in the target area himself.'

'Yes, Sir. The order was clear enough.' Essex was shaken. 'Sergeant Latham here can confirm it. He was standing by the signaller's truck at the gun end at the time. The guns were checked.'

'Must have been mad. Good officer, though. There'll have to be an enquiry, of course.'

By the time the enquiry took place, it had become an unfortunate formality. No-one said so, but it was just an irritant when there were so many other concerns: guns and trucks to waterproof, new equipment to process, a vast order of movement down to the coast. In fact, it looked like the real thing at last.

It was after the war had ended that I thought of that voice on the set.

It was so high-pitched, almost a shriek at the end. Audible and intelligible enough, but was it Chantrey? There had been no point in telling the enquiry."

chapter 20

The tiger rug

If anything marked a difference between Davis and McManus, it was their attitude to women. McManus was usually easy in company with women. He found them congenial and felt warm and happy when he was with them.

After he had left the elementary school, he had grown up with girls and gradually came to share and appreciate their deeper wisdom. In any case, it was foolish to stereotype them and he recognised in his own make-up a mixture of so-called male and female characteristics. He supposed this was the same for everyone.

It was not the same for Davis. To him, women were either goddesses, or doormats. They were either adorable, remote and mysterious, or sluts, whores and campfollowers. Seeing McDonald among the crowd of ex-officers by the bar reminded him of some early and perplexing encounters.

Someone had been talking about ammunition, he remembered. The CIDS, or some such, was coming to inspect the stuff soon. Was the army the first to invent those irritating, incomprehensible acronyms?

Anyway, whoever he was, he was coming to look at it all. It would have to be got out of store, cleaned and polished and, don't forget the primers, they said.

They were sitting around in the mess for "elevenses," having just returned from the gun-park where the daily parade had mustered the troop and "details" had been issued.

"Carry on, sergeant-major" was the order sufficient to move Gunner Stokes and Gunner Harris to the latrines where they could atone for being drunk and disorderly the previous night. That would please the sergeant-major.

Then Gunners Jones, Hidge and Henshit would be despatched to the cookhouse for the day's potato-peeling fatigue.

Once more, the rest were dismissed to maintain the breeches, crawling under lorries and tractors to inspect axle-bearings and oil levels.

"You want to get on an ammunition course, that's real jammy," McDonald had said to Geoffrey Davis when he had complained of boredom.

"After walking around looking at heaps of the stuff and having an odd lecture or two on fuzes and suchlike, you can clear off after lunch without being noticed and live it up in Bromley – not the brightest of spots, OK, but quite a bit of talent there with a lot of WAAFs nearby."

He did not think much of the idea. Women and ammunition, what a frightful bore.

He had been in the seaside town for a month now. It had the false reputation of being the most badly damaged town, for its size, on the south coast. Hit-and-run raids by young bloods of the Luftwaffe occurred from time to time to liven things up.

He supposed they were taught to conceive of themselves as some sort of new breed of aerial Teutonic Knights, bringing order and decency to the decadent west. At first they caused a few palpitations to the local inhabitants, but now people were learning to take them in their stride and were growing so accustomed to them that normal air raid warnings were treated with casual sang-froid.

No-one ever quite knew whether the raid was "on" or "off," raiders clear, or raiders approaching. Only the "cuckoo," a concentrated call, meaning raiders overhead and not the herald of spring, sent everyone scurrying to his hole, sometimes, fatally, too late.

As Davis took another sip of hot, sweet tea and without any warning at all this time, there came a great power roaring overhead. The sky was suddenly filled with Tigers accompanied by an ominous metallic clattering, the explosion of cannon shell, the splintering of glass and the gentle patter of shrapnel falling through the leaves outside. A bomb descended like the whinny of a horse.

The tiger rug

Everyone was prostrate. Some of them scuttled under chairs and tables, the mess sofa hid two others and one more plunged under the carpet. Twelve Focke-Wolfs swept over them in the space of three seconds and shot them up with satanic fury.

One had a whole sequence of involuntary thoughts on those occasions – like, "Am I going to die now? Is this the time and place? Can a cannon shell get through this wall I'm hiding against? I must show the others I haven't lost my cool," – as the infernal racket died away.

As pale and agitated faces appeared above the chairs and a shaken carpet-bagger visibly recovered his composure, it occurred to Davis that at least the event had given them some relief from the eternal routine of gun maintenance, ammunition polishing, or brightening up the regimental signs with oily rags.

Later he met McDonald again as they did their stint of orderly officers together in the cookhouse, staring with repulsion at the black vats of boiling stew, the sizzling fat and the buckets of peeled potatoes.

They watched the men patiently shuffling past proferring their mess tins. Flop, in one went mashed potato and thin gravy and, in the other, a dollop of rice pudding with a little red eye of jam.

Gradually, the tables filled up to the clatter and rattle of eating irons, mercifully not machine guns this time.

"I'm going to meet Valerie at the club again tonight. Coming?," asked Mac, one eye on the queue. "Not that I'm likely to get very far."

The prospect again was unappealing and Davis pondered on the alternatives, equally unattractive. "OK, I suppose." And then as an afterthought. "But it's no use getting there before eight, the bar is dead before then."

Apart from the Focke-Wolfs, the other distraction was the officers' club. It was run by Lady Drake, a lady of the kindest and most patriotic intentions who was doing her very best to win the war in her own way, the way she knew best, the maintenance of officer morale.

The Reunion

The task was an uphill one. For one thing, the premises were hardly promising. The club had been given rooms in one of the empty hotels on the sea-front and had about it an air of dowdy gloom.

There were potted plants of uncertain age in the former foyer just inside the old swing doors. The carpets leading to the bar, a well-trodden route, had a faded look. The Edwardian cane chairs placed in strategic corners had seen better days and the lights functioned unpredictably, especially during "cuckoos," and when they worked gave everyone a mildly under-nourished look.

In what had been the ballroom, the floor was still polished, but the palm court quartet had long since dispersed and been replaced by a lone gramophone that, surprisingly, did not have to be re-wound by hand.

The records, kindly donated by the good ladies of the town, were a mixed bag.

Victor Sylvester still had style. Harry Roy was decidedly out-moded.

Lady D. took a close and personal interest in the girls who were invited. The Valeries, Connies, Veronicas and Daphnes who turned up to the club were well-vetted, daughters of colonels and captains, generals and admirals serving far away in the global war.

The girls could be relied upon to be lively, chat at the bar, dance and even organise musical chairs and other innocent fun without being indiscreet, or "going too far" as Lady D. put it.

The blokes, as Mac put it, were far better off. Admittedly, they had their boring tasks like the officers and had to put up with that bloody awful food, but they seemed to make out fine with the town girls, the ones who spurned the officers.

With their tight little smudgy jumpers, pointed breasts beneath, their pert jauntiness and trim waists, the girls in the shops and factories offered delight only to those acceptably familiar by smell, sound or sight.

Davis and Mac reached the club about nine. It was now nearly ten. It was the expected bore. If anything was going to happen, it would have to happen soon.

The tiger rug

Davis had two pints at the bar and the two gins that followed merely added to his depression. It was obvious that Mac was having trouble too – with heavy competition, he noticed, as Valerie laughed knowingly at a rival's joke.

He wandered into the ballroom where four couples were experimenting desultorily with the slow foxtrot to the thin sound from the gramophone. He looked about cautiously. The slow foxtrot was almost as terrifying as the Focke-Wolfs.

"You look lost." He was startled as Lady Drake pounced.

"Not at all. I'm fine, really, thank you all the same."

"Now, let me introduce you to a really nice girl."

A "cuckoo" went up in his mind with a picture of one of Lady D's wilting flowers.

"Well – ehm, thanks, OK. Yes." He could do little else in the face of her enthusiasm.

"This is Daphne Winters. Now, your name escapes me."

"Geoffrey Davis."

"Geoffrey, meet Daphne."

He was right, exactly as predicted: glasses, hair in a bun of some sort, thin, almost scrawny, sharply protuberant teeth with a cutting edge.

"Do you dance?," she offered.

"Well, I'm not very good at it," he mumbled uncertainly.

"Let's try, anyhow."

It was painfully not worth trying.

"Why don't we just sit this one out." He headed her gently back to the safety of the bar. "What can I get you?"

"An orange squash, I think."

"Not something in it?"

"No, I'm afraid I don't drink alcohol, gives me headaches."

It was worse than he thought. Was it even worth pursuing? He looked around quickly while Daphne searched in her handbag. There was no easy way of escape. He had better make the best of it.

"What do you do in the WAAF?"

"Not much, really."

"Does that mean you're a plotter, or something?," pointing to the badge on her arm.

"Oh yes, that's right, but we're not supposed to say much about it – secrets, you know." She must be frightfully naive, he thought.

The talk between them wandered on and Geoffrey became more and more despondent. The gin and tonics tasted more of stale aniseed at every gulp. He grimly decided he could not abandon her now and would even have to see her home.

He waited while she went to the cloakroom and did those mysterious things that girls always had to do before they went home and that always took such an infernal length of time.

The blackness outside pressed against their faces. Here the blackout was taken seriously. It seamed to enhance the smell of the pines along the sea-front and, for a moment, he remembered walking in the Lakes in what seemed centuries before.

"Do you live far away?"

"Not very far. Mummy and daddy are away." She clutched his arm. "I asked for a posting home."

He would dump her at her doorstep and push off quickly. There was one of those bloody exercise early in the morning with the guns actually firing a few live rounds on the ranges.

They had come to the bungalow where she lived. In the dark it still gave an impression of ample prosperity. Suddenly in the silence came the impact of the cuckoo warning.

"Won't you come in?"

He hesitated. There was a long walk back. It was chill and damp and somewhere overhead were the raiders.

"I've got a bottle of daddy's gin inside, or there's whisky if you'd like it."

"All right then, just for a minute, just till the all-clear. Thanks." The last word came as an afterthought.

He was surprised when he got inside. Expensive chairs and tables had ample room to breathe. A large wall electric fire had been left on and the place was warm and softly lit. Shields and assegais from daddy's trophies vied with the antelope heads on the walls and his thoughts switched from the Cumbrian lakes to Kilimanjaro.

A huge chaise longue was strategically placed opposite the fire by a tiger rug, feral and flamboyant with a barbaric snarling face and splendid molars. He had never seen one before except in a museum.

"Make yourself at home." She had removed her glasses and had the slightly disengaged look of myopics when the image becomes blurred. "Would you like a whisky. There's some in the decanter over there. Help yourself. I'm just going in the other room. I'll be back in a minute."

He waited for her, sipped the whisky, added soda, having only recently learned the trick of the deft touch to avoid a splash. The tumbler was a perfect barrel and the cut glass caught the glint of the fire, making the eyes of the tiger seem to glow more brightly.

"Nothing like this has happened before," it seemed to say; or did it gleam with accustomed recognition?

"I love tiger rugs, don't you?"

She was standing at the door with assertive confidence, gown opened, hair loose, breasts surprisingly palpable, her pubic hair physically immediate. She was slender as a willow leaf, but her teeth reminded him, just momentarily, of the silent witness below.

There had been marks all over his back next day, but they could be concealed with a little ingenuity. It was the one on his neck that was as glaring as a mark of the plague.

As he shaved, blearily eyed and close to the mirror, he could even see the imprint of the teeth. He might be able to do something with a scarf and put it down to throat trouble.

"That's a nasty one you've got there," grinned Mac. "Didn't know there were vampires in town."

"No vampires, more like tigers." He muffled the scarf more tightly.

chapter 21

The crusade

"Have I told you the one about the Jewish couple registered in an hotel for their silver wedding anniversary?" Johnson sniggered. "An hour later, the wife is heard shouting 'Murder, Fire, Police.' As the detective is about to burst in, he hears her more plainly 'Furder, Meyer, please!'"

Davis was with the ex-officer group and was half listening to this, another of Johnson's appalling jokes. Without warning, an odd turn of phrase, the suggestion of a scent, a mannerism in gesture or laugh, can evoke sharp memories. Johnson simpered again and it brought total recall.

They were on a boat going to Normandy and it was the opening of the Second Front. They had set out from Tilbury, bound for the invasion beaches, and they were still at sea after three days.

The weather was execrable. There was no other word to describe it. They were experiencing the worst June storms in the Channel for half a century. The ship, grim, wet and cold, was stuffed with guns, vehicles, equipment and soldiers. It flopped about on the crossing under lashing winds and the lower decks were often awash.

Davis remembered the card school. It was pontoon. No-one had the inclination for bridge. The gathering was an unusual one consisting of the ship's second officer, the doctor, a young and very brash Johnson, a large gentleman from the Graves Commission and himself.

"Second trip for me," the second officer remarked. "The last time, I managed to get ashore with the infantry and had a pot shot or two before getting back to Tilbury." He sounded as if Drake was still in charge.

"I suppose you got across in 24 hours?"

"That's right. If we don't get there soon on this run, the bridgehead won't hold and they'll push us off. It could be worse than Anzio."

"As far as I'm concerned, the longer we stay here, the better for us. I've only got a few cases of mal-de-mer so far." The doctor could always be relied upon to make the best of things. He looked guardedly at Graves Commission.

"I'd no idea we'd need chaps like you as early as this. Just bury them where they were, I should have thought, not start to sort them into their permanent homes already!"

Graves was expansive and chuckled as if enjoying a life-long permanent joke.

"Well-planned operation this. Everything laid on from padres, candles, holy wine to K rations and contraceptives for the use of. All prepared for good Christian burials."

"Do you mean, they've already planned the cemeteries and started to think about the gardeners to keep them all in good military trim?"

Graves grinned conspiratorially as if he shared the secrets of MI5. "I'm not supposed to divulge, as they say, but – well – yes. I've got an extra supply of waterproof bags and lots of little markers. It helps to have been in the business in peacetime. When things are on the move, there isn't much time to do the job properly.

"The boys on the ground have to dig 'em in there and then, just where they find 'em. Can't always be sure to get the right bits with the right body, but who would know?

"The padres supervise and say a few words from the Good Book, if there's time. All we ask is they should mark it clearly with the standard issue cross, plus name, rank and number. They don't even have to decorate it with a steel helmet, though that helps to find 'em when there's a lot.

"There are times, though, when they have to be left for some days, even weeks or months, especially after a retreat, but, when the ground is recaptured and it's a bit more pleasant, we rustle up some janker parties."

"What do you mean, janker parties?"

The crusade

"You know, deserters, blokes on a charge, drunk and disorderlies. Shove 'em right out in front, where they deserve to be. Get them to do the first burials and at night whip 'em back to the cages. Also, of course, it's not our job to sort out the personal possessions. The adjutant of the battalion, or whatever, has that responsibility and, these days, they don't send the whole bloody uniform back to the next-of-kin as they used to."

He giggled derisively. Except Johnson, the others looked sick.

The boat shuddered with them as another squall hit the side.

Davis remembered laughs like that, futile expressions of fear mingled with relief. It was one way of managing the dead. In his fashion, Graves did it well. "Not me, oh Lord, anyone else, but not me. Not now."

That same laughter he had heard when they had been back in transit camp in Tilbury waiting to embark. The regiment had not had much sleep that night, standing in the slit trenches and listening to the moaning syrens.

Radial searchlights scanned the night sky and beamed on to slow, slug-like objects following the course of the Thames towards London. There was the thud of AA fire, but, in curious contrast, the shells burst in the sky silently.

From the rear end of the slugs came trails of incandescence like sinister comments. They moved with throbbing uncertainty. Then suddenly, the sound from them ceased, their engines appeared to stop. And down they plunged, unseen, far off in the night.

Momentarily, the countryside was lit up for miles around as they exploded with a hideous growl.

It was all a free show for the men in the trenches. "Another one down," they cried with delight. "What are they, the last of the Luftwaffe?"

Someone else had bought it, not them. But the slugs were not obsolescent aircraft, piloted by German Kamikazes, but the first of Hitler's secret weapons finally off the ground.

The Reunion

Who knows, perhaps that was why the Second Front had finally got off the ground too. With the secret weapons, it was them or us. The crusade against the Atlantic Wall had begun.

For years they had been preparing for it. Stalin insisted, but had been stalled. The Americans kept pushing. It could no longer be put off. The regiment had practised again and again. As Graves said, it had to be a well-planned operation to have any chance of success even now.

Once, indeed, they had done everything except actually embark. "At last," they had said with nervous relief, "At last, it's on."

The guns and trucks had been waterproofed with canvas, grease and oil. From the back of the vehicles came long pipes like bizarre chimney pots for the puff balls of exhaust.

Slowly and deliberately in extended and dedicated files, they had traversed Kent stopping for nights in Wealden woods and hushed in radio silence.

They slept under canvas and were convinced they would soon be thrown against the Nazi western wall. Davis had overheard the blokes talking as he made his rounds, the tents giving their occupants an illusion of isolation.

"It'll be a fucking blood bath, half of us won't reach the beach," he heard one of them say. One or two had broken bounds and gone to the pub to forget their fears, but he did not report them. Later they stumbled back, belching grossly, too frightened to desert.

They fumbled for the canvas flap of the tent, got caught in the guy ropes, but tried not to disturb their sleeping companions. "Fuck it," they muttered under their breath, considerate still.

Davis had been in charge of battery headquarters then, comprising the batmen, cooks, drivers, specialists, clerks and the sanitary orderlies.

He arranged for them to have the weekly bath in a barn where they sluiced themselves with buckets of water. Afterwards, they hopped about naked, shriven and cleansed.

The crusade

As their bare feet touched the cold, stone floor, they shouted at one another to hide their embarrassment.

Soon, they would be ready for the sacrifice.

One curious incident at this time Davis recalled vividly. It was a Saturday afternoon and he had left the guns in a wood and gone with Johnson for a stroll into the nearby village. It was hop-picking time and the chestnuts were just starting to fall.

At the end of a row of cottages stood a small, neglected congregational chapel. As they passed, they had been stopped by the pastor, a hoary old man in his eighties, hands shaking as he spoke.

Would they like to come to the tea-and-bun social on Thursday evening and, maybe, read the lesson? They had looked at him in awkward silence. Who knew where they would be on Thursday, an age away?

Talking to civilians was like talking to someone long left behind in some previous life. No? Ah well, he quite understood. But, perhaps, they would give him their names. He kept a pocket book of names recorded under birthdays. Then, he declared, he could pray for them, one name on every day of the year, to keep them from being killed, or mangled.

God would look after them. Reluctantly, just to please the old boy, they had told him and watched, with mute compassion, as he meticulously wrote their names and the day they had entered the world in his little book.

The next day was the church parade "to commemorate the opening of the Second Front and to re-dedicate themselves to the cause," as regimental orders put it.

They had all objected. The men had to change from their denims and shirt-sleeves into best battle-dress for the ceremony and then change back again. It would be another palaver just for the padre and the general.

But they lined up, as ordered, in the morning sun. Nobody liked the padre much. They reckoned he was a pompous little toady. But their faces made no sign as he faced the parade, his boots and gaiters peeping incongruously beneath his white cassock, and announced proudly that the general would read the lesson.

Now the general believed in the mission of Bible and sword and was not without respect, but this time there was a submerged chuckle as he came forward to read that favourite part of St Paul's Epistle to the Philippians, adjusted his monocle and lisped his Rs.

He always chose the same verses. There was nothing like good routine. "Be careful for nothing; but in everything, by prayer and supplication with thanksgiving, let your requests be known unto God."

The padre resumed his cue and gave his standard sermon too. There was a time limit on the service. The army was sensible about such things. The men must be back on the guns by twelve.

In the meantime, they must endure the padre's dissertation on duty. "It is our duty, personal and social, to see the war through to the finish and for each and everyone to carry out his job, however boring it might be, the job God has allocated to each one on this earth to overcome the forces of evil.

"And now, to God the Father, God the Son and God the Holy Ghost . . . be all majesty and power this day and forever more. We will now sing the hymn 'Abide with me.'"

And they sang in cracked, untuneful voices and remembered football crowds long before. They lowered their heads and prayed as instructed saying to themselves "Not me, oh Lord, not me."

Davis, bemused by the warm sun, could think of nothing but the grasshopper that had appeared at his feet and must have jumped a full yard, right across a tiny rivulet and minute wall of stones.

They had stayed for two weeks in Kent. Then they drove to the water's edge at Newhaven to be told that the whole thing was just another practice run after all. One more year would elapse before the night at Tilbury when the crusade could be put off no longer.

The crusade

In the bar, Davis looked at an aged Johnson across the table. He was telling another of his stories. How long now would God listen to the pastor? "Not me, Oh Lord, not me, not yet."

"Did you hear that one about the man in the train watching an old maid undressing in the berth below? She unscrews a wooden arm, wooden leg, takes off her wig, removes her false teeth and a glass eye. Suddenly she sees him watching. 'What do you want?,' she cries. 'You know damn well what I want,' he says, 'Unscrew it and throw it up here'."

Johnson laughed. The others smirked politely.

chapter 22

The cavalier

"Good to see you, James. You look well." Davis saw Brigadier Edgecumbe, Ret'd, glowing with health and energy, his abundant white hair confirming his cavalier appearance.

He was reminded of that prayer they always had at Fairlight, the one used by Sir Thomas Astley at the Battle of Edgehill. "Oh God! If we forget you this day, don't you forget us." Or something like that. "How are you?"

"I'm very well."

Davis shook hands vigorously. They shared secrets.

Edgecumbe grinned. He could have carried a cutless in his mouth.

"You must meet my wife."

"Is she here? Surprise, surprise!"

"My dear, this is Geoffrey Davis."

"How do you do?"

"How do you do?"

"You've been sailing in Corfu, I hear. Lucky you. Did you play cricket as well?"

"No, but James did. They still play so enthusiastically, but the wickets, he tells me, are abominable."

"But it's a green island. I've been to Kyrenia. Isn't that the place where they have those little broughams to take you round the town and isn't there a monastery, a beauty spot, in the middle of the bay?

"I remember it because we had a mad taxi driver who drove like the clappers across the island, putting his trust at every turn in the St Christopher dangling on the windscreen.

"I am pleased to say the saint did not let him down, otherwise I shouldn't be here. Anyway, what's it like being married to a cavalier?" Davis asked.

"Fine. My three kids and his two get on well together."

"It's a second marriage for both of you?"

"That's right. We really enjoy life now. James does his sailing and the boys are at boarding school."

"I see I shall have to go back to Corfu if you're there."

Edgecumbe was looking on still grinning, but now with a more proprietary air as if he had just returned from a successful skirmish and taken one prize prisoner.

Davis went on, "Great man, your husband. No sense of danger. Used to go around as if he was one of Prince Rupert's patrols, or a cowboy in a western, loosing off his pistols to make us all jump to it."

He turned to Edgecumbe. "Do you remember the first gun position in Normandy? You came charging up to the gate of the field and fired two shots into the ground to show you were there. In the hedge was a dead Scotsman from the 15th Divisional attack the previous day. Cheux, that was the place."

Davis did not go into details of the repulsive attraction he had found in the first dead body he had seen, the man's papers scattered all about it, the P45 pay book lying in the dust with a photo of the wife and kids.

The man's legs were strangely twisted so that his knees faced each other, an accidental invasion of privacy. "Can't remember much of it at all, Geoffrey. They keep telling me different stories of what happened, but I can't remember any of it."

"Lucky man. I remember it much too vividly."

He placed Edgecumbe in an event that happened two months afterwards, when they were "battle-hardened" and it was the beginning of the Normandy break-out at a place called Cahagnes.

They had been given those bloody awful American half-tracks: great, ungainly, rectangular steel boxes, always getting stuck in the narrow lanes, or grinding to a halt as you tried to cross the tall field boundaries that constituted, each one, a natural defence line.

Old Church was there, Signalman Church. He had just seen him with a group of drivers and signallers, with a belly like a barrel and a pint in his hand. It must have been about 4 o'clock on a late August afternoon.

The whole battalion were to go down a narrow leafy tunnel like somewhere in Kent except the chalk dust had the unmistakable smell of dead flesh mingled with the chlorophyl.

Everyone was cheerful at first. The Germans had started to retreat at last. "Just keep them on the move, that's all. Opposition will be slight," they said.

And then, it was all hell. German 88s cracking like infernal pistons, the burst of impact almost contemporary with the thud of discharge, air-bursts above the trees sending down showers of deadly splinters among the falling leaves and Tigers, which could out-gun, out-manoeuvre and out-defend any tanks of ours.

The forward company were limp with fear, clinging to the ditches, their hands well down, and the narrow lane was blocked with screaming blokes who had lost arms and legs, or had white hot rods in their thighs, blokes who had suddenly entered night when they knew it was still afternoon.

"Stretcher bearers forward." They bent double as they scampered down the tunnel to ease the blokes onto canvas litters and get them away until some of them were knocked off too. "Oh, fucking Christ!"

Davis, with his half-track and its crew – driver, signaller and specialist assistant – was waiting on the country road with the rest of the battalion transport at its junction with the lane. Signaller Church got out and stood for a moment in the road. He was the colour of pale straw, white under his tan.

"Bloody awful mess, Sir." He was shaking with terror. "They always tell us there's no opposition."

"We've got to go down there somehow. I just hope the half-track will make it."

Church looked doubtful. If wishing counted, he would make damn sure the thing got stuck.

Davis reached for his map. What was the bloody map reference of the target? Then there was all this ridiculous "farting about" with encoding it. He would have to forget that and send it down in clear.

His thoughts were interrupted by a sharp rattle of fire, two or three bullets from a Sten quite close by, and there was Church hopping about the road like a madman.

As Davis ran to him, Church fell on the ground, grabbed his foot, shouted and sobbed, mouth opening and shutting, eyes screwed up with pain.

"What's happened? What's the matter?"

"The fucking thing went off in me hand, right down through the boot." Church was gasping as his blood seeped through the welts into the pale yellow dust.

Had he shot himself? Was it an accident? Would he be for the high jump? It seemed pretty obvious in some ways, but stens were cheap and nasty weapons so that the catch easily became dislodged when it was hanging down from its sling round a man's middle, barrel pointing down.

It could have gone off like that sending three bullets into his foot.

Davis would never know. "Give the poor sod the benefit," he thought.

He ran towards the end of the small column of stationary, abandoned trucks, their crew pressed down hard in the road-side ditch. "Stretcher bearers, here!"

They came running, doubled low, mortar bursts checking their path. Who were they? Conscientious objectors, artists, poets, Quakers? Their non-combat role, so-called was a damn-sight more dangerous than that of thousands of squaddies in the rear echelons of the depots and supply lines, the town majors and staff captains who composed the six to every one at "the sharp end."

"Careful now. Keep his boot on till he gets to casualty clearance. Let First Aid decide whether he wants a shot or not. Probably he can hang on."

Church was groaning, his eyes closed.

"Send up replacement signaller. Gunner Church wounded." Davis spoke down the mike and the message was acknowledged, but by the time young Nelson, the replacement, got there, it was dusk and the wretched situation had not changed.

Time had lost its meaning. Davis would rarely live so intensely again.

The initial plan, like most plans had gone to buggery anyhow. Sod ruled and they decided to wait till dark before resuming the attack. Brigade was pressing the infantry battalion commander to make another "go" straight away. Division was on their backs and Corps were complaining of the slow advance.

"We are encountering heavy resistance. We'll go in at 23.00, not before." The infantry colonel knew he was respected and they would take him at his word.

Darkness shrouded the fields and orchards where ripening apples hung in the trees like decorations at a children's party. Things gradually quietened down and the moon rose slowly and full, a great eye on the absurd.

It seemed hardly the best time to go in again as the moonlight shone clearly, but it could be that the Germans had pulled back.

"C Company with Morris will probe forward. You, Davis, will have to go on foot with the 'T' set. There's no way ahead for carriers, let alone half tracks, and it's probably all mined anyway. Usual drill if you meet trouble. A and D companies will do a right and left flank. Any questions?"

Humping the 'T' set on his back, Davis went down the dark tunnel of the lane. The twigs cracked like small sparks of a fire and spiky brambles scratched his face and hands as he gently climbed the hedge at the far end and the company emerged on to the edge of a moonlit field.

They seemed to be in a vast mausoleum under the vault of heaven. Away out in front, a forward patrol had already taped a path through the minefield. They could smell the stinking sweet horror of dead cows and dead men.

Davis was reminded of the little Samuel Palmer pictures of an apocalyptic Kent.

They walked silently, in single file, seeking reassurance from the man in front. Tree shadows made eerie branching patterns across the meadows. Moonlight caught the profile of a dead German soldier, twisted on his back, head of a doll, jaws open in frozen agony.

They found the farmhouse wrecked and deserted and entered two more fields bounded by high banks sprouting tall beeches, each one a natural barricade. It was in the far end of the second field they caught it again.

A staccato Spandau, with gold and red tracer arcing above them, splintered the night's silence and gave them a pretty, but lethal firework display. The company commanders were called for an order group under the hedge. Davis had forgotten the time and just knew it was cold.

They pored over the map that was lit by a hand-shielded torch giving a sallow spot. It was while they were peering at the map trying to find exactly where they were themselves before they could hope to position the enemy that a patrol reported in, panting with exhaustion and fear.

"They're on the top of the hill, dug in behind steep hedgerows, Panzer SS. Can you stonk them?" The colonel turned to Davis.

"It's a bit difficult, Sir. The wireless has failed. We can't get through the static."

"Well get back to your carrier, man, and get it through there. My chaps need help."

"Right, Sir. I'll do my best."

But, suddenly, he didn't care, best or no best. It was 4.00am. He had taken some benzedrine the night before and its effects were starting to wear off. The whole enterprise had become empty and had lost for him whatever meaning it ever had. His head ached and he felt ill.

Spandau were still firing vigorously when he got back to the carrier across the fields. Predictably, it was stuck fast in a hedge gap. The driver had done his best, but it was immovable. They had all given up and sensibly gone to sleep, huddled in their greatcoats, slumped over the whispering wireless set, the maps and the bren gun.

He shook them awake and they moaned, so he let them be and got on the set himself to the guns.

"Hallo 15. X-ray."

There was a short pause before the bemused reply.

"15 Roger."

"Hallo 15. Battery target. Map reference 453521. Enemy concentration. Fire by order. Five rounds gunfire."

"15 wilco." The voice was more certain.

Davis waited. Exhausted as he was, he felt the sense of power.

At his command were 40 rounds of high explosive and, if he wanted, ten times as much. Unlike the poor sodding Germans, we had no shortage of ammunition.

They prided themselves on a quick response at the guns even at this God-forsaken hour. They would need a few minutes to work out the range, angle of elevation, angle of sight, apply weather corrections, call out the orders to the sleepy gunners and get the guns on line.

He was not wrong. It was quick. They were getting skilled craftsmen.

"Hallo X-Ray. Ready!"

"Fire!"

He heard the reports two miles away and then the noise of sad, sighing wires overhead as the shells passed over him, giving music to the frightened infantry huddled behind hedges and walls.

They landed, all 40 of them, some singly, some in great bursts, but 400 yards to the front on what must have been the hill top, their blue flashes lighting up the trees and hedgerows. It might all be hit and miss. A map reference could be out by two or three hundred yards and, in any case, the patrol might have got it all wrong.

But it was not wrong. Dawn greyness revealed the smashed bodies, stained with blood and dust, disembowelled and with the slime of brains, a lingering smell of stale garlic and sweat before putrescence, lying broken and battered in the ditch.

They'd been caught all right. Davis had done his best.

That was when he had seen Edgecumbe.

"I'm taking over. The CO has sent me up." At least he was not quite so breezy, waving his pistols about like some manic schoolboy.

"You go back and have some sleep. Leave it to me."

Davis must have looked relieved. "Go on. Get moving." Edgecumbe was jocular, looking forward to some enterprising cavalier work. The war was his time. This was his metier.

By the time Davis got back to the gun lines with the carrier, it was getting hot, August at its prime. The sun had brought back the flies and the flowers in the hedgerow and the ochre cosmetic of dust churned up by passing vehicles.

Sweat prickled his face, which was unshaven for three days. He stopped the carrier and forced himself over the side into the ditch, dragging blanket with him.

Two dozen Germans aged between 16 and 19, hands on their heads, were being hustled down the road at a jog-trot by a couple of infantrymen. The young Germans jeered at him impudently as they passed.

He had driven the nail of hate harder into human affairs. There was no forgiveness, or reconciliation this way. Somehow he and the others would have to atone later.

With profound relief, he lay down, pulling the blanket over his head in warm and dark intimacy, shutting it all out, and losing consciousness almost immediately.

chapter 23

The hill of Calvary

June is Lammas time in Normandy, the time of the hay harvest. In most years, by then, the grass is long and lush. The cattle browse all day in contentment, unless the sun gets too hot and they are driven to shelter under beeches crowning the field walls.

Here their tails flick the flies that nip their hind quarters and their eyes are encircled with distress.

In the first days after landing, the German coast defence had been blasted from the sea and McManus and Davis, with their guns, had moved forward with exhilarating speed over country that remained sweet.

Now, twelve miles inland, they had come to a dead stop. The cows were upside down, their legs stiff stilts in the air, the grass uncut, but pressed down in a thousand tracks, the flies profane. It was still only half an hour in a jeep back to the sea, but the guns of HMS Rodney, which could blow a Tiger tank upside down, were out of range.

Jerry was tough. It had taken a whole division of the Scots to clear one small village. The German 502 tank regiment, with just twelve Tigers manned by battle-hardened veterans from the Russian front, had caused devastation and their fame had spread fast.

Montgomery's boast, that he would be in Paris by August, looked more and more like a schoolboy's bravado.

"Tank alert."

The message had come from Regimental HQ via the battery command post and McManus shouted it to the guns. He had feared it ever since he had landed.

The Reunion

The big sloping field of green wheat stretching in front of the gun position had been trampled and littered by the infantry the day before. One Sherman tank was still smouldering among the half a dozen wrecks out in front and you could still detect the small hunched figure of one of the occupants half out of the turret where he had died in agony.

But there were no signs of German armour up to the edge of a low wood five hundred yards away.

He walked along the gun line, checking on the four guns of Baker troop arranged in W formation, well dug-in about 30 yards apart. On "Tank alert," each sergeant in charge of a gun took independent command.

Hayward was steady as a rock, Baker a bit jumpy, Gibson careless and Donovan big and stupid.

"Change your No.3, sergeant." He did not trust Gunner Blythe, the No 3 on Donovan's gun, whose task it would be to get the tank directly into his open sights before firing. "And, while you're waiting, get some more sandbags in front of your gun-pit."

He knew they all dreaded it. They had all stopped talking. Some thought of the practices they had had on the ranges at Lydd back home. It was bad enough then, when they had fired at small canvas screens moving across their front. The noise was deafening as the armour-piercing shells had slammed into the targets, or, much more frequently, sent up showers of sand and shingle in the beach behind.

But at Lydd, the target screens could not reply and they weren't Tigers what was more.

The silence was comparative, of course. There was plenty of machine-gun and mortar going on beyond the wood and, away to the left, the rumble of a heavy bombardment.

Donovan's 5 and 6 were humping sandbags and some of the others were cleaning their gun-pits of haversacks and junk so that the gun trails could be humped about in their arc of fire more easily.

The hill of Calvary

"How's it going, sergeant-major?" Davis, command post officer and in charge of the gun position of both troops, looked anxious.

"We're OK, Sir. What's happening on the big plan?"

"Generally OK, they say. We are supposed to be holding down the Germans here while the Yanks are going to break out on the west.

"We always get the rough end."

Somewhere in front, the infantry of 130 brigade were forming up, poor sods, for their first real go as advance guard for taking Hill 112, the key to the capture of Caen and then, according to the plan, pushing on to the River Odon.

"Tank – front 30 degrees." McManus' speculation came to an abrupt end. Yes, he saw it. It was creeping out in front of the wood, its long snout of a gun like an evil antenna.

"Hold your fire." He called out. But the blokes were shocked by the impact and velocity of the 88mm projectile that landed just behind No 4 gun. "Have a go."

The strain was relieved by all four guns pumping, as hard as they could, 25-pounder, round after round.

The smoke cleared and they saw the great beast pause, as if mildly disconcerted by the pin-pricks all round it.

It shifted lazily to another position and was joined by a fellow from another part of the wood.

McManus shouted, "Tank No 2, front 31 degrees."

Before this one could fire, there was another startling interruption, this time from behind and up above. With the suddenness of shooting stars, our Typhoon fighter-bombers, their roar blotting out all sensation, curved down to the wood and unloosed a salvo of rockets.

The Reunion

The earth shook with thunder and the Typhoons rose steeply, leaving feathery trails of smoke behind them.

The blokes in the gun-pits cheered and laughed and shouted, Donovan slapping his sides like some big bear. "That's buggered 'em. Christ – did you see that?"

There were still some anxious looks as the smoke cleared. Two Tigers could have put paid to the lot of them and they knew it. But there was nothing to be seen. The Tigers had gone, cluttered off back into the wood still seemingly unharmed.

McManus thanked God they had complete air cover and that the Luftwaffe had been virtually swept from the sky. He could afford to feel admiration for the Germans with no air support, relying upon the Waffen SS, volunteers from half the countries of Europe, with a hotch potch of convalescents, beardless youths, over-fifties, held together by the hard core of a few Russian-hardened tank men and the Tigers.

He could not bring himself to hate them. It was still astonishing to him that any real harm lurked in the world, so tender and so supportive was his upbringing.

He was brought quickly to attention. "Uncle Target. H.E. 112 charge 3, zero 15 degrees. Angle of sight 2 degrees . . . . . Intense fire." The orders came through on the tannoy.

Something serious must be up. Intense was six rounds a minute. The guns could not keep this up for long as the barrels became red hot. Before long they were firing like maniacs.

"No 2, stop firing – cool barrels." The gunners of No 2 poured water from canvas buckets down the muzzle while the shattering noise of the other guns continued.

For ten minutes they kept it up until ordered to stop. It was only later the news filtered through. The 7th Hampshires had been decimated in the orchards of Maltot and 130 Brigade, or what was left of them, had been pulled out.

Two troop commanders at the OP were dead. Davis had left the gun position to replace one of them and later that morning went up with the colonel to Chateau Fontaine to recce.

The hill of Calvary

They had seen Paul Newman, a kind and considerate officer, lying motionless on his stomach in a slit trench covered with an old bedding mattress from a nearby farm.

They could not believe he was dead at first, with his eyes open, vacantly staring at the ground, but a German ranging air burst had caught the trees above and shrapnel had fallen vertically straight through the mattress and straight into Paul Newman's spine.

"Couldn't have felt much." The colonel was laconic. Newman was his favourite officer, but there was no time for regrets.

"Take over. There's an order group at the farm now."

Davis found the senior company commander surviving, now in charge of the battalion, with representatives of the other companies gathered round a wooden table in the outhouse, its roof shattered and open to the sky. There was dust and rubble on the table and they were trying to look at maps.

Every few minutes, a near miss sent them scurrying for shelter. A young subaltern, dishevelled, sweating from stomach and armpits, looked the colour of slate.

"Ah, Davis, you've come at last."

"I've just been . . . watch out . . . another bastard . . . I've just been telling them we're going to be part of 129 Brigade's counter-attack at 14.00. Have a look at it. But we shan't want you 'till 12.30. I should make the best of it while you can. Get back to the guns if you like."

Davis recognised Captain O'Hara, a phlegmatic soul even in these times, a mercenary soldier who claimed a generalship in the Paraguayan army, having been in charge of the machine gun corps in the Chaco war.

And so Davis had left them, making his way back through the green corn, by abandoned weapon pits, the rubbish of battle, water bottles, ammunition pouches, crumpled webbing, cases of ammunition, spilled cartridges, rifles and broken wireless sets and bodies already moving with maggots.

Every now and then a burst of mortar fire sent him jumping for safety in amongst the shit and flies of the platoon latrine, or any other hole, or ditch, or refuge. In one he left a young soldier, knees drawn up, hands over his face, crying as if he would never stop.

He crossed a great slope into the shattered village like a spread-out rubbish tip and noted the Christ figure still intact, if lopsided.

McManus was glad to see him when he reached the gun position.

"How's the men, sergeant-major?"

"OK, Sir. We had another tank alert after you left, but no casualties."

It was 11.30am and Davis felt unutterably tired. "I think I'll get down for some kip if you don't mind. I'm due back up there at 12.30. It's hell."

McManus was thankful it wasn't him who had to go. He was glad he was not an officer, the casualty rate being what it was. In any case, he could not treat it all as they did, like some kind of competitive game, or a rather more deadly cricket match.

What did Captain Butt say, laughing when the end of his penis was taken off. "Still good for its two jobs, sarn't-major." Some of them had a certain honour and style about fighting still, like a Spanish grandee.

Hadn't an ancestor of Butt's fought at Crecy? All fine, until he had lost his head, and not metaphorically, while standing up inside his tank. They all seemed like a lot of schoolboys, noble in a way, not like those Scottish bastards who hated the bloody Germans and shot them down after they surrendered, he'd heard.

To him it was all sobering, senseless and sad and, as such, he supposed he was a natural servant. As when Franks, previous battery commander now wounded and sent home, had gone round the gun position with him complaining about the blokes' sanitary discipline and had put Gunner Foot on a charge for crapping outside the latrine.

Poor old Foot had been identified by an envelope addressed to him by his mum.

The hill of Calvary

Gunner Foot had been called up at 42 – an old man – unmarried with only his old mum. But Franks would have nothing of it.

"Put him on a charge, sergeant-major. Section 40. Conduct prejudicial to good order and military discipline. That'll put a stop to it."

Davis had made for the space under his carrier to sleep. They always used this when there was no time to dig a hole.

"I hear Captain Newman is killed."

"Yes – air burst. The trouble is you can't see anything up there. It's on a reverse slope and there's no view unless you climb a tree. A medium-gun chap came down pretty fast when they plastered it though. We're putting in a counter-attack at 14.00." But he was wakened by McManus at 12.00.

"Sorry to disturb you, Sir, but the CO wants you on the blower." Davis was too bemused at first to take it in.

"Is that you, Geoffrey? You're not wanted after all. They're pulling us out, for a day or so."

It was a day or so later that Davis heard that the whole lot of them round the table had bought it, a direct hit about a quarter of an hour after he left.

It crossed his mind that someone in Paraguay ought to be informed.

chapter 24

The trap

"Captain Davis isn't it, Sir?"

To Davis the face was vaguely familiar, although smudged with creases and disfigured by tiny warts. It had sprouts of hair in the nose and ears and down the owner's turkey neck since he had seen it last.

"Sergeant . . .", Davis stopped himself and thought again. "Mr Steel, isn't it?"

"That's right."

"What are you doing nowadays?"

"I've retired and about time too. My daughters are married and I've sold the shop."

There was an awkward pause. Across to one side at the bar Davis could see the youngest sergeant of them all. "Boy Madden" they used to call him. Now he was a ripe man of 65, but still trim. He was the best gun sergeant of the lot.

Out of the corner of his eye, he could also see Sergeant Fairbairn with the two dishy daughters he always brought to these affairs to show them off like a couple of sports cars. He wondered why they came with dad. Perhaps it was some tale of his that made them curious to see the young bloods of his youth and now have the chance to smile at their spry gallantries.

"Oh yes, I remember. You told me before. A bakery and confectionery, wasn't it?" Davis returned to Steel.

"You've got it. That's right. We did well. Do you remember the time I made that oven?"

Davis was never allowed to forget it. The story varied little from year to year. Steel, unabashed, continued. "It was a hot day in Normandy. We'd actually stayed put for 48 hours. That was a change from being on the move all the time.

"It was 'Prepare to Advance'. We had hardly got the guns down for a round or two before it was another, 'Prepare to Advance'. But I thought to myself, 'The Captain would like a nice bit of rabbit, baked rabbit. There was lots of clay in the river bank and Marchant said, 'Let's build a mud oven. We can bake it to a turn and we'll have some real roast potatoes from the field to go with it, none of that tinned muck.'

"And Marchant and I knocked off the rabbit, skinned 'm, got the fire going and there it was all doing nicely when the orders came through again. 'Move!' And the whole lot, the whole bloody lot – tins, stoves, pans, the blowers – all had to be thrown in the back of the 15 cwt and me and Marchant, black as soot, lyin' on the top. I often wonder who had the rabbit."

"War was like that. Change all the time. Always have a contingency plan," Davis consoled him. "But you made up for it later, I remember, in Germany. We had some magnificent meals in the mess. And your cakes were really grand. Great tiered works of art – fit for a museum. It was almost a pity to eat them."

This was the signal for Steel to produce his pictures. They were getting faded now, but the cakes could still be identified. A new crack had appeared across the upper candles obliterating their flames.

"Magnificent. A pity cakes can't last forever."

Davis felt he had to get away and speak to Madden. A bright lad, that one. His gun was always ready first and he was well liked by his gun team as well.

"I'll be back in a minute. I must go and have a word with Madden." He left his pint unconsumed and went and stood by Madden who was in wrapt conversation with a friend, Sergeant Gibson, grizzled, genial and high-flushed with the best of them.

They became aware of him, standing nearby.

The trap

"Hallo, Sir." Madden turned on his stool, faced round from the bar and gave him a smile of genuine welcome. "What can I get you?"

"No, let me get you one. And how are you, Mr. Gibson?"

"Not so bad. Just the wife and me on our own now. All the kids are gone. Got plenty to do though, what with the garden, house and keeping the car on the road myself."

Madden continued: "We've just been talking about Gunner Ives. You remember him?"

"I shall never forget him. I've still got a picture in my mind of that time on the island. I went back there a few years ago. It took me ages to find it, but after going round and round the place on the back lanes, I think I identified it, although it was much changed.

"We were cut off at the time, surrounded. The Germans had cut our lines of communication in the rear. With more aircraft and tanks, it could have been a minor Stalingrad for us."

Davis sensed once more the dream that constantly recurred to him that the war would never end. They were trapped in it and there was no escape. Six years it had lasted, but in dream it was still going on. Only in death could there be release.

What he called the affair of Ives had started when they crossed the Nijmegen bridge. It was an old-fashioned construction – like something out of Victorian England, or the first bridge of iron at Coalbrookdale – but bigger, with a broad metal arc spanning the river.

Far below, it was the Waal itself, fast flowing in whorls and torrents round the bulky stone piers. Two blackened corpses, the mortal remains of German snipers, hung in the girders above, the shards of their uniforms fluttering vainly in winds that blew prematurely cold towards the North Sea.

He wondered if the bodies would crumble and drop off, or would someone later on make the hazardous climb and lower them down in all their stink and decrepitude,

The Reunion

for decency's sake, to where they belonged. Like Cromwell's head on London gate, they were a warning to all who passed beneath them.

A line of trucks of every description stretched across the bridge. From time to time they stopped, shuffled forward a few turns, then stopped again. Some were stacked with ammunition, some pulled guns – medium, field and anti-tank. There were staff cars, armoured cars, carriers and tanks.

It was late September and autumn had begun. Every now and again, the bridge was pounded with mortar and artillery fire. Then everyone fell flat, sheltering as best they could behind any kind of cover.

A piece of iron, like a projection from the bridge perhaps, or a kerb in the road, would do in lieu of anything more substantial.

They pulled their arms over their faces, hunched down and squirmed round trying to protect their vitals with their legs.

When the bombardment stopped, they got up slowly, convincing themselves they were still intact, puffed a quick Woodbine and nodded to the next bloke down the line, but sometimes the bridge still smouldered where the tar had been set alight and, here and there, were what looked like old pieces of rag and equipment where someone had been hit and hustled off, but had left remnants of his blasted body, or clothing behind.

It was a nasty place, the bridge. The Germans had got the measure of it, "stonked" it at irregular intervals and Davis was relieved when he got across it, with alarming interruptions, with his guns and tractors following.

They descended steeply down the opposite side and, stretched before him, were the dull, wet fields, flat and bare, of what came to be known as "the island."

He had followed the truck in front off the main road soon after leaving the bridge and found himself in a narrow lane, ditched and banked, a few feet above the low level of the surrounding land.

It was now just possible to make out the faint line of hills above Arnhem and hear the noise of guns as the parachutists were being severely pressed four miles in front

The trap

of them. Occasionally, the whine of a medium shell passing high above their heads announced it was feasible to give some help to their beleaguered comrades.

Edgecumbe, the regimental second-in-command, whom they all respected, was waiting for them at a crossroads as Sergeant Gibson, standing up in his tractor, head above the conning tower, bent to hear what he was shouting above the noise of the engine.

"Keep up. Get a bloody move on, sergeant."

"Sir." He acknowledged, but it was not worth passing on to the driver.

They would have to find somewhere off the road before night-fall for a gun position, or there would be a right "fuck-up" with the ground so soft and no camouflage to speak of.

One felt so exposed above the level of the land. It was not surprising that the tanks had come to a full stop, they said, high along the main road. They had been sitting targets up there and they just could not get off it.

They passed small bungalows and farmhouses with neat gardens and fences, all sited near to the lane and approached from it by narrow, sanded paths, all three feet below road level and all squared off by neatly cut dykes, sufficient to trap any gun, or tank attempting to cross them.

It was a dank evening, with mist crawling in the dykes, when Madden finally got his guns into position off the lane in front of a tiny orchard, one of the many plots of fruit trees on the island.

A weary line of Polish paratroopers under their General Sobowsky had just passed by. They were drooping, hangdog with the weight of their equipment, plodding back to Nijmegen, having made a frontal assault across the Rhine up ahead to try to reach the beleaguered British, all without avail.

Madden got the gun on to its right lines, facing north across the river, and then it was time for the brew-up.

The battery command post was in a large barn near a farmhouse. Madden could not understand why they had chosen an orchard for the guns and the farmhouse for headquarters. He thought both were much too conspicuous and asked for trouble.

The farmhouse was neat: he could see all the marks of a respectable, bourgeois life with a patterned carpet, polished table, china cabinet fully stocked, the antimacassars on chairs and piano and the framed pictures of the family.

There were few signs of the ravages of war here and Davis had put the command post in the barn nearby rather than molest its sanctity with soldiers' muddy boots. There was even a hint of remorse when the sandy gravel of the path was disturbed by staff cars scrunching round to the front.

The barn itself was as gloomy as a vault. Constructed of solid timber, ladders led uncertainly into dark lofts. The only light came from cobwebbed windows, vaguely illuminating bundles of straw and apple boxes in the corners.

They rigged up the artillery board and the wireless sets. Sergeant Steel and the cooks found a place at the back to pump up the petrol stoves to roaring heat for the tinned soup, bully beef and vegetables stirred together for dishing out into mess-tins in measured blobs when ready.

"Grub up. 20.00 hours," went out to the gun sites.

"Roger, what is it?"

"Duckling à l'orange with fine peas and new potatoes – what d'yer think?"

By 22.00 the guns were quiet. There was just an occasional starshell, or rocket far away ahead. Fifty miles back, the single road to Belgium had been severed by the Germans. They wondered if their turn had come to be caught in the bag.

Davis had got his batman to put up a camp-bed in one of the lofts below the tiled roof. In some ways that was foolish, he thought, but it gave him a good view of what was going on down below. He piled some apple boxes round the bed, six feet high on the enemy side, and got under the blankets.

The trap

He had not slept for 24 hours and there was a chance for a quick "kip" before the big barrage due to start at first light.

"The Dorsets are making an attack across the river, forming a small bridgehead so that a relieving force can take over from the parachutists. The whole operation is daft, if you ask me," said the doctor who was straight out from England and involved in his first battle.

"Here we are, strung out like bait at the end of a line the width of a road. It's madness. Typical Monty. What with him and Butch Thomas together, they'll have us all in the can." Both army and divisional commanders were noted for their keenness.

"We've got no alternative now but to press on, I suppose. Across the Rhine it's empty, they say. You can then just turn right and drive straight to Berlin. But I agree, it doesn't seem to make much sense if the parachutists are having such a rough time. I don't like it much, same as you."

Davis wished the MO would shut up and let him get some sleep. He shouted down to the others below, "See that as many blokes as possible bed down, sergeant-major. It's stand-to at 0400 for the barrage. And have you checked the sentinels on the gun lines? By the way, are the AA guns out? There aren't many German aircraft around these days, but there were one or two low fliers yesterday. Oh yes, and did you get that DR (Despatch Rider) down at the cross-roads for the ammo 3-tonners?"

He could not leave it alone. But there were still three hours. He might even take his trousers off to avoid a sweaty crutch. He had not had them off for a week.

He shared the watch with Jackson and the sergeant-major. He could hear the low voices and the radio spluttering on with strangled messages, saw the heads bent over drawing boards and maps illuminated in yellow patches by the spidery spot-lights and then, gratefully, he gave up consciousness with the ease of utter fatigue.

He reckoned he must be in a glass house and someone was pelting it with stones. The glass was shattering all around with deadly splinters threatening to cut him to pieces. He woke.

The dream was partly true. It wasn't a glass house. Mortar bombs and shell were hitting the roof of the barn with bewildering smacks. All round were cries of amazement, pain, yells and men swearing. "Cor, fuckin' hell. They've caught us – good and proper."

Above this could be heard, at short intervals, a strange sobbing noise like an animal.

As Davis franticly pulled on his trousers, another three hit the roof bringing showers of tiles, a curtain of dust and more cries. Instinctively, he ducked, then lay on the floor, panting with terror. Was the next lot his? At first it was shit-scaring, but, when you're not hit, exhilarating.

He got up unsteadily. He must try to get their bearings so the guns could retaliate. He scrambled down the ladder to the ground where all was confusion.

Meanwhile, on the gun position, Madden was getting it really bad. Twelve bombs had landed in amongst them. There was drifting smoke, tattered bits, an acrid smell of cordite and someone screaming. "Finish me off. I'm done for."

Gunner Blair had both legs and his genitals blown off and was staring down, unbelievingly, at the bloody wreck below his stomach. There was no pain. "For Christ sake, finish me off."

Madden was thinking, "What the hell had they been up to, choosing this position." The Germans, with air burst ranging, had got them very accurately before they had time to fire their barrage.

Davis got outside the barn with his compass to take flash bearings when another shattering burst of mortar and heavier stuff came down all around. Who was that, screaming for his mother, down by the barn grating. Gunner Ives, poor sod.

There he was wrapped up in his warm, grey blanket and one had landed right outside, blasting its deadly muck straight through the iron mesh and straight into the sleeping Ives, into his stomach and legs, and there he was, a hand hanging by one ligament, sticky red stuff all over the blanket, screaming his head off for his mum.

Where was the bloody doctor? White faced, as scared as they all were, the young MO appeared through the dust. A shot of morphine and a quick cut of the scalpel to remove the yellowing hand, with Ives going on about his mum, "My mum," like some bizarre record stuck in the wrong groove.

"Get him into the truck. Away. Fast."

They lifted him, still wrapped in his blanket, the blood flowing too fast to staunch, onto the 15 cwt, back to RHQ and the casualty clearing station. The MO turned to Davis, shaking his head. "Not much hope, loss of blood, shock. But you never know – if they can get him there fast enough."

Everything had gone suddenly quiet. People had started to think straight. The wireless was still working. From regiment came the message, detached and unruffled. "Report casualties. How, big a strike? Did you see their flash? What bearing? Range accurate, you say?"

Ives and Blair had died before reaching casualty clearance. There were five others, but Davis could not remember their names. It occurred to him at the time that they had all got out of the trap.

chapter 25

Intermission

"I certainly remember Ives," Davis paused, circling a finger round the rim of a beer glass and watching its contents bubble to the surface as he recollected Madden was still there before him.

"Why did he have to put his bedding down just inside the grating where the blast came straight through?"

"Yes, and why," thought Madden, "did we choose that exposed position anyway and why the bad intelligence about the whole operation, or was that intelligence deliberately concealed from the airborne division?"

Operation Market Garden it had been called, a bloody euphemism dreamt up by a literary-minded gent at the staff college no doubt.

It had all ended up in a ghastly stalemate outside Groesbeek in the late autumn, a strange intermission in the course of the war. It was wet and soggy in the pine woods east of Nijmegen where there was a vast laager of guns, lorries, tanks and other military junk.

The Germans, a little further to the east, were standing firm on their frontier. Hitler had instructed them not to yield an inch on their soil, the soil that for so long had been a symbol of blood, iron, racial destiny, mythical divinity and God knows what.

The allies were gathering their strength for the break-through to the Rhine which would still have to be crossed. The Germans calculated the war could be won by rockets and missiles, which, given atomic heads, could still enable the greater Reich to last for a thousand years.

As the gun-pits and foxholes were dug, the damp sand needed shoring up with logs and plaited branches like revetments of Napoleonic times.

Parker, Davis' batman, and some others dug a rectangular hole about four feet, covered it with thick pine, floored it with boards and draped the narrow entrance with rags to keep out the cold. The old camp bed was put up, there was a hurricane lamp or two, some tree stumps for a table and, with a big gun tarpaulin over the top, the dug-out was as snug as a second home.

At the end of a day plodding round the guns, Davis returned to it feeling like the ploughman from Thomas Gray.

At night he had to keep his clothes on under the blankets, in case of a sudden alarm, only discarding the muddy boots.

It was raw-damp inside the hole. The rusty Hurricane, with its tiny triangular flame, made flickering shadows on the brushwood walls. He could have tolerated conditions like this for years and he had a feeling that the Germans, a mile or so away, felt likewise.

The war was, of course, grinding on and he felt duty-bound to keep it fitfully alive, like the Hurricane lamp, by firing a few rounds on fixed lines from time to time. Harassing fire, they used to call it, aimed at cross-tracks in the forest, clearings that might be used for vehicle parks, or the few former hunting lodges that some fool might have taken over as a headquarters.

The Germans gave return presents at uncertain hours. All that was understood, but an almost chivalrous accord grew up between both sides. It reminded him of the notice put up outside the bedroom door when sleeping with a woman back in Brussels, "Do not disturb."

Even so, it was rather shocking when some ENSA girls had come as far forward as regimental headquarters and, after drinks and chat, had been offered the entertainment of seeing the guns being fired.

From the windows of the high lodge, they had witnessed 24 flashes, cracks and smoke puffs, as the shells howled like so many demons high over the conifers across the

Intermission

frontier into Germany. The girls had not seen a firework show like that before.

"They're organising a passion waggon into Nijmegen every night, Sir," said Parker one afternoon when the dying sun was throwing bright chevrons through the pines. "Sergeant-Major Williams is laying it on. Eight to midnight. They've started a NAAFI canteen there. Only six per night can go, but it's something."

"What about the officers then?"

"That's up to them, isn't it?"

"What about a jeep once a night?" Davis turned to Jorkin, the young Dutch interpreter. "Do you know anyone in the town?" Jorkin had been a law student at Utrecht, had joined them voluntarily when they had taken Nijmegen, got bored at headquarters and often came down to the dug-out where they would have long and knowledgeable conversations about Russian intentions after the war, or the extraordinary differences in the shape of women's fannies.

"There's the Mook sisters, I know, and the Scheerings, they're OK. And they have parties. I could introduce you. They're the right sort." Young Jorkin seemed to have connections in all the Netherlands.

"We would have to be back by midnight, but we could have a rota. Wade, Bentham and I could take turns. We could go first, you and I, to pave the good way. What do you say?"

"It sounds fine to me."

They set out that night, having first checked with the colonel. The jeep, without lights, ground slowly, but confidently along the sand tracks until they reached the dark suburbs of the city. Wisely, no-one was abroad. There was a curfew for civilians.

Jorkin directed the jeep to a large, brick house, damaged by bombing, with its windows boarded up, which stood at the end of a small lane. The door was opened and in they went to the light inside.

The sight was unbelievable. They had forgotten what it was like to be in a warm, furnished apartment. There were real carpets, pictures, upholstered roomy chairs, little shiny ornaments and girls! Girls with blonde hair and long shapely legs who laughingly reproached you, in quaint English, for your clumsiness and dirty boots while mouing with melting lips and clemency in their eyes.

"I must leave at half-past eleven sharp." Davis was talking to an attractive lass of 19 or so, warm and intelligent, and wondering how he could date her again.

"You have a story, a fairy story, where the woman has to leave the ball at midnight, so?"

"Cinderella, you mean. Something like that." Davis was still using the clipped, military style. He would have to soften up somehow, he thought.

"Next Wednesday afternoon I might be able to slip away with the jeep and meet you somewhere. That's if nothing happens in the meantime. Would that be all right?" He was still shy and could feel his heart racing for her answer.

"I would like that very much. You call for me at my house, meet papa, and I know some old places for picnic – we go before the war, not far away."

He smiled gratefully, not believing his luck.

She must have been only about 13 when the war started. He could picture the family with a basket of cakes, the lemonade for the children and a bottle of German wine for father.

"Smashing. Spot on." He held her closely and kissed her lightly on the mouth.

"If anything happens so I can't make it, I'll get Jan to pass on a message."

Soon they were back in the forest, five miles up the road and then along the twists and turns of the track, password to the sentries and to bed. It was a change not to sleep immediately as her image stayed in his mind. The time to Wednesday could not pass quickly enough.

The Mook house, with doctor papa Mook very much in charge, stood in a row of solid, bourgeois residences on the road to the railway station. Half of the row of houses had been wrecked by American bombs that had been dropped, 20 miles wide of the target, on the wrong town in the wrong country.

It was then that the Mook house had lost most of its windows and many of its tiles.

There were four girls, all different, all attractive, from Laura, the youngest at 17 and still at school, Koos, 19, the blonde at the party, to Lana and Hilda, the eldest at 25. Papa Mook ruled them all like an eastern potentate and mama aided and abetted him by her subservience.

They were finishing lunch when Davis arrived, all seated at a long table. The girls, unnaturally subdued, threw a glance in his direction every now and again, with Koos smilingly placing a finger on her lips. Papa changed to English, a courteous recognition of Davis' presence.

He spoke like an old Boer, bewhiskered, proud, condescending, but ever the correct host.

"We were talking about identical twins and a new work on heredity and environment. I have made a study of twelve – how you say – sets of identical twins. Even when they separate after birth and are nurtured by different foster parents, they share many qualities, the two of them, to a quite remarkable degree."

He looked at mama as if at one time his studies had taken a more practical turn while she went on serving the soup looking humbled and depressed.

Davis was surprised by the bizarre contrast of this conversation and their surroundings. Upstairs, the sky could be seen through gaps in the rafters and broken tiles. The floor was dusty with plaster from the ceiling and the table had remains of some rye bread and thin vegetable soup from a previous meal.

"I have heard vaguely about that and found it very interesting."

Mama broke in. "You haf not asked the captain if he wants anything to eat."

Davis, who had done quite well on biscuits, ample slices of corn beef, tinned soup and tinned rice pud, did not fancy the sour bread and the vegetable soup that smelt faintly putrescent.

"No thank you. I have eaten. I might be able to get you a few tins of soup myself and some American K ration."

The old man's eyes grew fierce with interest.

"We have had a bad time under the Germans. Anything you could do would be welcome. We are very grateful to you."

"I can't promise, but I'll do what I can."

"And ver are you going?" He looked severely at Koos.

"We thought we would go along the road towards Plasmolen, where we used to have picnic. We shall not be late. If you will excuse us." She left the table and went over to kiss him. He touched her on the shoulder.

"You vill take care of her." He gave Davis a penetrating look. "Do not go far. The Germans are close and may still come back."

The possibility that the Germans could make a comeback was very evident when they reached the bottom of the stairs and were forced to duck down in the porch. With an uprush of air, three very large shells hit the street two blocks away at intervals of two minutes like minor earthquakes.

They waited for some time afterwards before daring to move outside. He held her hand and felt her soft fingers interlocking with his. He felt vigorously protective towards her. How could he ever let such unblemished skin come to harm?

He saw her neck was pale and delicately entrancing and her breasts invited his caress.

The shelling ceased and they ventured across the rubble to the jeep.

People were coming timidly on to the streets as they passed a cloud of smoke and dust and some men were making the first attempt to clear a way through fallen bricks and shattered beams in a side street.

Davis and Koos did not hesitate, let alone stop, but sped out of the city to the east. After crossing a canal bridge and the outer suburbs, they reached a forest where the trees still retained a few brown leaves like tiny flags. There were gentle hills and Koos called it the little Switzerland of Holland.

"Where are we going? You decide."

"I know a lovely place with beautiful wood paths and a little stream. It's a lovely place and not far."

They were three miles out of town and everything was very quiet. The little chalets and bungalows bordering the road were empty and there was noone to be seen. The road looked as if it had not been swept for months, littered with tree branches and dead leaves, with pavements cracked and pot-holes untended.

Davis was getting anxious. "Is it far now? I don't know where this leads to."

"We're almost there." She did not seem to be aware of the warning signs of a no-man's-land. Her hair blew in the wind and her eyes were rapt with joy.

"Here. We can park under that tree."

As the jeep stopped, they were covered under a great cushion of silence. It was so still, the sharp crackle of broken nut shells where they walked caused a tiny echo.

"Down there. At the end of the lane there is a little – how you call it – clear place."

"Glade. OK. You lead."

She led him by the hand. The opening at the bottom was not far and they peered through the branches at it.

It was a graveyard, a graveyard of gliders, piled up in odd, pathetic postures, some on their heads, tails in the air, some totally upside down with wings broken off, or twisted. There were bits of clothing on the trees and torn scraps of yellow silk curled inconsequently round metal spars.

The whole place had become a junk yard of glider bits. All those spares, he thought.

She turned to him questioningly and did not notice that something, almost indefinable, had attracted his eye. It couldn't be, detached like that. But it was.

A man's hand, yellowing, edged in blue, lay on the bank, fingers half-gripped, one ringed, exclamatory. What other horrors, he thought, would be lying amongst that heap of decaying flesh and metal?

"I think we've hit upon a place where the Americans crash-landed when they first went for the bridge. Let's get out of here. We'll find somewhere else. It's not for us."

He gently hustled her away, placing himself between her and the dead hand.

The sky had darkened and it had become cold. They returned to the jeep, but the light had gone out in them too. They seemed to became part of some ancient sadness and their brief bid for joy was over.

They become aware of their part in an ageless tragedy of destruction. There would be rapture again, love negligent and attentive, but, for them, it would always be framed within a remorseless destiny of impotence and death.

chapter 26

Search for oblivion

Davis caught McDonald's eye again. The eye looked doubtful of itself and still mildly ashamed. "I won't give you away if you do the same for me," it seemed to say. McDonald had not come to the reunion before, which was hardly surprising since he came from Fife.

"Hello Mac, fancy you coming. Is it the first time?"

Mac nodded. "Good to see you. How's things?"

"Fine. No complaints." Geoffrey Davis thought of the time they used to patrol the men's mess together as orderly officers and ask the standard question. It was rare that anyone complained even when the food was disgusting.

They exchanged usual politenesses. You could always do that while preparing yourself for the next thing to say.

Davis remembered their last meeting vividly. The circumstances were unusual.

It must have been some time in the winter of '44, he reckoned. Antwerp had been taken, but there were still long, sogging battles on the flat mud banks of the Scheldt estuary to be fought before it could be used for supplies.

The Germans had clung grimly to the islands, causing Allied supply lines to be extended as far back as the old Normandy beachhead, a distance of over three hundred miles.

The battery had been in the filth and mud of a brickyard at the time. Around the yard, the trampled snow had brought mud, lots of it, everywhere, on hands, hair, blankets and even up the nose.

He and Mac had gone, with profound relief, on so-called recuperation leave to the city itself for a long weekend. Peter Little, the battery commander, had gone back there beforehand and organised an officers' "rest home" by putting an option on a clean, respectable and quiet flat and an elderly lady to look after it.

Flats like this were going for a song at the time, as Antwerp was still none too safe with the Germans dropping V2s on it. With no warning, the rockets came out of the big grey sky. There was a God-almighty crash and a street block would be blotted out in one go.

A few days before, a V2 had landed, slap bang on a cinema, right in the middle of a performance. Hundreds must have died instantly. All in all, Antwerp was not a very healthy place.

Davis and McDonald were due back at 1.00pm on the Monday. From the brickyard to the city was a comfortable morning's ride by jeep and Mac had got away earlier and spent the previous evening in the flat. The idea was that everything was specially arranged to bring a girl back for the night, but Mac, being a shy Presbyterian Scot at heart, had been totally unsuccessful in this respect and had slept solitaire.

"Drinks, I think? Down the road?," Davis suggested when he had settled in on the Saturday as the afternoon began. "I saw one or two comfy bars as I came in." And down the road they had gone.

The bar was warm and dark, with deep red furnishings. The stools had a polished brass foot rail. It was close and companionable, a satisfying contrast from the brickyard.

A few Belgians and an American were knocking back generous measures of Scotch and although it was well after 2.00 in the afternoon, there was no barman to call time.

The American bought them a round and explained he was a deserter, but was using his time wisely by building a sound capital base for future development on import and export, in the meantime keeping the police at bay by using a small part of the proceeds. A long line of similar entrepreneurs would stretch from him through army bases in Korea and Vietnam in the future.

"What are you guys looking for?"

Search for oblivion

"We've only just got here. Don't know our way around much. Mac here is not doing too well. He spent all last night with no girl anywhere near." With all their battle experience, they felt like a couple of church novices.

"Why didn't you say so. No problem. There's a place at the end of the street. You turn left at the bottom and it's on the next corner: 74, Rue Gambetta. They'll fix you up real fine." Mac looked dubious. "Well, why don't you try it. There's nothing much more going on in this fucking, crap town on a Saturday afternoon, let me tell you guys."

"OK, if you say so."

"Just quote me, Captain Cornick. They'll know the name. I procured them some K ration last week and some booze. Say I recommended you."

"Will do. So long then." They shook hands and Davis left with Mac following mistrustfully behind.

"What's it going to be like?"

"No idea. No harm in trying though."

They reached it. 74, Rue Gambetta, he'd said. They checked the road sign again. It was right. But the place looked like a merchant bank, or financial trust house. There were imposing oak doors shut fast, a small pediment above that. The large brass door handles decorated with Neptune heads were immoveable. It gave the austere appearance of a Scottish insurance office.

"It must be the wrong place. Let's go back to the flat and wait there for evening. Maybe there's a dance or something somewhere."

Mac was as nervous as if he was going on patrol.

"There's a bell or something here. Come on, no harm done." It was an antique, the kind you pulled that tinkled on the other side of the door like the time of the host at mass.

They waited until the sound died away and were surprised when a small wicket gate opened. An old man looked out.

"Désirez?", he asked testily.

"Le Capitaine Cornick nous envoit," Davis stumbled.

"Ah, bon. Entrez messieurs. Vous avez patienter un peu. Je vais chercher madame."

They crossed a small courtyard and entered a tiny ante-room with a fitted green carpet and one red leather chair. There was also an exquisite Louis XIV bureau where the old boy had obviously been reading, his glasses left on the paper.

"Weird do," said Davis. Mac looked utterly perplexed.

"What gives?"

There was little doubt about what would be on offer when madame arrived. She was the complete conventional proprietress of a house of joy, just as Toulouse-Lautrec would have portrayed her.

Dressed in black silk, which rustled as she walked, coiffeured in a style that made no attempt to conceal her age, she entered through a door from the passage and looked at them quizzically. She could have been any age from 40 upwards. She might even have been 70, there was no knowing.

She had done well and wore a gold pendant to prove it. The inset rubies were worth every penny of £2,000, whether paid in marks, dollars, or francs.

"Ah, officers . . . yes. This is an officers' house. You know Captain Cornick, I think?" The voice, tipped with Gallic, had a captivating flavour as well as being slightly archaic.

"He recommended us to come."

"A great friend of mine. I am pleased to welcome you. If you would not mind to follow me, we can sit comfortably, rest and have a drink until the girls are ready.

Please do not be afraid." She could see Mac beginning to cringe. "They are all very charming and we are delighted you come."

They were led into another room with the same leather chairs and green carpet now rosed into patterns by sunlight coming from a stained-glass window. They could have been waiting for an audience with the bishop.

"Would you like a liqueur, or perhaps a small cognac? Captain Cornick has been able to get us some 3-star cognac for guests. We will not keep you waiting long."

Mac sat awkwardly, hunched forward, giving little glances of alarm. His newly-grown moustache looked even more uncertain of itself. Davis felt like a procurer. From outside the room came occasional ripples of laughter and soft voices rising and falling.

They sipped the cognac in silence, too embarrassed to speak.

The door opened. There were two girls. Davis sized them up quickly and took the initiative. Neither could be described as beautiful. There were small defects in both of them. He chose the chubby one and left Mac the other. They had entered the lists with only the articles of war between them.

"May I, darleeng?" Chubby pointed at Davis' lap to sit down. "Of course." He did not hesitate. After all, she wasn't too bad at all. Blonde, luminous eyes and perky, about 19, he reckoned, maybe younger.

She was dressed in a grey shift, well-cut, slit at the side and exposing delicate, well-shaped legs to the thigh and well-turned ankles. The phrase to describe it came to him suddenly. It was impossibly, totally, fin-de-siècle.

She sat and wriggled into him, one arm immediately going to the nape of his neck, lightly touching him. She worked automatically with the assured manner of a practised artist. "And what is your name?"

"Geoffrey."

"Geoffree. That is nice. They call me Nicole. You like it?"

"I love it." In for a penny, in for a pound, he thought.

"You buy me drink and we play, no?"

"Sure, I'll buy you a drink. What do you want, champagne?"

"Champagne, that is nice. But perhaps later, when we go upstairs. You see, if you like me, we go upstairs and then Colette she bring us champagne and we drink alone."

Davis had become oblivious of Mac, just noting that he was still sitting awkwardly in the corner, talking in halting French to angular nose. He could feel Nicole's hard little bum wriggling restlessly on his lap, while her perfume was going to his head fast.

He risked one hand on her breast and was surprised when she helped him to caress her.

"You are ready, darling?"

"I'm ready all right."

"There is just little, how you say, arrangement we have if you like me. Outside near the stairs you see a statue of a god, a Buddha." She looked up at him with all the coquetry of France going back to the Middle-Ages and beyond.

"You put the money into mouth of the Buddha. Madame asks for 3,000 francs. If you buy me present, or champagne, you pay again."

Davis nodded as happy as the Buddha. He would have doubled it were he asked. It was an impossible farce.

She led him like a child at play, lightly touching his fingers, and, as they left the room, he saw that angular nose was making very slow progress.

Outside the room it was unexpectedly bacchanalian. A large, carpeted staircase, balustraded and with lamps, was the scene of splendid animation. A dozen Canadian,

Search for oblivion

American and English subalterns, captains, even a colonel, he noticed, were obviously enjoying themselves with tremendous gusto.

One of them was chasing a whispy, half-dressed girl up the stairs. A Canadian, looking mildly the worse for wear, stumbled and groped as his girl tweaked his great moustache with shrieks of laughter. Below the stairs, two couples danced affectionately, one of them a naval commander with flowers in his hair and with a girl like a Greek slave. Other couples fondled each other on sofas.

He slipped the money into the nodding Buddha, making it nod more approvingly, and they walked upstairs like two lovers going to their nuptials. On the top step a very young subaltern was sitting and talking very seriously to a ravishing girl, arms clasped about her knees. Davis caught his eye and they smiled at each other ironically like old men.

It was a suite of rooms, when they reached it. At the centre was a large high apartment in pale rococo green with gilt mirrors and a magnificent draped bed as its centrepiece.

There was an ante-room with Chinese rugs and, by the wall, a Louis XV table. Attached to the suite, the bathroom had gilt taps, he noticed. They shut the door and the noise of the frolic outside was stilled.

"Geoffree, je t'aime." She held her arms round his neck and pressed her body close. He was already like a rampant stallion.

"Mais peut être nous avons des temps libres – tout l'après-midi. Madame, elle nous ne voudrait pas jusqu'à six ou sept heures. C'est formidable, n'est çe pas?"

She looked reassured as she watched him, and went on reverting to her attempts at English. "Colette, she has, what you say, herr week orf quand elle nous servira. I ring."

She pushed a tiny button on the wall and soon Colette, attired like a Lyons tea-shop nippy from a boudoir by Ingres, knocked discreetly before entering.

"We have bottle of champagne." Nicole was mock imperious and Colette regarded us tolerantly, colluding our misdeeds.

The Reunion

Davis had never had champagne before, except the occasional glass at Christmas when it was saved for the roast turkey and they all wished each other a happy what-not and auntie became tipsy. Now it was served, wrapped in its napkin, the neck protruding like a decorated phallus from the silver bucket, and poured into two slender glasses which Colette left on the table before making a mock curtsey and softly closing the door.

The champagne bubbled at the brim. As they drank, he could see the reflection of her eyes as their glasses almost touched. He felt aristocratic and debonair, swashbuckling and elegant, like all the romantic heroes that ever were from Anthony Hope to Alexandre Dumas.

"Et maintenant, nous faisons vraiment l'amour. Tu me viens, darling."

He felt ridiculously incongruous as she did as he bid, undressing carefully behind the screen as if it were part of some religious rite. He emerged from the screen still too ashamed to take off his underpants.

She was waiting for him in the wide bed, naked except for a small silver chain with its cross of forgiveness lying idly across breasts of delicate charm. His eyes consumed her. To him, she was admirable beyond belief.

As he lay down beside her, she deftly removed the pants. "No darling, tu n'as pas besoin de ceux-la." Her hands felt his stridency. He felt proud and unashamed and could scarcely believe it was a source of delight to her as well.

There was to be no waiting. The spurt of love from him was too strong. She understood and gladly received him, her legs wide, toes curled, drawing him down to her while their tongues kissed, twisted and searched. "Vite. Je te console."

He lay on her exhausted and she told him to rest. "Dormes-tu un peu. We love again slow and you stay with me. Afternoon, better."

They lay side by side, his hand resting on her breasts, feeling their embraceable curves. Far away there was a low rumble as another V2 hit the city. The windows rattled for a moment, but he felt hushed and safe.

"But why do you do this? Pourquoi fais-tu ça?" He was discourteous to ask and she placed a finger on his lips, slid gently on to his belly and pressed her thighs on his until he lusted for her again.

They made love slowly and he was introduced to esoteric and arcane things that gave him wonder and delight.

"Tu viens encore?" She looked pleasingly as they dressed. It was getting dark.

"You come in the afternoon. It is better then and we have more time." He smiled and agreed and kissed her lightly on the cheek.

"Yes, of course."

He never did. The whole event was a cliché, a parody of itself, but he had been oblivious of the war.

Mac was waiting in the hall and seemed to have been there for some time. They went out into the street together and neither spoke until they reached the flat.

"Well, how did it go, Mac?"

Mac looked guilty and hunted. "She told me some interesting social facts. According to her, the Canadians have the most money, the least talk and the dirtiest underpants of all the troops in Europe, not barring the Germans.

She came from Massachusetts of all places, land of the Pilgrim Fathers."

"Yes, interesting, but did you get anywhere?"

"Certainly not. I made it quite plain I was not interested in sexual intercourse. Do you know what she said? 'OK, honey, but suppose I want to rape you!'"

Davis studied him for a moment. She must have had a generous soul after all, in spite of her angular nose.

chapter 27

Winter attack

> "It was not in the winter
> Our loving lot was cast!
> It was the time of roses
> We plucked them as we passed!"
>   – Thos. Hood.

McManus had spent a long time talking to ex-specialists who had joined the small group in the corner of the bar. There was Douglas for instance. If anyone had been lucky to survive to come to the reunion, it was he.

For months he had been the observation post assistant and in battle, as the OP party was usually with the leading company of infantry, it took the heaviest casualties.

"It's the pity of it," he was saying. "I am always so unnerved by the sight of the cemeteries filled with 19 and 20-year olds. I remember Captain Armstrong. I was with him in the winter of early '45 when at one point we were just inside Germany.

"Some people made their wills, or wrote letters to their wives. They had had so many escapes, they reckoned their luck simply could not hold. Captain Armstrong thought he carried a charmed life and had every confidence he would get through."

McManus recalled the incident well. "He gave me a letter to send to his wife. I was Quartermaster back at B Echelon at the time."

Around them the conversation was warming up as the pints of beer went their rounds, but the group in the corner was silent for a moment. They remembered.

"Here's some tea, Sir."

The Reunion

There was a short pause before Peter Armstrong acknowledged the smeared mug full of the thick brown stuff. He always tried to be quick in grateful thanks for Douglas' little acts of kindness. Solicitous as always for the party, Douglas had brewed up and followed a custom in war as important as the supply of weapons and the plans of generals.

"Sorry, Douglas. Dreaming. Are we in touch with RHQ? And what about the battalion net?"

"Yes, just through, Sir. Not much interference." Young Molyneux was a keen and efficient signaller.

"Just give our position. Here's the code. And then I think we can leave it for a few hours. Just keep in contact every half-hour or so."

"X-ray 7 to Sunray. We are in position. Closing down till 02.30."

"Wilco. Out."

The ear-phones, two padded discs with their trailing cable, were hitched over the rafters of the cellar and continued to crackle and distort the message of other units nearby.

In truth, Armstrong was not thinking of radio communication when he had paused before. It was fear he had come to acknowledge. Fear, gnawing away inside him like a ravening wolf. He had had it for days and it was getting worse.

It was not just the usual concern and vague apprehensions, but something physical, deep in his guts. He had a job to stop his hand from shaking as he took the tea.

He had dodged their glances in case they might see it in his eyes. He found himself bent and shuffling and it was not just the low rafters of the cellar, or the lice-ridden straw on the ground.

The cold did not help. It was cold, cold, never stopped being cold. Upstairs, the snow had partially melted into puddles on the stone floor. It had blown through what remained of a roof, the rafters retaining here and there an oddly suspended tile.

Winter attack

In the street, snow moved horizontally at the command of fierce easterlies. Down in the cellar there were three small haloes of sallow light where the spider-lamps gave sufficient illumination to read a map, or decipher a message.

"We have four hours before we move on to the start line and we'll take turns to man the set – an hour each. Nelson, you first, Douglas next, then Blake, and I'll do the last hour. Wake me if anything happens meantime. I think we should get down to as much rest as we can."

Armstrong unbuckled his two blankets and laid them on the straw. He knew he was optimistic about sleep. His feet ached interminably.

He had tried jumping, or moving his toes inside his boots, but he gave it up now and resigned himself to suffer it. Sweat was frozen into the bristles on his face and his nose was a dab of ice. But at least he could feel a small breath of warmth as he hugged the tea mug with his mittens.

He reckoned it was an impossible plan. This time he could not hope to get through. The odds had shortened and there had been too many near misses already. This time his name was on it. The premonition had been growing for days, ever since the plan was announced.

"We have this task of straightening out this German salient and pushing them back to the Roer before the Rhine crossing. The attack goes in at 06.30 on the 22nd. There are heavy minefields in this sector, but the Luftwaffe has been virtually destroyed since the Ardennes failure and Jerry has no air cover. Although the left flank will be exposed, we are not expecting much opposition."

He had heard that one before. They had said the same at Maltot when half the battery's officers had been knocked out. Intelligence always had it wrong. The Germans were persistently under-estimated.

"The infantry will go in on foot, or in Kangaroos, ten men to each one," the colonel went on. "You will bring covering fire along this line with HE (high explosive) and smoke for these church towers. After taking Putt and a brief consolidation, Phase II begins for the next village, Waldenrath, with the new start line just beyond Putt timed for 11.00 hours. Any questions?"

The Reunion

To Armstrong, it seemed like suicide, what with the minefields, the distance from start lines to objectives and this great left flank totally exposed, but he dared not say so.

He laid down on the blanket, pulling the other one up over him, and bunched his legs to his stomach. He shielded his face from the light with one hand, but the radio muttered on like some senile geriatric. Sleep was impossible.

He knew it would be his last day. As a boy, he had been told about death warnings. How his grandmother had dreamed of a black coffin floating on the sea when his great uncle had gone to the bottom with Admiral Tryon on the Victoria.

"Asleep, he was at the time, below decks, he couldn't have known a thing," she'd said.

He remembered the letter he had written. He had been too scared of what they might think to give it to anyone before, but, this time, he'd given it to McManus, the quartermaster, behind the gun lines before he had gone forward to the OP.

"Dearest," it read. "I'm just writing this in case something happens. I know you'll never read it, but just in case. I love you, but want you to promise to start a new life with someone else as soon as you can for the kids' sake. You won't have much trouble, a good looker like you. It's been wonderful, but now it's goodbye and no regrets. Love you, dearest, Peter."

"Do me a favour, Q? If anything happens, you know, could you post this on? I know it won't, but just in case." McManus had given a short nod. It was not a matter for words.

At 6.00 they gathered their blankets together and carried the wireless upstairs. Preparations were minimal and there was not much to pack into the carrier outside.

The wind had stopped. It was clear and cold and still dark. The move to the start line was as silent as they could manage, but it was not possible to prevent the metallic clatter of the starter as the carrier dipped and jerked into movement and its tracks slid on the black ice of the village street.

Winter attack

There was a soft grinding sound as the serried wheels of the Churchills moved to their positions. Then came the tracked Kangaroos with their huddled crews. The infantrymen in hooded snow suits, like white monks, plodded to their allocated places in single file and were briefly silhouetted against a background of shattered houses.

Some of them wore rags around their feet in a futile attempt to keep out the cold. There were those with bazookas slung across their shoulders, others carrying heavy, heart-shaped spades. A couple bore a heavy machine-gun with a follower to lug the box of ammunition to go with it.

All were trundling the impedimenta of war, all praying they were somewhere else, but all gripped by an inflexible fate. Their movements were slow and deliberate as if they were still asleep.

It was iron cold as the pallor in the eastern sky spread imperceptibly to reveal a frozen plain. It looked like something from a picture by Bosch.

The tall grey sides of flail tanks edged forward in stops and starts as the massive wheels in their sterns rolled over and over and their maces flogged the ground.

Crocodile flame-throwing tanks followed, with the armoured Kangaroos behind them as the attack began, the whole hellish thing set in motion by the whistle and whine of shells overhead heralding the smoke screen.

Armstrong could just discern the church spires now, far off to the left. Gradually they were being blanketed from view by the smoke and split from time to time by bursts of high explosive.

Driver Blake drove carefully in the track that had been flailed clear of mines by the tank in front. The flails could not always be trusted especially when the ground was frost-hard and afterwards thaws could be dangerous.

There was some Spandau and tracer fire coming from somewhere ahead, but it looked as if the remnants of the German 346 Division were offering only token resistance notwithstanding Hitler's frenzied order that every inch of German soil would be defended by the master race to the last drop of blood.

In this nemesis of self-will, hell was hot as well as cold and those who obeyed orders faced a hideous bubble of fire that burst from the Crocodiles, now in the lead of the attack. It was not a clean flame, like blowlamps, but a scorching, searing squirt that stuck and smouldered obscenely in blasts.

They screamed with pain and did not last long.

The few defenders left alive, emptied of their minds, staggered out into the open, hands on their heads. They had been truly wasted. The carrier stopped with a skid turn.

"Stay there. I'll be back in a minute. I'm just going forward to the next start line." Armstrong jumped out of the carrier. Time must have passed quickly. The fear had gone. Even the cold was only just beginning to impinge on his senses once more.

They had reached the first objective. All glory! Putt had been taken, a miserable collection of farm buildings and a little, blackened church. In peacetime this countryside was poor. There was a small heap of potatoes and mangolds dusted with snow by the outbuildings. The yellow metal road-sign was defaced with runnels of rust. All around the purpled bodies of the dead, crooked postured, looked more grotesque in snow, objects of sad irrelevance.

The infantry were being marshalled for Phase II when the counter-bombardment began. Bursting on the outbuildings with a sudden, splitting sound, it sent everyone to the ground fast except the battalion commander who remained upright.

"That was very naughty." He was Anglo-Irish and the response was in the finest tradition of Wellington himself, but the others were glum. Jerry had had plenty of time to range-in well and, as usual, the fire was accurate and devastating.

His particular burst was ten yards away on the roadside in among the slush. The clout in the face was like the kick of a mule, but it did not knock Armstrong over.

He realised he was still standing and could still see. Blood in streaks was running down the snow-suit, carmine at first, but changing fast to rust. He made his way unsteadily back to the carrier.

"You've got one in the face there, all right, Sir!" Douglas was as heedful as ever.

"Lets have a look. We'd better put something on it."

"No, don't worry." His face was stiff, but he felt euphoric and suffered them to dress it with a yellow lint and bandage tied round his head. It looked much worse than it was.

"Tight enough?"

"Fine," he mumbled, "but you'll have to use the set. Can't speak much. They wouldn't understand anyway."

His face felt frozen, but nothing else mattered now. He felt free and the fear had gone. That was the one meant for him and he had got away with it on the cheap. The gods had been deceived. He had an overwhelming presentiment that all would be well.

They would get to Waldenrath and, no matter what the Germans threw at them, he would be fine, forever reprieved.

They trundled behind the leading platoon into the next village. The counter-fire hotted up somewhat, but the distance did not seem great. Hastily, they sheltered in another cellar, leaving the carrier outside in the street once more.

Clumsily they thrust the set onto an old wooden table down below. It was covered with dust and bits of plaster like the inside of a neglected birdcage. A thin light penetrated the cobwebbed window.

Jerry had retreated, but was certainly letting them have it hard. Great bursts of counter-fire shattered the street, splitting the more violently in enclosed spaces. Bricks and tiles erupted dangerously as he ran from door to door on his way to Company HQ, but he knew they could not harm him now.

In what had been a shop front, the battalion commander was huddled over the command wireless set. "We've made it. Waldenrath occupied 11.30 hrs., but heavy counter-fire." He handed the microphone to a signaller and looked up.

The Reunion

"You've got a nasty one there, Peter. You'll have to go back. I insist," as Armstrong started to protest for the sake of form. "There's a Weasel standing by taking the wounded now. Just get in, there's a good chap. I've been on the blower for a replacement. You'll be OK. Thanks for the support. The barrage worked perfectly. They got it right for once. You've no idea how much good it does for our chaps." They shook hands.

The Americans had thought up a whole collection of useful tracked conversions like the little Weasel outside. There wasn't much room as there were already two others inside, one poor sod inert on a stretcher.

The big red cross in the white circle painted on the side gave them an extra feeling of safety. The bloke sitting upright was quite cheerful.

"Have a fag, Cap?"

"Thanks. I can just get it in at the side." He took a long, if awkward, draw. He was only 26 and life would always be good. We'll meet again, don't know where, don't know when.

That other poor bastard wouldn't though. It was shrapnel in the spine. He was lying on his back on the stretcher, head on one side, spittle at the corner of his mouth, as they jerked inanely, re-crossing the minefield, back to safety.

What was that bit in the Talmud? On judgment day, all would have to give an account of the good things they had seen, but not enjoyed. His account would be a short one. He would live up every single blessed minute.

It was thawing as a weak sun began to disperse the mist. His face was stiff and numb. There was no pain and the blood had congealed. Dead lucky he was. Gradually there was a suffusing sense of warmth and he slept, dreamlessly.

She opened the letter. The address on the envelope was streaked with rain. She had not got over the shock yet. The news had come three weeks before. She recognised the writing. What was the army post doing? At first, she could not understand. Was he still alive? It became clear as she read the note inside, the handwriting ill-formed.

"Dear madam, I thought I must send you the enclosed as Captain Armstrong told me to and I promised. I don't think he could have felt much pain as the truck he was in blew up on a heavy mine when he was on his way back after the attack. We all miss him a lot. The CO will be writing, but I wanted to say how sorry we are. Yours faithfully, J.McManus (Quartermaster Sergeant)."

chapter 28

Theatre of the absurd

They were sitting down at table, all 70 of them, still arranged by rank in old hierarchy like a body of Knights Templars, the purpose of the order long forgotten. At the top of the table, as guest of honour, sat the general.

On each side of him were the brigadiers and colonels, mostly in their 70s and 80s, long retired, some chairmen of parish councils, others governors of schools, some in trouble governing their wives.

Below them came the ex-subalterns, none less than 60, some through second marriage, or, an unfortunate chance, still seeing the last child through university before settling down in an outer suburb to morning rounds of golf, a snack lunch and beer and a quiet snooze in the afternoons.

All these had lasted rather better than the other ranks. It still counted to belong to the middle classes in spite of the so-called social revolution they loved to prattle on about.

As for the blokes, they stood awkwardly at their places at the long tables, stubbed out their fags and adjusted their faces for the solemn ritual that was about to follow.

"Gentlemen, shall we say grace? For what we are about to receive, may the Lord etc." It was the standard phrase that cast a glance aloft for continued good luck.

They paused for a moment and, following the first sound of movement, shuffled their chairs, sat down, and arranged their napkins, some fitting them in their collars.

"You'll have some wine, my dear chap?" Davis found himself next to Robin Pendragon.

The Reunion

"What have we got?" The menu, as usual, had been printed discreetly under the old divisional sign. "Ah yes, chicken. White then, I suppose."

"The general continues to look well. He must be getting on. Wasn't he in Korea as well?" Pendragon was not too familiar with the progress of the regular army, having been a journalist before the war and since.

"He must be over 80 if he's a day. I remember him as a battalion commander. If I am not mistaken, he came to the Dorsets as CO in '44. I was with him at that extraordinary time when the Germans flooded the Rhine. Five miles wide the water was at some points and the Dorsets were holding a line on the main dyke with all that water behind them and the wide extent of the main river in front."

He could still envisage that great, glassy sheet of water flooding the plain, sliding and sucking to the upper branches of trees, and the shattered eaves of farms with dead cattle and sheep floating awash among the reeds.

The sky was mournful and perpetually overcast, threatening to augment the flood. They had used a Cat, a small amphibious tracked vehicle, to get to the OP from the gun lines and had set out. It lapped above the grass of a damp meadow and stretched out far away across the trees and hedgerows to a watery grave.

He felt so incongrunous. It was about time they had something more to do now that the German fleet was no more and the Battle of the Atlantic won. Perhaps, with the marines, they could form a special naval brigade like the one Churchill had mustered to defend Antwerp in the First War, or maybe they could float up some of those flat-bottomed Monitors like the Austrians had used to shell Belgrade from the Danube.

Water, a wet November, and war on land was an unnatural mix. It must be some kind of comic mistake. The infantry, dug in below the top of the dyke in disgusting water holes, expressed it rather differently.

Winter afternoons are quiet at the best of times in those deserted reaches of the great Rhine. Now it had the silence of death. To put one's head above the level of the dyke was an open invitation to have it blown clean off.

Davis peered through a primitive periscope across the great wash in front of him and

Theatre of the absurd

observed the dyke line on the opposite bank, a mile away and equally isolated from the mainland like a thin causeway.

"Bloody absurd, sticking us out here," the company commander was saying.

"Can't do anything. They're there and we're here. And we're here because we're here."

"But Jerry comes across at night in small boats. They lob a few grenades over the top and try to get a prisoner or two. Very ungentlemanly of him, I reckon. And the blokes lie around here all day in these mud holes getting bloody cold with bleedin' pneumonia."

"Isn't that the frontier?," asked Davis.

"Yes, that's it, I suppose. The Fuhrer has told them to guard the bloody Reich to the last man and let no-one enter on the sacred soil. A lot of it's washed away, judging from what you can see from here."

Davis watched the little boat that he had rowed from Battalion HQ and tied up to a post at the bottom of the dyke. "If we could only see what they're up to, it might help. But the only place to get a view above the dyke is the church tower."

The gaunt medieval spire rose behind them, a severe skeletal digit that had served as a look-out point against Spanish marauders long before.

Davis continued, "I certainly feel like jerking things up a bit. I'll see what the CO thinks about it." The place was so quiet, he felt he was able to risk it. It was a chance for him to show how venturesome he could be without great cost.

The CO had installed Battalion HQ in the top half of the pastor's house in what was left of the village about three hundred yards behind the dyke.

They had made themselves comfortable like all good soldiers. There was a large table with a freshly laundered cloth from one of the many cupboards. Limited battalion stocks of food had been supplemented from the pastor's wine and schnaps store. From the look of things, he had made a hurried departure.

The Reunion

Tilly lamps purred and cast ovals of yellow light. It was just sufficient to reveal murky walls and pictures of disapproving pastors and their wives crudely painted by travelling portrait artists.

"Good to see you, Davis. Make yourself at home." Cody was a reassuring commander who never flapped and always made the best of things. "Try this for size." He poured out a liberal portion of schnaps. Davis gulped it down.

"Good stuff. Warms you up." The remark was redundant. Their faces were lit from within and glowed like those of Dutch peasants from a Breughel painting.

"Of course, we would like to know what they're up to." The infantry lived in a perpetual state of unknowing, making the best, but fearing the worst.

"Yes, well, 'um – I had an idea I might take a look from the top of the church spire tomorrow. If I make certain there is no glint, or perceivable movement from up there, they shouldn't know what's up."

"You know the whole of the ground floor is awash, don't you? It's a good ten foot deep, I'd say!"

"Yes, but if I could get a boat through the west door and get to the bottom of the tower, I could trail a D5 up to the belfry."

"Sounds worth trying. Don't take any unnecessary risks, though." Cody was known as a man-carer. For him there was always some unpleasant duty prescribed by "the politicians," but compassion was never far from his eyes.

"In the meantime, try some of this roast pork. Smith found it upstairs in the barn."

The night was quiet. There were no raiding parties. In the early morning, a damp watery sun matched the scene as Davis got ready for his "Boy's Own" adventure.

With a signaller and an assistant, he rowed up the village street and edged the boat into the great nave of the church. Pillars rose solemnly from the flood and the sound of the splashing oars echoed in the high vault. Two starlings clattered out from behind the altar and there was a scurry of rats. Davis felt the disapproval of the God of Noah for games of war.

The spiral staircase of the tower was much narrower than he had bargained for. There was only room for one. He told the other two men, who had been silent up to now, to stay in the boat while he went aloft. Maritime expressions came naturally to mind. Both men were sleepy and obviously thought the whole enterprise irresponsibly daft.

Hauling the cable of the D5 wireless set behind him, he climbed clumsily. A dun light glistened on drops of condensation seeping down the stones. At each turn, he had a vague feeling he would meet someone, or something. He experienced a sense of the forlorn, of a tower empty of man if not ghost.

Bird droppings and dirt littered the belfry. Rubble had fallen from the decaying steeple high up. It was bitter as a pale draught blew through the vents, too thin to move the huge bells.

He made his way carefully to the vent on the German side, making sure to keep out of sight, and looked across the mirror of water through his binoculars. It was like "Alice through the Looking Glass" seeing the unknown world of the enemy.

There was a German dyke, clearly visible, and the flood stretching behind it to a distant smudge of land. They had dug themselves in much more thoroughly than the English. There was nothing new in that. They always spent more time making themselves safer, with more home comforts.

For one, he detected a really posh lav, down the line on the far side of the dyke near the water's edge – a four-seater from the look of it, one where you could have a nice social chat with friends while protected from the icy blast by some tatty brown hessian. And there, before his very eyes, was an actual enemy.

It was rare to see one alive and well, except as a prisoner. Heavy in his grey-blue greatcoat, he was picking his way, a trifle unsteadily, to the "bog." At times, he slithered down the slope of the dyke and, when he reached his goal, he sat down, visibly relieved, took off his helmet, put it carefully by his side and scratched the back of his head.

Across the entire German line, as far as Davis could see, all was tranquil and at rest.

Davis never forgave himself afterwards. He didn't want to kill the bloke, he told himself. It was just that he felt like a puppet master. He would make the bugger jump.

He whispered down the telephone as if they could have heard him right across the way.

"Troop target, HE115, charge 3, zero 23 degrees, angle of sight zero 3500, fire by order." There was time to work it all out, no panic, like arranging a target at practice camp with no instructors to worry you with problems of blind crests, or impossible map identifications.

The message, relayed by radio from the little boat, went back across the waters to the four guns on the edge of the recent sea and back came the reply.

"Ready."

"Fire!"

There was a short pause, a vague sigh overhead, and then, surprisingly, about three hundred yards beyond "the bog," a quite distinctive splash of the ranging round.

"My God, " thought Davis, "this is something straight out of Jutland." The bloke on the bog came sharply upright from his contemplations.

"Drop 300, one round gunfire. Fire!"

Two landed on the dyke and two in the water behind. Jerry, a bundle of loose trousers and greatcoat, scuttled like a scarecrow to the safety of his hole, leaving the steel helmet abandoned on the seat.

Davis remembered the time when, showered with mortar bursts, he had dived for his life into a Normandy latrine, full of shit, flies and little mementoes of brown-smeared paper. "Paid the buggers out," he thought.

His revenge lasted barely two minutes. From at least four points on the dyke, like homing rockets, came the response. Something nasty and very fast crashed through the belfry wall, bringing hazy clouds of dust and plaster. Mortars were coming at him again, as well as crumping into the village below and smacking onto the roof of the church itself.

Davis suddenly felt as if he was on the high wire, one foot slipped and no safety net. He scrambled for the stairs, grabbing the telephone in a confused mess. He was the puppet now, no master.

He shied and banged and slid and fell round and round to the bottom. Would the boat still be there? Would they get out fast enough?

The last turn revealed the boat. They had not left him. He'd deserved it, but they hadn't left him. He must keep some dignity.

"Bit too obvious up there."

They did not respond. It confirmed their opinion of the blithering idiocy of the whole bleedin' lot: the war, the army, the Germans, church towers, officers, and, in particular, officers dotty enough to climb church towers.

O'Leary untied the rope with weary patience and they rowed across the nave as another packet of bursts hit the roof. But then it became silent, sensibly silent again.

The enemies had become friends again, if only for a short time, with a mutual pact of undeclared silence full of authority. It was a silence that hushed the great flood and the two dykes, a mute comment on the stupidity of such gross meddling with the ways of man and beast, tree, plant, land or sea.

"Anything going on?," asked Cody when he got back. There was just the trace of a smile as he said it.

"Pretty dead – stirred 'em up a bit. But little sign of general activity otherwise."

Was Davis mistaken, or was Cody a conspirator, conniving the silence?

chapter 29

Big men and little men

Company headquarters was in a barn. German barns are huge and draughty at the best of times, but now broken tiles and jagged rafters allowed the cold winds of early spring to pierce and moan.

The Canadians had relieved them from their watery positions on the Rhine dykes and they were on the move again.

The Scots had had a terrible time in the Reichswald, losing their way, stumbling and cursing in the darkness and mud of the forest. Many of the maladjusted of Strathclyde had met their match with the disturbed aggressives of the German 6th Para, battle-hardened from Russia.

As Davis reported to Vines, surprisingly still C company commander, he could not rid himself of thoughts about two young subalterns, scarcely 19, killed the previous day. He saw in the mind's eye their baby faces, taking it all so seriously, keeping strictly to their officers' manuals on how to look after your men and all that. Now they were both gone with no-one to look after them, shattered and burnt alive in tanks suffering direct hits from German Tigers.

Christ, it was cold, bloody cold. Davis shivered. He felt thin, laced and honed by the wind, though still insufficient to do more than muffle the noise of another Tiger blasting away on the edge of woods five hundred yards in front.

"Bloody cold!" The observation was unnecessary, but it convinced them they were still in one piece.

"Just right for the wine though. Here, look at these." Vines had found some bottles of Hock, cobwebbed, some broken, but some, like them, still miraculously intact.

"Hock, sparkling 'ock. Here, give us your mug." Vines poured it into Davis' mug where it babbled and greened the black chipped enamel and reminded him, for an instant, of mussels and white wine in summer suns.

"Fill it up then." Vines was measuring it out like the precious fluid it was. A treasure trove of diamonds could not have been better.

"They're all down there."

"What d'you mean?"

"What I say, the whole bloody family are down below in the cellar, simpering in the corner under piles of duvets and stuff."

Davis allowed himself the beginning of a smile. "Poor sods. Of course. They've nowhere to go now, they can't be evacuated any more. And now they're right in the middle of it."

He paused, took long draughts of the sweet wine and felt it warming and smearing his mind. His watch told him it was three o'clock in the afternoon and he had not eaten since six that morning. He felt drowsy.

"Have they got anything to eat down there? Better go and see." Davis could not bring himself to hate them, much as he felt obliged to try to. He moved towards the head of the wooden stairway leading to the cellar when, without warning, three explosions in quick succession, impacted the roof and walls.

An almost instantaneous burst, after the initial report of firing, indicated they were German 88s. Everyone, except Brooks, the latest in a succession of battalion commanders, had curled up like snails under any cover: old tables, bits of farm machinery, cattle byres, straw, anything.

Davis' mind cleared wonderfully. Only Brooks, a worthy upholder of his Anglo-Irish past, remained standing, laughing at them all.

"How very naughty." He brushed the dust from his shoulder and shook himself like a confident old sheepdog.

Big men and little men

"There's still two Tigers in the wood. 13th Panzer Grenadiers are putting up a stiff fight. You'd think they'd know it was all over, the silly sods. Davis, I want a good stonk on them and, after that, a couple of bazooka patrols can get round via this hedge to the far side of the wood and try and shift 'em out from there."

He pointed to the map, with black finger nails protruding from filthy mittens. Brooks was truly a big man. The blokes adored him.

Whether the stonking was effective or not, no-one knew. Judging from the past, it was unlikely. The fact remains, however, that by morning the Tigers had gone and the 5th Para and 15th Panzer Grenadiers had retreated behind the Rhine.

Along the entire front, the way was clear to tackle the last great obstacle to the heart of Germany. At Arnhem, six months before, the allies had failed, but this time they were to make doubly sure.

As March turned from cold rain to dust and gleams of sun, the great armies of the west collected their strength. McManus watched the enormous processions of amphibious vehicles – Buffaloes, armoured bulldozers, pontoon tractors, tanks, bridging equipment, 6-ton lorries, the dumping of vast quantities of ammunition – altogether a collection of the paraphernalia of war second only to the preparation for the Normandy landing, but this time virtually unimpeded by the Germans.

On 23rd March, the guns of the regiment joined with hundreds of others in a stupendous bombardment, laying down a smoke screen of immense proportions.

To the cheering soldiery, a great armada of 4,000 Dakotas, Stirlings, Halifaxes, Lancasters and Flying Fortresses darkened the sky and bombed with steady and saturating intensity.

On the receiving end, old men in their 50s and 60s, hastily given uniforms and arms, formed into scratch units by a manic Hitler, stood dumb with astonishment at such a display of might. They deserted in droves, the "Stomach," "Eyes," and "Ears" battalions disappeared in the night and the Dutch and Belgian SS vanished.

The hopes of the secret weapons department close to the Fuhrer were stilled, even though they dared not yet reveal what they thought. Only determined and scattered units of the 5th Para and 15th Panzer Grenadiers continued to fight on with fierce and crazy determination, more than a few making single-handed and suicidal attempts to stem the invasion of the homeland.

When Davis and McManus crossed the Rhine, it was the memorable day when the big men came to visit them. They were risking their necks, it was said, though Davis and McManus could never quite take the point.

They were together when they caught a glimpse of the motorcade. There was no mistaking the fat cigar, the stubby fingers with the "V" sign, and the other one with his beret covered in badges, like a couple of prep. school boys out on a spree.

Davis remembered his toy soldiers in the garden long before when he hid them behind tufts of grass, dug little forts and made tiny rivers for them to cross.

He used to put the general right up in front.

McManus saw the men responsible for Archangel, the Dardanelles, Crete, the Gold Standard of '25, the man who had never travelled in his life on public transport, the man who thought of ordinary blokes as a cross between Doolittle and Andy Capp, but yet had made that decision to resist in 1940.

He spotted Captain Davis. "Here, sergeant-major, personal orders to the troops from the commander-in-chief."

McManus looked down and read. "Having crossed the Rhine, we will crack about in the plains of North Germany, chasing the enemy from pillar to post. The swifter and more energetic our action, the sooner the war will be over, and that is what we all desire, to get on with the job and finish off the German war as soon as possible. Over the River Rhine, then, let us go. And good hunting to you all on the other side. May the 'Lord Mighty in Battle' give us the victory."

"Oh, and by the way, this is your proxy voting paper for the election." Davis gave him the brown card and envelope. "If you don't mind my asking, who are you going to vote for?"

"I don't mind your asking and I don't mind telling. Atlee, as a matter of fact."

"What, that little man?"

"It's a case of horses for courses. Perhaps the time is coming for little men, Sir."

Davis curled his lip in disbelief. To him, McManus had got it utterly wrong.

chapter 30

Games of chance

"Gentlemen, I give you the fallen."

They rose unsteadily, some with little wine left in their glasses, and acknowledged the toast.

"The fallen."

The word was archaic, associated with stained glass windows of knights in armour in old country churches, memorials by grieving fathers to youths of 18 slaughtered on the Somme. For a moment, Davis pictured a teenage boy clutching his breast and falling balletically while playing soldiers.

But what word could be used? Atomised, liquidated, mutilated to death, decapitated? "Gentlemen, I give you the atomised." It did not sound right somehow.

Whatever it was, fallen, atomised, obliterated, they had all wanted to avoid it, keep out of its way, dodge it, especially when they were about a month from the end of the war in Europe.

Germany was caving-in fast. Bremen had been taken and they were driving the old 15th Panzers right up against the Danish frontier and the North Sea. There was still some token resistance by groups of die-hards and desperates, but, generally speaking, it was an orderly retreat on their part using mines to cause delay. Let the Westerners come through, hold back the Russians, they were saying.

But you could still be decomposed by a mine, or rendered impotent for life by a psychotic 13-year-old with a brain bent askew by the Hitler youth. So everyone was getting cautious. The definition of unnecessary risk was widening daily.

Dobson was one of those who stood back a bit and calculated the odds. He was a thin-faced, sanctimonious man in whom burned secret fires and he had a strong regard for number one. Nobody liked him much, but he was efficient at his job and he got much more careful with his wagers after the incident with the gun-position sown with anti-personnel mines.

Mines were everywhere, planted with no apparent plan. Davis had been with the forward party, reconnoitring the place. It was a bright April morn, with the dew not yet blown from the new grass and a westerly breeze with a trace of the warm sun. Things looked promising.

"Let's get on with the bloody thing," he'd said to the truck driver as they came off the narrow country road. Dobson was in the back with young Chapman as troop officer, just sent out from England and as green as the grass itself.

They had been delayed by sea mines, wicked steel-bellied monsters dug-in below the little bridges across the dykes and needing very careful handling if they were not to carry trucks, guns and tanks straight to kingdom come and leave scarce a trace behind.

Time was short. It could only be about another 50 miles to the Danish border and the neck of the peninsular, which formed the scene of battle, narrowed fast the further north they penetrated into Schleswig.

The truck was brought to a skidding halt near the middle of the field. They all knew the drill well by now: director to take the angles, gun flag markers out, give the map reference on the radio, a crash action.

"Move it," Davis shouted. The guns were only ten minutes behind and they might have to fire straight away. "Ordinary staggered position, Dobson. And Bombadier Adams, that church spire can be aiming point."

Adams was a sleepy, but intelligent youth, another replacement from England, but, like all the new ones now, well trained. He sloped out with loping strides. And then there was an explosion.

More a puff, it was, not even as vicious as a banger on fireworks night. But Adams was lying, screwed up, on the ground, shrieking and sobbing. "My bloody foot," he gasped, "it's gone into the ankle!"

For a moment they were like statues at a childrens party. "Hold it," cried Chapman, "I'm coming."

He ran out and had got about ten yards when there was another horror. A puff, another dragon's tooth, with Chapman on his knees, holding his head with both hands, blood pouring from his face making a sticky mess all over his shirt and tunic and a curious, whimpering cry.

Davis looked again not believing what he saw. There was Chapman's eyes and Chapman's nose, but below his nose, nothing, all gone, just a smashed pulp. Jaw blown off, teeth, tongue – gone!

Davis was shaking with terror himself. Dobson and the others stood motionless by the truck. The film had got stuck. Adams was still shouting and there was this half-human, half-faceless thing kneeling, ten yards away swaying gently from side to side making animal cries.

Davis grabbed the mine detector. "Steady," he thought, sweeping it in great swathes 180 degrees, inch by inch, in front of him. Make sure. Make sure. Yes, there. One there. Watch it. Another bastard. The ground was sown with dragons' teeth, no lanes and no obvious plan.

He made a path, zig-zagging slowly. "Get the tape. Mark out carefully. Tread in my footsteps," he called to them behind. "Don't go off my tracks, not an inch." Were they children, avoiding cracks in the pavement like it was a century before?

"Bring up the stretcher. We'll get Lieutenant Chapman first."

How long was it before they reached him? He would never know. An eternity, a microsecond? There was just the staring eyes of Chapman and all that blood and bubble-spit as they got him awkwardly on the stretcher. Face upwards he was, or what was left of his face. And then, keeping carefully within the narrow path on the stepping-stones of safety, they edged him back to the truck, expecting another deadly puff at any moment.

"No risks – now again – keep to the tracks exactly – carefully does it," Davis reiterated as they got to the moaning Adams. Painfully and slowly they got him back as well.

"Radio for the ambulance, but warn them not to go into this field. We'll steer the truck out first. Don't want any more. I'll sweep a track back for it. Don't turn round. We'll back it all the way the same as we came in." Slowly it ground back to the road while Dobson in the back gave morphine from the first-aid.

Davis had never seen Chapman, or Adams again. They had never come to the reunion. Someone told him once that Chapman had had 23 operations on his jaw: marvellous surgery, best in the world. Built up the jaw, piece by piece, and then the flesh. He could even mumble a few words, they'd said.

Dobson had been quite right to play it cagily. There had been a tacit agreement on that score three weeks' later when, in a small cottage belonging to a lock keeper by a remote canal, they heard the news.

There would be peace at midnight.

They had put up their camp beds upstairs for a change in a little cold room and just slept and slept and slept while B company, on the other side of the canal where they had dug in on the previous afternoon, still kept watch and sent up an occasional rocket.

At midnight, with a fizz, the sky was streaked with Verey lights, which momentarily redeemed the darkness and revealed meadows and trees just budding into leaf. No fireworks night would ever be like it.

A week or so later, in the middle of May, they took over a Schleswig village in charming rural surroundings untouched by war. There were capacious farms, their upper windows draped with white flags, containing huge barns for cattle and straw.

Horns of oxen were fixed to the great gables, ancient Saxon symbols of fertility and a reminder of times past and times to come. The chestnuts, bursting green from sticky buds, were showered with a light powder of dust as the guns were drawn up on the village square.

They would not be fired again in anger for a British cause, but would be painted a fresh olive, with the blue and red signs refurbished for the victory parade, a march of the conquerors without slaves. One tribe of Saxons, though wary at first, took quickly to the other tribe and admired them.

There was beer from the peasant girls and more besides. As they talked with a whiskered veteran from Verdun, they discovered a common heritage and the fact that the Germans are our natural allies.

There came a time when Davis was called upon to accept the weapons of the conquered. They were not battle axes, or double-handed swords this time round, but Spandaus and Mausers, beautifully cleaned and oiled, each one with its neat pile of ammunition arranged on canvas like exhibits at a museum.

A retired Saxon major, head of the local Home Guard, proudly picked up a piece to demonstrate its perfect condition and offered its barrel for Davis' inspection in dutiful anticipation of praise. What better demonstration of friendship between similar tribes?

The last elements of 15th Panzer were marching to a ceremonial surrender in the little town when Davis visited headquarters. The men were without their caps, hands on their heads, their officers in front.

With boots gleaming and accoutrements shining, they goose-stepped down the country road under the chestnut trees. It was not exactly with drums beating and colours flying, but as near to it as made no difference.

Davis, aware rather more than usual of his muddy boots and the holster that drooped from his belt like an American pard, turned away in disgust and made for divisional headquarters.

Drinks for divisional officers would be served from 17.00 to 19.00 hours with plenty of Hock and the champagne that some enterprising Saxon had lifted from France three years before. A scratch band of Palm Court army musicians played uncertainly on the platform in the corner of the dining hall.

The house was a substantial one and had belonged, until recently, to a cattle merchant, a local party official, now hustled off for interrogation to a nearby camp. The dance floor was empty. As yet there were no QA (Queen Alexandra) nurses, VADs (Voluntary Aid Detachment nurses) or Wrens to entertain the troops.

The band played on thinly for its own sake and Davis wandered to the salon and from there to the lounge. Apart from a small poker school, everyone had gone.

"What gives?"

One of them glanced up at him from studying his hand. The brigadier and most of them are upstairs."

He found them in what must have been a large bedroom. They were sitting around on cane chairs, legs dangling across the arms, deeply engrossed in volumes of embossed green leather – encyclopedias, he supposed. Twenty or more, some opened, were scattered round the room.

"Here, come and look at this." Dobson beckoned him over.

There were photographs, slightly smudgy in black and white, of two girls mutually masturbating, with sleepy pre-occupation, heads to tails.

"Filthy bitches," he exclaimed, his eyes gleaming with the prurience of the fourth form remove. "Look at it, stacks of it. Old Sammy there has got two of the best to take home, they're too bloody heavy for me. Burn 'em I should say."

That would be a pity, thought Davis, as some of the text was in old German script and the production showed considerable artistry.

"Let's have a drink at the bar."

Davis waited, but there was no response. They turned the pages with the absorbed silence of researchers at the British Museum while he went back downstairs. James, the brigade signals officer, was gloomily drinking alone. He was a young electronics expert, itching to get back home and make his way in the new industries.

"Hallo, what will you have, there's some good Scotch."

"Fine, a double, just water." They paused and studied the liquor display at the back of the bar.

"Not bad, considering it's only been over for a week or so."

"First things first." James gave him a hint of a smile. "But even before that, we've got our hands on a Boche rocket team. Bright boffins they are, specially guarded with good rations, all ready to start up in business again back home. Oh yes, and by the way, there's going to be a party in a fortnight's time.

"They're getting some QAs, and VADs up from base and bringing casualty clearance right forward now. No reason why not, now it's all over. They can take over the German hospital, deal with just a few cuts and bruises, I suppose, and give the boys and girls a good time. Anyway, we're getting a whole crowd of them to come Monday week. If you care to show up, perhaps you could help to ferry one or two over."

"Sure, delighted. Better in the flesh than in the mind." Davis nodded upstairs where the silent vigil was still going on.

He took Dobson and one other with him when the time came. It meant travelling by jeep about 20 miles across country, with roads pitted by shell-fire and frost, unrepaired for years. There were wide slushy cart-tracks on either side of the decaying metalled centre.

Dobson had been reluctant to come at first, but eventually had agreed. "Nothing better to do. Never one for women, myself, but the divisional mess is bound to round up some good liquor now the God-forsaken war is over."

The band were jazzing it up right jauntily this time when they arrived, having practised hard in the previous fortnight, but they were still a long way from American standards. They were all anxious to work their demob. too and get back home, start their own groups, and cease being court musicians to an army brigadier in a one-eyed village out in the North German sticks.

All but a few of the girls had already been taken up and the dregs of the QAs looked forbidding. Davis met James and they drank lugubriously at the bar. It was a situation depressingly familiar. By ten o'clock, conversation between them had become more and more desultory. It was then that they realised Dobson was missing.

"Seen Dobson around?" he asked people at the bar. "No sign of him."

"Well away when I saw him last. Had a QA. Both pretty far gone, I thought."

Vines was obviously having a great time with a flushed, bright-eyed young thing who said she needed a long cool drink and was obviously stating a truth.

"A weird one, that," Davis averred. "He didn't want to come and now he's disappeared."

At 1 o'clock it was time to go. The nurse he had brought had found her way with somebody else upstairs where lucky couples had gravitated. Outside, Dobson's jeep had gone. Davis found himself mumbling. The door of his jeep was being particularly awkward and at first he drove forward with the brake still on.

"Might have told me he was going off: a bit casual that, not like the careful Dobson. He didn't risk a cut finger a month ago, not if he could have helped it. 'I'm going to get through the bloody lot, stuff 'em, he'd say.'"

The jeep went very well on alcohol. It was a damp night with curls of mist in the sad woods. From time to time, as he crossed stretches of marsh, the headlights hit the fog like a grey wall and then, suddenly, it would clear and he could see the road ahead with a low moon shining on the muddy slime of the cart tracks.

Now and again, he felt the jeep sliding and was forced to pull himself out of a half dream. He wanted to surrender too.

It was after one of these jolts of last resistance that he spotted the small red light in front. At first he thought it was moving, but then decided it was the effect of the mist. The road was straight at this point and the light must have been three hundred yards away.

As he approached, he saw it was stationary after all. It was the rear light of a jeep lying on its side in the ditch by the slimy edge of the road. He stopped and got out unsteadily. Everything was still. The giant firs, half concealed in mist, were like the hoary tree gods of Saxon tribes.

He saw that the front lights were smashed and the windscreen was a shattered mess, but, strangely, the rear light worked like a forgotten warning. The man at the wheel had been thrown clear and was lying on his back, his head contorted at the neck.

A torch showed it was Dobson all right, dead cold, glass splinters everywhere, dark stains down his left side. One very long and accurate sliver of glass had cut his jugular as neatly as any slaughterman could want.

Dobson hadn't got away with it after all.

chapter 31

The betrayal

"Gentlemen, you may now smoke."

The dinner would soon be over for another year. They could look towards a declining future with dwindling numbers as more and more of them became too old, or enfeebled to bother to come.

The senior officers and NCOs were already fading away. The one certitude of life is death and they would be the first survivors not to survive. Following these, would be those from Scotland, Belfast or Wales, withering far out on the vine.

McManus found himself at table opposite Griffiths, a thin taciturn man, who had been another battery sergeant-major without becoming quartermaster. Griffiths usually managed to conceal his deeper feelings under a derisive exterior. He had been soured by Welsh rain and baked hard by Indian sun. Joining the regular army as a boy to escape the mines, he had later been drafted into the territorials to stiffen them up. After the war, he had served out his time with stoical resignation.

McManus nodded him a greeting in which many unspoken experiences were shared. He could not remember seeing him for a very long time.

"Hallo, Taffy. Is this your first time?"

Griffiths nodded again, took his pipe from his mouth, knocked it on the ash-tray with slow deliberation, and refilled. He liked to take his time.

McManus persisted. It was an unnecessary question. "Have you left the army now?"

Taffy curled his lower lip over his upper, indicating he thought the question unnecessary too.

The Reunion

"How do you like it now?"

There was another pause. "I like it well enough. I've got a cottage and smallholding in Powys. The children have married, but live close by. Its a good life. What about you?"

"Can't grumble. I'm still teaching in a Comprehensive. I come here every year. Make a point of it. This time I came with Davis. You remember him?"

"Captain Davis?"

"That's right. We come from the same town. Sometimes we have a round of golf together and we're both keen on cricket."

Griffiths lit his pipe with care, stubbing it gently with a measured thumb.

"Wasn't he your troop commander at one time?"

"He was. I was quartermaster sergeant then. Years after the war finished, we bumped into each other quite by chance. We found ourselves living nearby and the friendship has grown ever since."

Griffiths considered this. He looked at it from various angles, as if judging the merits of a horse before a race, and then he lent forward. "I'm surprised."

"Why? Those old differences of rank mean nothing now. Anyway we found we share a lot in common."

Griffiths cast his eyes to the top table to see Davis in close communication with the colonel, turned back to McManus and raised one eyebrow quizzically. "I'm still surprised."

"Why so?"

Two long puffs of smoke curled up contemptuously. "I seem to remember you had some trouble once with some missing stores. In Germany, wasn't it?"

The betrayal

McManus took time to answer now. He was wary. This was touchy ground still. He remembered the affair all too clearly, but did not care to think about it. It continued to bring a sense of shame.

The war had been over a month or two. Every day a fresh batch of men had been released to go home in order of their age, service, or whether they could claim to jump the queue, to do a much needed job in a Britain starting to recover. It was also the time of the big fiddles.

The destitute and sullen Germans wanted food, coffee, cigarettes and alcohol, coal, wood, petrol and cars – all the basic stuff to get a modern economy going again – and they were willing to pay a high price. On the market were family heirlooms, pictures, jewellery and furs, cameras, Mauser pistols and grandfather clocks, anything not already looted by the victorious allies as they swept across the old frontier.

German girls had offered themselves as easy lays for a tin of coffee. The men traded first editions for a box of K ration. There were all kinds of kickbacks, deals and rackets.

Generals acquired the Mercedes cars of their erstwhile rivals and tried to ship them back home. Town majors ran silver-fox farms and made profitable deals with merchants in Hatton Market. Sergeants flogged the mess whisky and the squaddies made a bit from the weekly free issue of fags. It was a happy time and a free market had flourished.

McManus recalled it with humiliation. There had been an unaccountable loss of petrol from the dump, a hundred gallons or more, and he had been held responsible.

The odd thing about it was that he was such a careful man. He had prided himself that the inventories were kept in much the same order as before D-Day and the Normandy landings. Every item had been named and numbered, from the watches and binoculars to the gun caps (canvas, muzzle for the use of), all set out neatly in the correct columns.

He checked them once a week. Of course, they had not bothered too much when they were in action and things had to be written off quite quickly, but now he appreciated that the army wanted to be sure to count up what it was left with.

The guns would be greased and lined-up in long, lonely store parks, collecting dust and rain until they were sold off to an emergent African nation, or a petty Central American dictator.

No doubt some were still doing service even now against some miserable Pathans on the North-West frontier. But 50 jerry cans of petrol had gone and were unaccounted for.

He had had to report it to Davis and Davis in turn had told the colonel, noted for despising the fiddles, the peddling in the black market where men grubbed about like muck beetles.

McManus sensed he would be accused and his self-pride was damaged. He saw that Griffiths was studying him closely.

"Some missing stores, wasn't it? Rations? No, I remember, petrol, jerry cans of petrol. You were in charge."

McManus assented, "I was in charge all right, and the stuff was missing. It was kept in the wired compound in the next village. There were two keys. We had one, the troop commander had the other. The store clerk opened up with mine sometimes for issuing it out, but I was responsible."

McManus still felt he was in the dock. "You'll remember I was cleared though. I left the army with a clean record. They were all strictly fair. Davis spoke up for me on character, I remember. Good bloke, Davis."

Griffiths considered this before he spoke. "I was surprised the charge was ever brought in the first place. If they had wanted to set an example, there were many more, much clearer ones to go for."

Griffiths hesitated again as if he thought it inadvisable to continue, but, like many of his countrymen, he enjoyed passing on the gossip. Perhaps it came from living too long in his youth in those God-forsaken valleys they are always imploring the Almighty to remember.

"I don't think the colonel would have brought the charge had it not been for Davis.

The betrayal

I was with the battery clerk and they didn't know I was there. Davis and the colonel were together."

"How so?" McManus tried to conceal his interest. It did not matter now, so why bother? And yet the shock of the court martial had been hard to bear.

"There had been an order from Division about clamping down on fiddles. The Germans were beginning to get the idea we were a lot of materialistic oafs. Not far wrong, if you ask me. But they were already being seen as our future allies.

"The colonel asked Davis about you and Davis should have stood firm. Perhaps he had his reasons for not doing so. 'Unaccountable losses again. We shall have to make an example this time. If necessary make it a court-martial.' I can recall his words. 'McManus? What's he like? He's your troop. You're responsible. You haven't kept a close enough eye on him.'"

McManus was intrigued. There was no doubt that Griffiths was speaking the truth. The army had become worried about falling morale. Even before the fighting had stopped, it was becoming scandalous. Whole platoons had wandered away, looting German houses, in the middle of attacks.

Since peace had been declared, it had got very much worse. Six sergeants had been court-martialled for suspected looting while searching for weapons in a farm. The local town major, a veteran from the First War, on to a good thing as the military governor of the district, had been quietly sacked for his rake-off from the coal merchants.

"What did Davis say?" Griffiths smiled. "Good reliable man. First-class record. Would never suspect him, normally. It was the 'normally' I remember, and then, 'He might just have done a deal, I suppose, not suspecting the spot check.'"

"You're suggesting he might have been tempted," McManus thought. "Davis must have sensed the betrayal. If he had stood firm, the colonel might have got round to his own implication."

Griffiths continued. He was enjoying this. It was better than the chocolate mint at the end of the meal. "Davis was questioned closely, I recall, but was just that little uncertain. 'It's doubtful, but one can't be sure,' he said.

"You realise we'll have to charge him?' 'Is that absolutely necessary, Sir?' 'Divisional orders give us no alternative now. Will you do it, or shall I?' 'I'd prefer not to. He's in my troop.' 'Yes, well if he elects to go to court-martial, it will be a fair trial, and, whatever happens, it will do everyone good pour encourager and all that.' "

For McManus, it was like an old wound giving trouble again. He felt besmirched.

The case had gone on all day. He remembered the hut, the plain wooden tables, the tiny clouds scudding over the tops of the fir trees through the window, the smoke fumes creeping from the leaking boiler in the corner, his boots clattering on the bare boards.

"Stand . . . Attention. Quick march. Left right, left right. Squad . . . halt. Right turn. Cap off. No. 326570, Sergeant-Major McManus . . . Sir!"

The regimental sergeant-major took a pride in his presentations.

"Stand at ease, McManus." The colonel could show his compassion and magnanimity now.

"You are charged under Section 40 of the Army Act with conduct prejudicial to good order and military discipline in that you, on 2nd June, 1945 failed to account for the loss of one hundred gallons of motor spirit, the property of His Majesty's Government, and committed to your charge. You have the option of summary punishment by me if you plead guilty. What do you say?"

The colonel, with the little gleam in his eye reserved for these occasions, indicated how lenient he would be if people were only sensible. Far better for a man to get if off his chest, saving all the bother of blasted lawyers, witnesses, advocates, friends of the accused and all that. The adjutant was already much too busy to have an awkward case like this on his hands at this time.

McManus stared straight ahead. The picture of George VI, slightly askew, showed

The betrayal

his majesty looking dreamily on the proceedings. The Hanover Germans were asking to come under his sway once more.

"Well, do you plead guilty, or not guilty?"

"Not guilty, Sir."

"You realise, McManus, that this will mean waiting for three weeks and you will be under open arrest until we can organise the court martial."

"Yes, Sir."

"It's far better, man, to acknowledge the offence now, if there is one. The punishment of a court martial can be severe if a man is found guilty. Do you still wish to keep your plea?"

"Yes, Sir."

"Very well, McManus. Carry on, Mr. Stephens."

"Squad . . . Attention. Cap on. Left turn. Quick . . . march, left right, left right."

Three weeks later, Major Benson from the Judge Advocate's Department and two officers from local units had been called to sit and judge the case in the school hall.

Best battle dress was the order for the day. Captain Jefferson from the other troop had defended him and had done it well. Archer was the prosecuting officer.

They had questioned the store clerk, but he had not had the key all week. The guard commanders and the dozy guards on the dump, one by one, had sworn on the Bible and given their evidence.

No-one could account for it.

Jefferson, in his closing speech, had referred to the possibility that the cans of petrol could have been taken one night from the cage. If the place were insecure, it would be wrong to make a charge of culpability.

Jefferson himself had taken the trouble to climb over the iron mesh fencing. It was ten feet high, but possible to climb. Also possible, with a team of men, to pass the cans over the top. It was not impossible. He left it to the keen sense of justice of the court and referred them to Captain Davis' good reference.

They had not been long coming to a verdict.

"Sergeant-Major McManus, we have considered the case before us very carefully, and, while we consider there has been some inefficiency – after all, one hundred gallons of red petrol don't just vaporize, not even in this warm weather (old Benson had chuckled, but noone else had thought it worth a grin) – in view of your excellent character and long service, we find you not guilty of the charge, but would recommend, however, a much closer vigilance on everyone's part. A day-to-day check of all your stores would not be out of place. Case dismissed."

They had stood to attention in silence as old Benson and the supporting cast had shuffled back-stage for the long-awaited gin, and then it was all over.

Afterwards he had been congratulated. Sergeants and officers, his own troop commander, Davis, had come shaking his hand. "Come round to the sergeants' mess. There'll be a real soak-up tonight. Have you met Erica, the new barmaid. She's a Latvian. Her father's a professor, or something. They've all been working in a factory for the Germans, displaced persons. There's some rumour the Russians are ordering them back, but they don't want to go. She's really something."

They had left the dinner table, but were still at the bar. McManus sensed Davis' hand on his shoulder.

"You all right? Can I get you a drink?"

"No thanks. I'm doing fine." He could not bear to face the man. Could he ever bring himself to speak to him again after what Griffiths had told him?

chapter 32

Islands

"No man is an Island, entire of itself;
every man is a piece of the Continent,
a part of the main."
- John Donne.

The old comrades were drifting away. The girl behind the bar rattled the glasses to be washed with annoyance. Those who were staying the night in the hotel retreated slowly, with maundering Scotch and fading reminiscences. John McManus and Stanley Griffiths took their drinks to a side table.

"I wouldn't say war settled nothing, John," refuted Griffiths. "It just changes the spotlight to a new conflict. Friends become enemies and vice-versa. At one time we thought the Germans could never recover. The first big order group we had, after the war was over, when he gathered the officers and NCOs together, contained a statement from the colonel which went something like this:

"'In the final phase, as the Germans lost control of internal security, some Polish displaced workers formed gangs, took to the forest and, from hideouts deep inside, went out to raid surrounding farms. They are still looting, committing rape and even murder in the countryside. Intelligence suggests that arms are hidden in the camps. At 06.00 hours tomorrow, B troop will carry out a search of huts 7 to 12 at the camp. All weapons found will be confiscated and anyone suspected of having any firearms will be apprehended and brought to headquarters for interrogation. Elements of the newly formed German police will collaborate.'"

McManus remembered how, in the dawn light, he had jumped out of his truck. The troop was not used to this sort of thing and it all went against the grain. It was all something of an overkill to storm the sad, mouldering, wooden huts, originally built

The Reunion

on islands of wasteland to house prisoners of war. Now they harboured the human wreckage of six years of it.

The people inside were known as displaced persons, DPs for short: the depersonalised, though no-one drew this parallel. Years before, they had been persuaded, many forcibly, to leave their towns and farms to slave for a German war effort.

Now many had crumbled away, all effort gone from them. Before long, many who had lived within the extended boundaries of Soviet Russia – Ukrainians, Latvians, Lithuanians, Estonians, the Crimean Tartars, ethnic Germans of the Volga and many other groups – would face a more terrible slavery when they were compelled to return to the cold embraces of great mother Russia.

"Harris, Jones, you go with Sergeant Vaughan to the rear of hut 8. Bombardier Taylor, with Deakin and Scutt, will be ready to get anyone trying to escape on this side." He repeated the orders for the other huts.

"Don't move until you hear the whistle. Then, altogether, push the door open. No shooting. Make it quick, but don't miss a thing and don't forget the inside of the women's thighs." They grinned knowingly at this. "Anyone found with arms, hold 'em and send for me straight away. Any questions?"

He would go himself with the party for hut 7. The morning was grey and cold. There was a vague drizzle. When he blew the whistle and they burst inside, he could scarcely see to the far end of the hut.

A naked light had been left on all night and it revealed about 40 men and four women lying on treble bunks, one above the other, in a vast untidy dormitory.

He smelt a mix of urine and stale cabbage. A few dejected people raised themselves on their elbows and peered at him. An old man edged out of bed and made for the pot in the middle of the floor.

At the far end, a girl of about 15, swollen with child, slowly disentangled herself from a youth, not much older, in a narrow bunk. Both were expressionless.

He wanted to get out of the place quickly and felt ashamed of his useless mastery of the situation. Thomas walked round the bunks, vigorously displaying a notice in Polish and Ukrainian, explaining what they were doing. It created very little interest. No notice could bridge the distance between the English and people from Eastern Europe in circumstances like these, but the search proceeded implacably.

Pathetic little heaps of personal belongings, like driftwood, were carefully turned over. A youth, disparagingly, gave up a Verey-light pistol and was marched off.

Through the grimy window, McManus saw a man lugging a sagging suitcase of loot to a waiting truck. He was summoned to see a former Polish soldier, still in stained uniform, who had somehow kept his rifle.

Another pregnant woman was discovered with a carton of silk underwear. All had the blank look of automata and were wan with soldiers and their neighbours alike. They were people who had exhausted their suffering. They had an indifference mingled with suspicion for the capacity for sympathy.

McManus thought about it during the church service the following Sunday. The words that had shocked everyone in the padre's sermon were about the need to "Come to Christ as a DP, stripped of all insignia of rank, whether crowns, stars, or stripes." It was already becoming a common assumption that the Germans were bad enough, but the DPs were an unmentionable and verminous lot, hardly human and not to be allowed in church for Sunday parade.

The Germans were there and looked down gloomily from the gallery onto their English conquerors in the nave below. To them also, the words were an affront to decency. As the congregation all stood for "God Save the King," the 70 black crosses on white linen on the west wall, commemorating dead village soldiers, offered silent injury.

By this time the "non-fraternisation" rule had been partially repealed. The English soldiers were told that the Germans were "an open-air-loving race and every opportunity should be taken to organise parties for young children and to indulge in all sorts of sports."

This had brought a laugh or two, but it was plain that there was an intention on the part of the Higher Command to encourage the seduction of German girls on the heath. That would occur naturally and without encouragement, but visits to German homes were forbidden as it was felt that this created too many opportunities for more fiddles.

After parade, senior NCOs were invited to the officers' mess where the sermon became the object of guarded comment. Normally, religion was barred as a topic, but everyone felt outraged.

"That man must go," pronounced the colonel to his senior commanders. "I shall just refuse to take my men to another church parade if he's there," responded a battery commander, adding to his favourable score with the colonel.

"The trouble is," the colonel went on, "his posting will take some time to get through. I'll have to get on the blower to the divisional chaplain and tell him to buck his ideas up and get the man shifted. Can't stand 'im, myself." He was always forthright and you knew where you stood.

Subversive attitudes, uncomfortable thoughts had been crawling out unsuspectingly in all sorts of ways, like lice from under the wainscot, ever since victory two months previously. For the colonel, the first priority was to maintain morale, keep the chaps occupied and keep the Germans in their place.

The Germans were useful to run things, but there was no need to stand any bloody nonsense. Ideas were always dangerous and were best avoided. Alcohol helped to fudge the mind and Sunday drinks would drag on to mid-afternoon. The need for reassurance diminished after the third Scotch.

"I was taken round the museum by a German curator chap the other day," observed the divisional commander whose presence always had an inhibitory effect. "I've forbidden the exhibition of thumbscrews and those other instruments of torture. They'll only encourage the Germans in their wrong ideas." The conversation altered still more.

Comparatively isolated, the English lived in islands of privilege, reinforcing concepts hoary with age and current with the Raj for generations.

The party broke up. Outside the mess half a dozen Germans, some hobbling on crutches, victims of amputations from frostbite on the Russian front, waited for discarded fag-ends, or some meat scraps from the kitchen after lunch.

Even so, the colonel declared that the village was lucky. It was largely undamaged and life for the inhabitants was a damn-sight easier than for those who, at daylight, crawled out from cellars under the brick hills of the near-obliterated city.

It was times like the church parade, or when the tatty circus came, that the English left their island. The English soldiers were ushered through lines of the conquered Germans to take their places in front. If they enjoyed the act, they chucked whole packets of fags into the ring with condescending approval.

Alternatively, they jeered at the clown whose jokes they could not understand.

As the two girl acrobats came on, painfully thin in scanty costume, the whistles and yells were overtly patronising. A skeletal pony tottered on its hind legs in the middle island as one girl raised her whip. For them it was a struggle to feed the one pony and almost a relief that the Russians had commandeered the rest.

"We'll take a jeep to Schwarmstedt tonight," said Dick Grant to McManus. "I've got a bottle of champagne and Harrison, the mess waiter, is making up some sandwiches."

They had been travelling together across country the night before and had picked up two girls for a lift, Anna and Eva. They had gone 20 miles out of their way when the girls had surprised them by revealing they lived in a castle. OK, it was a small castle, but not a chance to be missed and something certainly worth following up and far enough away not to be discovered as a breach of the non-frat rule.

He remembered how, that night, Anna had told them about the last month of the war for her. She had been in a company of girl plotters for the Luftwaffe, but, as the German airforce died, had been drafted to strongpoints outside Magdeburg, issued with Panzer-Fausts and faced up to the Russians.

Grey with terror, they had watched the tanks approaching across the flat fields as night fell. When the gunfire hit them, a girl nearby with her thigh blown off, had died through loss of blood. That same night Anna and some others had escaped and made their way home to the castle.

McManus had no way of knowing whether the story was true. Certainly her father, prematurely aged with frail hands, had the dignity and appearance of the baronage he claimed. He still possessed one room in the castle for himself while the rest of it housed some 50 refugees and DPs.

Ragged tapestry hung incongruously from the walls and small pieces of glass from shattered windows lay unswept on the floor. The baron's room was bare except for a table, three chairs and an oil lamp that gave a glow like a Rembrandt painting.

There was again a frowsty smell of unwashed flesh and urine mixed with cabbage and onion as the DPs cooked up on little stoves on the floors of their rooms.

"Let's open the champagne and drink up." It seemed imperative to McManus to get the conversation round to a more cheerful tack and the baron had left them alone. "And here's some sandwiches to go with it."

"Oh, swell, that's great!," she exclaimed. The Americanisms went oddly with her surroundings. Both girls attacked the food wolfishly. There would be no chance of love-play until more basic wants were satisfied.

"What is the ration now? I'm interested." He wasn't really, it was just to keep the conversation going.

"Would you really like to know?" She was already showing a German archness.

"Well, for breakfast, I have two slices of rye bread and jam, two mornings a week with butter, and a cup of tea. At midday there is a soup of potatoes, carrots and cabbage with, once a week, a small piece of meat. For supper, it's the same as midday with a slice of bread and a cup of ersatz coffee."

Again he had no means of testing the truth, but it did not seem to matter as she rested her head on his shoulder and slept. The tapestry stirred slightly as a cool, fresh wind could just be sensed blowing from the heath.

John McManus ordered the drinks. He had been far away.

"Jane and I called at some of the old places last summer. The time lapse seemed geological. We have to watch our money now, with inflation and the mark below three to the pound. There are not many Englishmen east of Cologne holidaying nowadays and our van was an island of a different kind among the German luxury mobile homes whipping down the autobahns.

They have heraldic signs painted on the sides and they park them on little carpeted areas with coloured lights like amusement arcades.

"We went to Schwarmstedt. The castle grounds are properly landscaped now with the formal garden freshly sanded and the box hedges clipped and squared off like rows of toy Prussian guards.

"The building is a beautiful baroque picture renovated in pink and white. When the sun goes down, it catches the gilt on the garden statuary. There is a puckish charm about the putti who play in frozen mockery. The camp site is well away from the garden, of course.

"The showers and services are all first class, with exterior finishings in pine, all in unostentatious good taste. The restaurant has brightly coloured sun-shades. Many Germans are big people punching out familiar tunes with that steady rhythm everyone seems to enjoy. I could see the drops of sweat on the heads of the two gentlemen nearby as they got down to a big plate of Wiener schnitzel with lashings of chips.

"'Have you seen the prices?'. Jane looked at me in amazement. 'A beer costs near enough two pounds!'

"I remember we had to go back to the van and cook up the fried potato and cabbage left over from the day before. She had a small tin of meat to go with it."

McManus paused and tried to sum it all up. "And yet, if there are such things as just wars, I suppose it was the one against Hitler."

Stanley Griffiths considered this carefully before replying.

"That's looking at it now from our present point of view. Conceivably, we could be forced into a kind of national socialism ourselves before long. We could all become Little Englanders, get out of the Common Market, slap on import controls, make money from armaments, protect the currency, employ the out-of-works on public contracts, appeal to patriotism and xenophobia. Then we might change that judgment."

He had the look of a sardonic Welsh wizard. "It's time again for the history books to be revised. There's no knowing where we might find our new line in saints and sinners."

chapter 33

Reunion

There is a curiously deflated quality on Sunday mornings in hotels. Although there is a leisure and amplitude in the way breakfast is served, allowing time for the extra cup of coffee or slice of toast, this is only the calm before a sense of anxiety increases as Monday approaches.

The expectancy and fulfilment of Saturday is over. Ahead stretches lunch, sleep, evening TV and then more sleep as people charge themselves for the trials of another week.

At first, the posh Sundays give excellent cover, thick enough to ward off most conversational attacks, but there is a trace of uncertainty in the air that sets the teeth on edge as you bite the toast and marmalade.

Davis and McManus were late getting down to breakfast. As they were travelling back together, they sat at the same table. McManus looked at Davis closely as if for the first time. He had not observed how thin his top lip was before, determined but petulant, how his ears showed scaly-reddened skin at the lobes and sprouted indecent hairs.

Come to think of it, he did not like Davis very much. There he was stuck behind his Sunday Telegraph, confirming to himself all those comforting right-wing views that eased his doubts and salved his conscience.

McManus had not slept all that well thinking about his talk with Griffiths. In the night he had tried to forget and forgive. After all, it was so long ago. Why should he re-live in his mind experiences best forgotten, why should he want to remove the plaster from the old wounds and discover old betrayals and the little treacheries and deceits.

They exist even between those who live close together for a lifetime in the conventional marriage partnership. It was nearly 50 years ago and long forgotten until Griffiths had brought them back and revived memories which were best left alone.

But he had been kept awake by the shame, the worry, the loss of faith in himself and the stain of doubt he had seen at the time in the faces of the others even after his exoneration. But now they were going back home together, he could not bring himself to speak about it.

"What's the score? Is Boycott out?"

"Yes. Caught and bowled for 19." Davis did not want to be disturbed.

"Is that all?"

"The Australians are bound to get the Ashes. We don't stand a chance with this one."

"Brearley was a mistake, completely off form."

"Sound captain though. Gives the team confidence, good tactician, puts himself last."

They settled the bill, got into Davis' car and moved out of the town, which was just starting to pull itself together, with newspaper boys cutting corners on their bicycles as there was no-one about.

McManus started again. Cricket is as good a topic as any for comment without communication.

Strange we should be talking about the Ashes. As long as I can remember, I've talked about the Ashes. My father did too. It's like a tribal rite, very English. What are they? Isn't it something to do with the first time the Australians beat England?"

Davis' knowledge of sport was exceptional, of cricket encyclopaedic. He read Wisden for pleasure. "That's right. It was an obituary notice in The Times in 1882. A noteworthy game. England lost by seven runs. There were three splendid bowlers, Spofforth, Boyle and Palmer, with a great wicketkeeper, Blackham. 1982 was memorable – a century of great cricket!"

McManus looked at him with grudging respect. "How do you know all that?"

"I've made a point of it. These great events of cricket are about being English."

Davis thought about this before continuing. "They're like the 'News of the World', Gloucestershire cider, rooks in the elms, or . . .", he fumbled for another simile, "like pantomime, or the 'Army and Navy Stores'."

"Yes, I understand what you're driving at, but the elms have nearly all died, the 'News of the World' gives way to the 'Sunday Mirror' and the 'Army and Navy Stores' would long ago have gone into bankruptcy if it only relied on the foxhunters and sons of empire. I question whether any of the things they stand for are worth keeping anyway. Aren't they just cliches masking a deep disunity if you are offering them as symbols of nationhood?"

They drove on in silence for some miles and distanced themselves from the town and from each other.

It was McManus who threw a line across again. He could keep quiet no longer.

"I was speaking to Sergeant-Major Griffiths last night."

"Is that the chap with the long face who sucks his pipe and broods. I saw you with him. What had he got to say?"

"He reminded me of the court martial." McManus waited for some reaction, but none came. He hesitated before the plunge. It was like someone else speaking when the words finally tumbled out.

"He said you tipped the colonel into putting me on a charge."

"What does he know about it?"

"He said he was in the outer office at the time and overheard a conversation between you and the colonel. He reminded me that you had another key to the dump."

"He has a mighty good memory – too good."

The Reunion

The great down of Uffington stood boldly on their right. High up, Sunday walkers were climbing on the spikey limbs of the white horse, the same image observed by Celt and Dane and by an imaginary Tom Brown when he went off to Rugby school.

It was some time before Davis spoke again. He was a careful driver and kept his eyes firmly on the road.

"I can't remember too much what was said. I know we talked about the need to set an example and he asked my opinion."

"What did you say?"

"I said you were a very good man, example to the regiment, no doubts in my mind about honesty. Meticulous regard for accounting, if I remember rightly."

"I was charged nonetheless."

"Yes, but you came out stronger in the end. Didn't I give evidence as to character?"

"That's right. That's why I was astonished to hear what Griffiths said."

"Griffiths is a trouble-maker, always was. Like all Welshmen, they enjoy stirring up dissension. Forget it. In any case, the whole battery was under suspicion. It was better to clear the air. There were a lot of people making the most of their opportunities then.

"The war was over and the bright boys were beginning to play the market. You could start to build up some capital to launch your own business at home – and good luck to you. I don't know why you're still on about it. Why bother? I didn't know you then. Sometimes, there are higher loyalties than friends – the team, the regiment in those days, for instance."

Davis was not usually so disjointed. McManus felt prim as he spoke.

"Actually, it never crossed my mind to fiddle."

"Anyone can see that now. I certainly can. Chaps with integrity are so predictable, easy dupes when it comes to planning a deal. Men work for profit, or a cause and the ones who work for profit can win every time just by changing tactics."

"I don't think I want that much to win."

"That's your trouble, John. Everyone must want very much to win now, if they are going to survive. It's always been like that and it's going to get more like that. There's no place for nirvana among the living. Look at India, for example, the most religious country in the world, and where has it got them? Starvation, misery, disease, Holy men among the dead and dying. Compare it with Japan and remember the Indians had a head start with the British Empire. Anyway, let's forget it. We meet as usual in the Bear on Wednesday, right?"

"Right."

In time, McManus thought, even Judas must be forgiven.